IRREPLACEABLE

xoxo
Angela Graham

IRREPLACEABLE

Angela Graham

Editor—Jen Juneau
Book Designer—E.E. Long, Biblio/Tech

"It's often just enough to be with someone. I don't need to touch them. Not even talk. A feeling passes between you both. You're not alone."

—Marilyn Monroe

TABLE OF CONTENTS

Chapter One

SWEET DREAMS NO MORE

In a haze of raw, undeniable passion, his strong hands gripped the backs of my thighs, torturously working their way to my ass, where his skillful fingers kneaded and teased me into surrendering to his every demand. His breath was thick and minty, with a hint of bourbon, and left me craving more. Goose bumps flared over my blazing skin. The weather outside was a numbing twenty degrees, yet I was heated from the inside out.

A giggle escaped my lips when he lifted me from the ground, my legs finding their way around his waist as his seductive growl kissed my soul. My hands were relentless, snaking under his shirt and over the toned muscles of his back. My eyelids fluttered wildly in a vain attempt to hold his gaze. The harder I fought to watch his every move, the deeper I lost myself in our moment of hunger.

Everything inside me screamed for more and I ached, truly pained with anticipation. Grinding myself against his hard body, I rolled my hips, demanding every part of him. The cool brick wall dug into my back, the thick coat I wore seconds earlier now lying abandoned on the blacktop beside us.

A lurid groan spilled from my swollen lips when his hands dug into my hair, his lips nibbling the corner of mine, the searing passion between us uncontrollable. Forsaking all logical thought, I submitted to his reckless frenzy, my lips quivering as his hand slid down the front of my dress. He tore it open in one swift move, leaving me bare and at his will.

"I need you, Cassandra."

Oh God, I needed him. I burned for his touch. It was the closest to serenity I'd ever felt, and I never wanted to lose it. His lips ravaged mine, taking my breath and eliciting panting when they began their descent down my jaw. His tongue ignited a trail straight to my breasts, which were on full display for his eyes only. The scruff of his jaw scratched across my skin, further awakening every hidden emotion and greedy desire I possessed.

The world around us ceased to exist. He and I were all that mattered—all I felt, saw, and needed. Lost in the strength of his grip and power of his lust, I remained at his mercy, fisting his short waves of hair as he dropped to his knee.

My head fell back, savoring his tongue working its magic down my stomach. A delicious purr spilled from my open mouth, expressing everything my brain couldn't process into words. I wanted more. I wanted it all, but in an instant, the rough, needy clutch of his fingers and moistness of his mouth were gone; the indescribable emotions he'd awoken in me were no more.

Dazed, I whipped my head back and forth, desperately searching the darkness that now engulfed me.

"Logan?"

Panic set in, filling my veins with fear-induced adrenaline. I reached down for the pieces of my tattered dress, the frosty air now stinging my clammy skin in his absence, only to find they were gone as well. There I stood, naked and vulnerable, alone in the night.

"Logan, please…don't leave me."

I stumbled forward, struggling to adjust my sight to see anything other than black. My hands smacked into another wall, and it hit me.

The alley. I was in the alley.

The air was pulled from my lungs, legs quaking as the harsh words he'd spoken replayed through me.

"I want to fuck you. Here and now. I'm tired of waiting."

"Logan!" My hands shielded my ears, shaking my head to make it go away. Make it stop. He wouldn't say that. Wouldn't treat me like another whore.

"Come back! Don't leave me." My words dripped into a slurred sob as tears sprung from my eyes, distorting my vision further.

Where was he? Why would he leave me like this? He wouldn't—not me. He cared about me. He had to be there…somewhere.

"Logan, please!" I cried out, a cracked whimper pouring from my soul as I fell to my knees, helpless, terrified, and completely alone. Something in my heaving chest broke.

My heart. It had to be.

With my hands covering my face, palms pooling with salty tears, my ears rang with a buzzing horn. I looked up, squinting into the distance.

There was a light ahead. Someone was coming back for me. Logan.

It had to be Logan. None of it was real. He would never say those things. Never toss me aside.

The light drew closer, a blinding ray suddenly racing toward me.

I lifted my trembling hands over my eyes, tilting my head, anxious to make out the approaching figure. It was so bright, too intense, and glaring into the wetness of my eyes. I couldn't see, couldn't understand, until the car horn blared through the air. Suddenly it was on me, crashing, barreling my body into nothing until all I felt was pain as the unknown consumed me.

I jerked up, fighting to catch my breath.

The familiar dry air of the hospital room eased me back onto the thin pillows on the small bed. It was all a dream—a horrible nightmare I could never escape. Five long days trapped in tiny rooms, and every night I closed my eyes and found him waiting for me. Each kiss took away the painful memory of that night, slowly erasing it until I was lost in his arms in that dark alley. His touch and longing were all I felt, all I lived for there. But it wasn't real.

Nothing was real anymore—not the need to feel him, my body entangled with his, lost in each other. I wanted that while I was there, wanted him: Logan.

But then it was gone. The haunting memory of the accident—the fear, the cold, the cruel lingering pain—woke me and hurled me back to reality every time. He didn't want me like I did him. It was all in my head, exactly as it had been with Mark, yet I was too blinded by their charm to realize it.

"Hi honey. You awake?"

Of course I was awake. How could I sleep knowing what awaited me in my dreams?

I stared at the wall, facing away, but gave a slight nod. From my bed, I was unable to see out the tall windows, but I'd counted every single shape on the dull drapes over the last three days. I spent every waking moment too ashamed to cry. I did it to myself, and now I was enduring the consequences: anger, pain, hurt, betrayal, and loss. So many emotions consumed me, but only once did I shed tears for him.

It was the day I first awoke in ICU, a few days earlier—the day I opened my eyes and found him there, so broken and tortured. He had no right to be the one in agony, to beg me to forget. How could I?

I shook my head, unable to inhale a soothing breath for fear of the reckoning my bruised ribs would set upon me if I did. I never wanted to relive the heartbreak and devastation of that night again.

"I talked to your doctor, and he said you're doing great. The cut on your leg is healing, and it doesn't look like you'll need to stay past Friday."

The cut? I winced at her euphemism for the deep gash running down my thigh that ripped into my muscles and nearly damaged my nerves. *Luck*, the doctors had told me.

Funny. I didn't feel very lucky.

"Honey, did you hear me? You'll be going home in three days."

"Great." My voice wasn't my own. It was hoarse, and laced with numbness.

The patter of my mother's feet bustling around the room as she hummed a lullaby from my childhood helped keep my mind from spiraling into the ocean of melancholy I'd been drowning in the last few days. She was tidying up the room, even though it was no different from how it looked the previous day.

At least, not aside from the newest flowers that arrived.

"I see you got more flowers delivered. They're gorgeous. Logan, I'm guessing?"

Try as I had, the one thing I couldn't escape was the number of lavish bouquets that decorated the small, dreary room. Were they unbelievably breathtaking? Yes. Were they from Logan? I could only assume, since nobody I knew had that amount of money, or such impeccable taste. Only the first delivery came with a card, and it was still in place on a thin, plastic stick peeking out of the vase of pink peonies beside my bed. They were my favorite flowers, and he knew it. I didn't know how, but he did.

"I went to see him yesterday." Hesitation was heavy in her tone.

My ears perked against my will.

"Why?" It was all I could muster.

Hilary, Luke, and Caleb had been regulars there, but Logan was a no-show after he'd left me a crying, scared mess. I didn't know why I'd expected differently. He didn't care about me. It wasn't real—I told myself that constantly. I was a conquest to him, nothing more, and all he felt now was guilt. I could smell it in the flowers. But whatever he was feeling, it didn't matter anyway. It was over.

The bed dipped down behind me, and my mother's hand attempted to smooth out the rigid posture of my spine. I waited for her to explain, irritated I'd even asked.

"He called me, wanted to meet for lunch...and I agreed."

How lovely of her! I fought to quiet my nerves as I listened, fury stewing, unable to find my voice to tell her I didn't want to know any more.

"I don't know what happened between you two that night, but I do know that he looks like he hasn't slept since. Don't get upset, but...he's paid all of your expenses here, and...asked me to give you this. Or, more so, deposit this into your bank account."

"What?" I rolled over, ignoring the sting in my bruised ribs. She handed me a check, and I could only sit there with my jaw dropped, gaping at it. Fifty thousand dollars. So that's it. He doesn't come back to visit, but sends a check.

My blood boiled.

"You're going to need a new car, and—"

"I don't want his money, Mom!" I ripped the check in half over and over again, taking my fury out on the small paper until I could tear it no more. "Tell him no! The answer is no!"

I dropped the tiny pieces off the side of the bed, wanting to make it all disappear, but the insult was heavy on my heart nevertheless.

"Cassie, be reasonable. The other driver didn't have

insurance. It could take years to see a dime from that guy. He's an unemployed drunk, not to mention the cheap insurance you have isn't in a hurry to pay up." She sighed and took my hand. "I'm sorry, honey. I know you don't like handouts, but we'd never be able to afford this hospital bill or anything else that you may need. Let him help. We can save up to pay him back."

Turning my head, I focused back on the drapes and let out a ragged breath. Tears glossed my eyes and I bit my bottom lip to control my quivering chin.

I had nothing. I knew I couldn't afford the bill, but taking money from Logan was not the answer. After another deep, painful breath, I looked back at her, willing the tears away. Her expression was hopeful.

"I'll refinance my house. I can—"

"You will not!" Mom leaned back, scowling at me as though she'd eaten something bitter. "Your grandparents left you that house to live in and enjoy, not to mortgage and possibly lose if you can't keep up with loan payments. Your inheritance went to pay your tuition, so I know you can't have much left."

She stood up and began pacing the room. After a few laps, she stopped and approached the bed, frown lines set on her forehead. "You're out of work for at least the next six weeks, Cassie. You need Logan's help. I'm sorry, but I'm telling him you'll accept it, asking him for a new check, and depositing the money myself."

"I'm not a child anymore. I can take care of things my own way. I don't want his help."

My mother's face fell. "We'll discuss this later, but I'm going to do what is right for you, whether you like it or not. You're my baby, and I won't watch you suffer when you don't have to."

The room grew eerily silent for far too long before the door creaked opened. Luke strolled in, holding a small paper bag of food from Haven with his messenger tote slung over his shoulder, oblivious to his hostile surroundings.

"Oh…hi, Mrs. Clarke." I could tell he wasn't expecting to see her, but his cheerful smile didn't falter until he looked my way. "I can come back later if…" he started, concern creeping over his features as he stopped halfway through the doorway.

"No, it's fine," my mother replied, anxiety still etched onto her brow. "My shift starts soon, so I was just leaving."

She grabbed her purse from the chair beside me and leaned down, placing a quick kiss on my forehead. "We'll figure everything out," she whispered. "Just get some rest. I love you, honey."

"I love you, too."

Relieved she was going, I was grateful Luke showed up when he did. I needed the distraction. I couldn't stomach the idea of accepting anything from Logan; flowers were my limit. Luke shuffled out of the way as my mother passed through the door.

I noticed the smile on his face didn't quite reach his eyes. He'd visited every afternoon during his lunch break since I was moved from ICU. He would bring board games and sneak in snacks, and was the only visitor who didn't try to coddle me.

"Everything all right?"

With a shrug, I snorted. "One guess."

"Well, I brought your favorite: grilled cheese." There it was as he opened the bag: his sweet, all-teeth smile. It settled me so easily.

He waited for me to maneuver into a more comfortable position to eat, then handed me my afternoon snack.

"Not even three days and you already know my favorite sandwich. Stalker, much?"

Luke chuckled, and I couldn't help but crack a smile. He was so easy to be with—no drama, no expectations, no underlying tension.

"Are you familiar with these stalker types?" Luke raised his brows, humor in his eyes as he pulled his own grilled cheese from the bag.

My shoulders rose playfully alongside the grin on my face until I took a giant bite, closing my eyes and savoring the cheesy goodness.

"So, mind telling me why your mother left here looking like she just found out the doctors changed their minds about sending you home Friday after all?"

"You heard?"

"Yeah, Hilary made sure everyone in Harmony knew this morning after your mother called her," he explained.

"Of course she did."

Hilary had to be beyond excited. She hated seeing me there, and every visit ended with her in tears no matter how much I tried to convince her I was going to be as good as new soon enough.

Luke's lips twitched. "You know she means well."

I nodded in agreement.

"All right, so I have thirty minutes till my butt has to be back in my office chair. Your pick: Battleship or…" He pulled out a travel-sized version of the game and sat it down, reaching back into the bag with a wide, cheeky grin. "Candy Land?"

I let out my first real guttural laugh of the week, which was followed immediately by a tearful cry. My ribs rumbled in my chest, and my body dropped back against my pillows, pain slashing through me.

The chuckle grew into a nasty groan. I sucked in my bottom lip to control the scream about to burst out and fill the halls. It hurt worse than nearly anything I'd experienced before. Only one other wound claimed the most painful spot: my broken heart and fractured confidence in men.

"Sorry, you want me to get the nurse? Get you some more pain meds?"

My head shook just the slightest bit, not wanting to move

my body as the throbbing began to subside.

"You're too tough for your own good." He let out a relieved breath and ran his hand over his forehead. "Okay, let's try this again…slowly. No laughing. Battleship or…"

I sucked in my lips again, hands gripping the rails of the bed, but this time bracing myself to keep the laughter at bay. His face was so serious, which only made it harder.

"Battleship!" I whispered, biting my bottom lip to control my breathing.

"Good choice." He chuckled and cleared the tray table hovering above me to set up the game.

As he focused on placing his ships, he asked, "It was about Logan, huh?"

"What?" I looked up from the game, melted cheese stuffed in my mouth. He hadn't mentioned Logan the entire week. I honestly wondered if he even knew about him.

Luke's gaze rose from the game and locked with mine. "Hilary made it clear to Caleb and me not to mention the guy, but I saw him having lunch with your mother the other day. That's why you guys were fighting—because of him?"

I swallowed and took a sip of water. "I wasn't fighting with my mother. I just need her to understand that I can take care of myself. And I especially don't need Logan's help."

"I'm not surprised he would want to help you out. The guy's loaded, you know."

"So are you and Caleb. What's your point?"

His smile fell away for only a faint second, but I caught it. The Townsends were the wealthiest family in town—well, before Mr. Logan West strolled in, anyway.

"No, my father is rich. I make the same amount of money as any other college grad working for him. And Caleb…I've yet to figure out the story of where he disappeared to the past few years. But he definitely did well for himself."

"Good for him. I'm happy he's happy."

"My brother's certainly happy today. When I went in to get lunch earlier, Logan was there, and they were laughing about a poker game they had last night. Caleb won ten grand from him. So if Logan wants to help you, let him."

Logan met with my mother and went to a poker game all in one day? Yeah, he was really hard up with suffering for me.

"You know what?" I avowed, snatching up my last few ships and placing them strategically. "If Logan thinks he knows me at all, he's in for a big surprise. I don't need his handouts, and I'll be damn sure he gets that memo."

"Still the stubborn girl I remember." Luke smiled proudly. "Now, get ready to have your ships blown up in your pretty little face!"

"We'll see about that, Mr. Townsend."

——◆◆◆——

As we played our second round, a soft knock sounded from my door.

"Expecting company?" Luke asked, standing and walking over to open it.

I shrugged my shoulders in reply. Hilary was at school and my mom at work, and neither tended to knock, so I wondered who it could be. On instinct, I brought the blanket higher over my chest, hiding the bruises that covered half my body.

Luke opened the door, and there stood a bundled-up Oliver with a nervous smile on his face and his hand wrapped around Julia's.

"Hi," Julia said, staring straight at me, her expression clouded with apprehension.

I smiled, surprised but happy to see them.

"I better get back to work," Luke said, walking toward me. He collected the game, tossed it into his bag, then leaned down to hug me and whisper in my ear. "You have some serious explaining to do as to why I never met this girl before."

I gave a subtle nod and smiled.

Luke must've smiled at Julia as he left, because an answering grin played on her lips. Her eyes followed him, head turning just enough to watch him leave. *If it weren't for Mark, Luke and Julia would make a great couple*, I thought to myself.

A soft cough sounded and my gaze fell to Oliver, whose lip was twitched up at the side.

"Hi," he whispered, shifting his feet.

"Oliver!" I smiled so big my cheeks stung and eyes squinted. I was happy to see him, but anxious about what he must've been thinking. I knew I looked wrecked. "Come here and give me a hug."

To my surprise, he rushed over, but then stopped abruptly and stood beside me, eyes wide.

"Are you okay?" His voice cracked, and my heart melted. I wanted to cry.

"Yeah, I'm fine," I managed.

He looked curiously at the bandage on my arm, where I had a few stitches. "Do you hurt?"

I shook my head, a reassuring smile firmly in place, and gave the most believable lie I could muster. "No."

Oliver seemed convinced, as his smile broadened. "Here, I made this for you."

In his hand was a green piece of construction paper that was folded into a card. On it was a drawing of my tree house, with a bright rainbow behind it. I opened it and smiled at his large, careful handwriting: 'GET WELL SOON, CASSIE'.

"Thank you." I leaned over and pulled him into my arms for a hug.

It was great seeing him, but not if it meant he'd worry about me. With a slight intake of breath, I willed the beckoning tears from my eyes and watched him hop into the chair Luke had occupied moments earlier.

"I hope you don't mind us stopping by. Oliver refused to go to school until he was able to see you. Logan brought him home late last night."

Of course. Why would he bring his son home earlier if he had poker games to play and sympathy money to hand out? I refused to let it irk me any longer—especially during the few minutes I had with Oliver.

Looking at the young tot, I smiled. He had a way of pulling the optimistic side right out of me before I knew what was happening.

"I'm glad you came, but make sure to go to school tomorrow. Promise?" I held out my pinky, and he wrapped his around it.

"Promise."

"So, how was your time with your grandma?"

He rested back into the chair that overwhelmed his tiny frame, getting comfortable. "Great! She's fun, and I told her all about you and Scout. She wants to see you too."

I grimaced. Meeting Logan's mother was no longer on my to-do list.

"You really like flowers a lot, huh?" Oliver sniffed the bouquet closest to him.

"They were gifts. Flowers have a way of helping people feel better when they get sick."

I looked to Julia, whom I caught glancing at the door. She stood at the end of my bed quietly.

"Did they make you feel better?" Oliver asked.

I nodded, smiling, looking around the room at the dozens of vases. "Yeah, they did."

We sat quietly for a moment before he spoke again.

"Where's Scout?" he asked.

"At Hilary's. She's taking care of him for me till I can go home."

He scrunched his nose and looked down at his lap. "Oh."

"If you want to see him, I'm sure she'd bring him by."

"I wanted to watch him." He peeked up, disappointed.

"I'm not sure if your father would like that," I explained. "I'm not going to be able to really take care of him for a couple weeks, and—"

"I can ask him!" Oliver scrambled out of the chair and raced to the door before I could finish. "He's right outside."

My voice vanished, lost somewhere in my constricting throat alongside my held breath. Blood raced through my veins, leaving me paralyzed in silence.

Logan was there. Of course he was.

"Daddy!" Oliver pulled open the heavy door, struggling to keep it from closing on himself until a large, familiar hand grabbed the other side, holding it open from the hall. "Daddy, come in."

I froze, unsure of what to say or do. Logan was seconds from seeing me, and for some reason I was overly concerned that I looked like hell.

What was wrong with me? After everything he put me through, and still...I found myself attracted to just the thought of him. Maybe he'd come in and see the shreds of his check covering the floor. That lightened the heaviness filling my chest.

My hands gripped the blankets for dear life when Oliver grabbed his father's arm and nearly dragged him into the room. He seemed...different. He looked tired, and was dressed in faded blue jeans and a grey T-shirt that peeked out from his wool coat.

"Hello."

The word was entirely too soothing, and I felt walls beginning to encase my heart, protecting me and reminding me his voice was nothing more than a lie—a deceitful charm.

I sat silently. Oliver spoke up, tugging at Logan's coat.

"Can Scout stay with us? Please, Daddy!?"

Logan's eyes never strayed from mine as he answered. "Of

course, if Cassandra doesn't mind."

My head bobbed twice. That was all I had, and luckily it was enough. Oliver squealed, thanking both his father and me until Julia wrapped her hand in his and leaned down to whisper in his ear. It took all my effort to keep my eyes focused on Oliver, but by the uncomfortable tingling of my skin, I knew Logan was still watching me intently.

"Okay," Oliver answered Julia. He smiled at me. "I have to go so Daddy can talk."

Julia half chuckled, and I had a feeling he wasn't supposed to say that part.

"But you can talk to me, too," he added.

Before I could agree with him and tell him how much I wanted to talk only to him, Julia chimed in. "Why don't we go see if they have Jell-O in the cafeteria?"

Oliver's big blue eyes brightened. He looked at me and smiled. "Do you like red Jell-O?"

"It's my favorite."

"Mine too! I can bring you one."

"Sounds great."

Julia began to lead him from the room when he stopped and looked back at Logan. "Just tell her you're sorry, Daddy."

Chapter Two

STRENGTH

"You got the flowers, I see."

That was it? His first words to me after a shallow 'hello' were a frivolous observation about the flowers? How could he stand there and talk about flowers?

I met his gaze and gave a drawn out, "Mm-hmm." No way was he getting a 'thank you' out of me.

'Awkward' was the only word to describe the tension building between us the longer he stood there. He finally shifted his gaze, which flickered from the flowers, went once around the room, and landed on the floor beside my bed.

Confused, I watched the tormented look soften his face as the corners of his mouth curled up. He bent down, picking up a piece of the destroyed check.

Pride filled me. *That's right—I'm not one to be bought.*

"I see you'll be needing cash next time." His voice was sweet and almost humorous, nearly breaking my resolve to stay cool and urging me to act on impulse by chucking the vase of flowers beside me straight at him.

Grinding my back teeth, I narrowed my eyes. "Go for it, and you'll have some expensive confetti for your next orgy," I hissed. I hadn't realized exactly how pissed I was until I'd seen that damn grin on his gorgeous, unshaven face.

He held firm, unaffected. "Never been to an orgy. Not my

scene." He gave a tight-lipped, easy smile, as though we were enjoying a casual conversation.

"Julia could have brought Oliver herself, so why are you here?"

His gaze fell to my chest when I sat up further, a frown marring his once-calm expression. I tugged at my blankets, pulling them higher to hide the deep bruises peeking out.

He cleared his throat, soft and remorseful eyes rising back to mine. "A few reasons—one being my son insisted I come."

He's a good father, yet that doesn't change a thing, I told myself.

"However, it all comes down to the fact that I couldn't stay away any longer. I promise, I tried. These past days have been pure hell, my nights restless with nightmares tormenting me."

I knew all about nightmares. He got no sympathy from me.

"As hard as I tried to give you space and keep myself from stepping foot in this damn hospital, I can't do it any longer. I'm going mad not being near you, not knowing that you're really okay. That you're safe."

I had no response. His words cut through me, leaving me further muddled. Truthfully, I just couldn't deal with the emotions his words awoke inside me. Instead, I rolled my head to the side, facing the window, ignoring his movements around the room.

"You can go," I said finally, closing my eyes so tight that bright-yellow spots were all I could see beneath the lids.

"No, I think I'll stay a while. Oliver is coming back up with your Jell-O, so I'll wait here till then."

"Suit yourself."

Please leave, please leave, please leave. The ache from his presence was too much to bear. My breathing grew more ragged with each passing second as anger stewed within.

"Cassandra, I—" I heard him sigh, then felt the bed dip.

He not sitting on my bed!

I looked back and pushed him off. His face was stunned,

almost hurt. *Good!*

"Get the hell out, Logan! You've won, all right!?" He stood there, staring at me. "You proved I was just like every other girl you meet, ready to hand herself over for you to devour. Now LEAVE. ME. ALONE!" I yelled. My head rolled back to the side and I buried my face in the pillow, too numb to cry and praying he'd just leave.

I maneuvered my body to lie on my side, my injured leg still flat on the bed and my back to him. To my relief, he didn't speak again, but I could feel him inches behind me, my body soaring to life when his warm hand settled on the back of my neck.

Something inside me broke. His touch was so tender, so soothing; it devastated me that my body still reacted to it. I couldn't think, couldn't breathe. My throat constricted, heart racing as sobs bubbled inside me. I sucked in a deep breath, cringing at the agony my chest endured. Hot, thick tears sprung to my eyes, but I fought to hold control—fought to keep them from pouring out.

I couldn't allow him to see the real damage he did under the surface, beneath my bruised and battered body: the gaping hole he left in my heart.

Logan's fingers drifted down my spine and back up again, attempting to soothe me further. But the problem was that it was him causing the need to be soothed. His fingers slid down again over the fabric of my gown, enraging me, reminding me of the harsh reality of what I was to him.

Then, as his fingers landed at the small of my back, they slid back up, soothing the pain he'd just inflicted. Again and again. Pain and comfort. Agony, then serenity. My head was spinning.

"Cassandra, I never meant to hurt you."

With a swipe of my hand across my nose, I rolled back and held up my hand, shushing him, struggling to pull myself together just as the urge to urinate hit hard. An idea popped in that I felt was just the thing to get him to leave me in peace. I couldn't hear his voice any longer. I didn't want to hear any of his excuses.

With focused determination, I searched the blanket for the buzzer.

Logan grabbed my hand. "What are you looking for?"

I yanked it away, narrowing my eyes at him. "None of your business."

Once the buzzer was in my hand, I pressed the button. Instantly, a nurse at the desk answered. "How can I help you?"

"Yes, I need to use the restroom."

"A nurse will be right in to help."

Of course, Logan didn't get the memo that now was a great time for him to give me some privacy. Instead, he cocked his head to the side with a resolute stare and then, to my shock and horror, shoved one hand gently under my back and the other under my knees, lifting me from the bed.

"Put me down!" I shrieked in a panic.

He didn't listen, and I was too sore to get away. The blanket began to fall but I held it firmly, not ready for him to see the giant bandage covering my thigh, even though he might have felt it with his arms wrapped under me. As I held tightly to his neck with one hand, something yanked at my other hand holding the blanket, tugging at the tape-covered skin.

"IV!" I spit out.

He stopped immediately and grabbed the IV stand, rolling it beside us as he carried me to the restroom and kicked open the door.

My grip around his neck tightened as he bent down, lifted the lid, and rested me on the toilet. I wanted to die. My face burned, and I could only imagine the deep shade of red covering it. I maneuvered the blanket to cover my lap fully and sat there staring at him, wide-eyed.

Did that really just happen?

"I'll wait outside the door." He said it so calmly I was left speechless.

As my brain began to spark back to life, fury piqued inside me. How was I expected to pee with Logan right outside a door I realized very quickly was left a crack open?

Hell no!

"Close the door!" I yelled.

"Just pee."

"Not until you close the door!"

"What if you fall and I can't hear you?"

Was he really justifying leaving the door open enough to listen while I used the restroom?

"Shut the damn door, Logan, or I swear to God—"

"Is everything all right in here?" I heard Marilyn, the day nurse, ask, and relief flooded me. She was the sweetest but toughest nurse I had—always the one to force me out of bed to walk up and down the hall, with her at my side, to keep the muscles in my legs strong.

"Yes, can you please shut the door for me?"

The next thing I knew, the door was closed, and I heard the muffled voices of a conversation between Logan and the middle-aged redhead. The woman was ruthless; she would lay into him. I smiled at the image.

Quickly, I was able to focus on the task at hand. I'd never peed so fast in my life. After I finished my business, I heard the voices quiet. I struggled to lean forward enough to reach the sink and wash my hands in record time, then called for Marilyn.

"You ready?" she asked and, when I gave a quick affirmative, the door opened to reveal her laughing at something Logan was saying, her hand on his shoulder. He looked me over, as if I might've gotten hurt during the sixty seconds I'd been in there.

In two long strides, he was in front of me, smiling.

"Feel better?"

I rolled my eyes, snubbing him. I'd hoped Marilyn would be there to help me up, but Logan scooped me back into his arms. His scent was all I could focus on, committed to not making a scene. A part of me missed his natural scent: so masculine and clean. So Logan.

"It's safer if she walks," Marilyn complained, but he continued until he was beside my bed, placing me back down gently.

"Was that really necessary?" I sneered, not bothering to look his way as I smoothed the blanket back out over my legs. I swatted his hand away when he tried to help.

Marilyn laughed, earning her a sneer too, which she only shrugged at. "Well, I'll leave you two alone," she said, and left the room.

Back in place, I was ready for sleep to end my mortifying torture of the day's events—even if that meant enduring another nightmare.

I looked up at him. "Seriously, you can go. I'm sure Oliver and Julia will be back any minute, and I don't plan on having anything else humiliating for you to witness before then." I focused my gaze on the opposite wall, waiting for some wisecrack on his part.

Instead, his hand caught my chin, pulling my attention back to him very slowly. The moment my eyes met his, he released my face. I sat frozen from the agony written over his expression.

"I'm not leaving until you listen to me—until you understand that I'm never going to walk away from you again." His hand came back, his pointer finger running over my cheek briefly, but it only added to the agony on his features. His fingers withdrew as though they'd been burnt.

"I fucked up, Cassandra. I hate myself for it and I can't take it back, but I will spend every day and every night proving I can be the man you need me to be."

His eyes were so soft, voice so sincere, but I couldn't let it get through my defenses. I couldn't go there again. The pain was too much. He didn't really want me—it was only guilt he felt.

"Logan, I—"

He silenced me with a single tear that lingered in his clouded blue eyes before falling to his cheek. His eyes closed for a moment then opened, begging me to hear him out.

"Don't. Don't tell me no, or that it's too late. I'm already aware of that, but I won't give up. I just need you to know…I'm never letting you walk away from me again."

"I got Jell-Os and found blueberry muffins!"

I swallowed the fresh tears brewing and mammoth emotions buzzing in my gut, and smiled at Oliver walking in as though everything was always rainbows and sunshine. I wished it were so easy.

"Thanks," I said, pulling on a forced smile.

Logan backed away so Oliver could hand me the small plate and plastic spoon.

"Bet it's not as yummy as yours, d'ough."

I smiled. No matter how much anger I held for his father, Oliver was as sweet a child as you could find.

"We should get going. Cassandra looks tired," Julia said, sensing the tension in the room. I offered her a grateful but uncomfortable smile.

"I'll come see you when I get home, and I'll have Hilary bring Scout by tonight for you," I told Oliver.

He stretched up on his tiptoes and rested his head over my chest. My arms held him in place for a pause, relishing the comfort he exuded. I brushed a hand through his mop of blond curls. "Make sure Scout gets lots of love," I whispered.

He looked up and nodded. "I will. Promise."

He was such a good kid. Luck was definitely on my side when fate placed him in the house beside me. If only I could say the same for his father.

Logan walked back to my bed, and my posture stiffened

when he leaned down. "I'll be back tonight with dinner, and we'll finish talking," he murmured. "Till then, sleep well." His lips brushed over my cheek, lighting my soul on fire in spite of myself.

Closing my eyes, I sunk into the stiff mattress. *Sleep is exactly what I need right now.*

Chapter Three

CONTROL

A man of his word, Logan entered the room just past six that evening carrying a plate of food, but not from the cafeteria. As he drew closer, a relaxed look settling over his face, I noticed the plate held my favorite childhood meal: two chili dogs, with waffle fries and orange slices on the side. My mother had to have been to blame for his knowledge of it, and I wondered what other little tidbits of information she'd shared.

"Hope you're hungry," he commented, setting the plate on the tray beside me then wheeling it closer to rest in front of me, hovering over my lap.

"Considering the nurses never delivered my dinner, which I'm sure you had something to do with, yes, I am."

The chili dogs smelled delicious. My mouth salivated, and I couldn't help but snatch a fry. Oh, yeah—he was good.

I swallowed and looked up at him questioningly. "So what else did my mother tell you about her only daughter? The name of my childhood crush? Or perhaps the date of my first period?"

Stuffing my mouth full of fries, I hoped to disgust him as much as he'd disgusted me that fateful night. I refused to let him know how wonderful the meal was. Why couldn't he just drop off the food and leave, letting a girl eat in peace?

"No, but I can always give her another call." He raised his brows and pulled out his phone, earning him a deserved scowl as

I sunk my teeth into a juicy hotdog.

God, was it good. *Damn it.*

"Did you bring anything for yourself, or are you planning on watching me eat all this alone? 'Cause I'm not sharing."

His face lit up, amused at my hard tone. "I could watch you eat every day, sweetheart," he said with a smile, sitting in the chair beside my bed.

There it was: a name that once completed me, but now caused me to spit the rest of my hotdog into the cloth napkin. My appetite was gone. I wasn't his, and I never would be.

"Something wrong with it?" He watched with a mystified stare as I stuffed the napkin under the rim of the plate.

"No, but something is very wrong with you sitting here as though it's the most normal thing for you to do after I offered myself up on a silver platter and you laughed in my face."

His carefree manner was replaced with a distraught frown. "Cassandra, I never laughed—"

"Don't try to make me feel better, Logan. I made a fool of myself, and you know it! The truth is out there, and you can't take that back." I pushed the tray forward, needing more space to think, to breathe, before angling my head to the side, scowling. "You wanted to fuck me! If Natasha hadn't shown up that night, you would have, proving I was just like every other girl."

"Please, you have to—"

"No! I don't have to do anything. I don't owe you a damn thing, so you need to leave. Get the hell out of my room, and out of my life! Go enjoy another game of poker with Caleb!"

"I'm not going. And as far as that game of poker I played the other night, I don't know who told you about it or what they said, but I was there trying clear my head so I could think straight. I was miserable the entire night thinking about you, here, stuck in a damn bed!"

"I don't care!"

"Obviously you do, or you wouldn't bring it up. You think I'd rather play poker, a game I lost ten grand at that night because my head was focused on you, instead of being here?"

I didn't say a word.

"I'm staying. That's final!"

Who the hell did he think he was? With a sigh, I decided the best way to get him out of my life was to stop engaging him.

"Fine, then stay, but don't expect me to speak to you or even acknowledge you, for that matter."

I turned away and closed my eyes. I wasn't going to let him stroll back into my life. I wasn't going to be that girl ever again.

And so it began. Logan remained sitting beside me, quiet as ever, until visiting hours ended. Then he gave a soft but rueful goodbye before leaving me alone to wallow.

—◆◆—

The next morning, Logan arrived as though I was expecting him. I didn't believe he was really there to stay until he sat solemnly on the chair beside me for the next few hours without a word. He returned again later that evening with dinner.

"Still holding onto the silent treatment, huh?" he asked, setting the plate of food in front of me.

I didn't say a word. Silence was better than talking, because talking would begin a conversation that would lead nowhere good. The man was gorgeous and here with me, trying, but it didn't matter. My anger—not just at him, but at myself for being so weak—was deeper than he could imagine.

Logan slid off his coat, dropped it onto a small chair across the room, and walked back over. I wondered if he'd went to the paper to work after he'd left that morning, but doubted it, due to the dark blue jeans and long-sleeved grey Henley he wore. It hugged his arms and chest and looked a size too small, which was exactly what any hot-blooded woman hoped for.

The man looked good. *Too* good.

With a sigh, my eyes slammed shut and I lowered my head, shaking it. *Not good. Not beautiful, not sweet, and definitely not kind.* He was none of those things I'd once thought—at least, not to me he wasn't. I'd tried, put myself out there, ready to jump in, but he'd made things clear with the condom he'd thrown in my face. I saw exactly where I stood with him; looks had no influence anymore. Gorgeous or not, the man would eventually destroy me—I felt it deep down in my gut.

I stabbed a piece of meat and shoved it into my mouth as Logan sat in his usual spot in the chair beside my bed. I ate in silence, and was finishing off my bowl of fruit when the door cracked open and the male nurse on shift smiled.

"Sorry it's taking so long. It's been crazy around here with a few of the other nurses out with the flu. When you're done eating, buzz the desk and we'll get you showered."

I nodded, smiling as I chewed with a closed mouth. I watched his head disappear and the door close.

Just as I pierced another piece of melon, Logan was out of his seat, staring at the door. *What the hell is he doing now?*

"That's your nurse?" he asked, turning back and staring at me with a scowl burrowing between his brows.

"Yeah," I scoffed, shoving the melon into my mouth, irritated at his critical tone. "Got a problem with male nurses?"

Stalking toward the bed, he towered over me with a hard expression. "No, what I have a problem with is that guy thinking he's going to help you shower."

I rolled my eyes. *Is he serious right now?*

"Why? I don't have a problem with it," I replied, and there was a flash of not just anger in his darkening eyes, but something else, something deeper—hurt—and I couldn't stop myself from driving the stake in further. "Actually, he's kind of hot." I shrugged my shoulders, pushed the tray holding my plate away, and reached for the buzzer.

Logan's hand covered mine in the same instant and ripped the buzzer away.

"You're a horrible liar, Cassandra." His hand held mine and my heart raced, legs trembling.

Why did I still feel it—still react to him? I hated it, and my anger fueled the strength to tug my hand free. Logan stood unaffected.

"Using something as petty as jealousy to hurt me won't change a thing," Logan said. "If that's what you need to do, then I welcome it; we both know I deserve your worst." He walked around the bed and unplugged my IV stand. "But I won't allow another man to help you bathe."

"What are you doing?" I sat up further, clutching the blanket to my chest.

"Getting you your shower before that pervert comes back and I get myself arrested."

"What!?"

He was not serious. First, it was the bathroom so I could pee, now a shower? *Hell no. Not happening.* "He's a nurse, not a perv, you asshole! If anyone's a pervert, it's you!"

I could've sworn I caught a glimpse of an upturn at the corner of his lips, but it smoothed as quickly as it'd peeked out.

"Possibly. However, we're not talking about me right now, Cassandra. This isn't up for debate—if anyone's going to help you, it's going to be me."

My brows drew together. Did he just admit he was a pervert? That was a bit of information to store away and dissect at a later time, but not right now—not with Logan walking over to the bathroom. A second after he went in, I could hear the spray of the shower.

I watched with a tense posture and narrowed eyes as he came back out. He rolled his sleeves up, then removed his watch, placing it on top of his coat.

When he turned to face me, it took everything inside me

not to melt. I needed to work on that. I squared my shoulders and drew from the image of him in that alley on New Year's to restore my standing. Worked like an angry charm.

"Logan, you're not helping me shower!"

"We'll see. Now, do you need me to carry you in?"

Was I being punished? I mean, come on! The last thing I needed was for him to see how battered and bruised I was.

"Cassandra, we both know how much I enjoy carrying you."

At his first step toward me, I panicked, my stomach turning violently as I grabbed the buzzer and pressed the button hard again and again. There was no reply from the nurse, but to my relief, he was in the door a second later.

"You all right? Ready to get cleaned up?" As the nurse—Jeffery, his badge said—approached my bed, his eyes darted between Logan and me, then to the bathroom that was beginning to fog up. I honestly wasn't too keen on a male nurse helping me shower, but I was able enough to bathe myself. I just needed a little help getting in and out.

"Yes, I'm ready. This guy was just leaving," I said, nodding at Logan.

"No, I wasn't," Logan snapped, stalking back to my bed and standing between it and Jeffery. "I can help her in the shower myself. You can go."

With a glance at both of us again, Jeffery smiled. "I understand. Just make sure she sits on the chair in there and holds the shower sprayer to wash. I'll come in when you're ready to apply a fresh bandage. We don't want those stitches to get infected." My jaw dropped as I watched Jeffery smile once more over at me, then turn to leave.

"Wait! No—Logan, you need to go. If I miss out on a shower because of you, there will be hell to pay!"

"I'm sorry," Jeffery's eyelids lowered in confusion. "I just assumed you two were…"

"Nothing but unfriendly neighbors? Yeah, that's us, and he was just leaving."

"Like hell I was," Logan said, still glaring at the man who stood at least six inches shorter than him.

"Look, I wasn't planning on bathing her myself, sir. I just need to be here if she needs any assistance. But if it would make you more comfortable, I can send in a female nurse. It will be another hour or so, but it won't be a problem."

"That's not necessary," I blurted out, aching to get my first real shower. Sponge baths had not done the trick the past couple days.

"Yes, it is." Logan craned his neck, and with a serious and almost intimidating stare, he added, "Either me or a female nurse is getting you clean tonight—your choice—but I won't be leaving till it's done."

"Screw you, Logan. I don't take orders!" I spit, pushing myself up. "Can you help me?" I , tilting my head to look past Logan's powerful frame to Jeffery.

"Um…yeah, of course."

Great, now Logan had the poor guy scared. It didn't matter—I would prove he couldn't tell me what to do. I wasn't his girlfriend. I winced at the thought.

"You take another step toward her and it will be your last." Logan's threat was menacingly deep.

"Sir, Cassandra's my patient. If you stand in the way of her care, I will be forced to call security."

Go Jeffery! I was liking that guy more and more. Too bad he looked like one of Santa's elves with his tiny frame, short stature, and pointed ears.

"Logan, I'm showering. End of discussion."

He turned to face me fully, jaw clenched tight, hands balled at his sides so tightly the knuckles whitened. Slowly, he appraised my set, assertive stance. I wasn't backing down.

"Yes, it is," he replied, eerily calm.

Something in the way he spoke the words shot an icy shiver up my spine. Then, to my complete shock, Logan stepped out of the way and allowed Jeffery to wrap my robe around my back and help me to the bathroom. I was thankful it covered the laceration on my thigh and most of my bruises.

Once inside, Jeffery watched as I sat on the toilet lid, then kneeled down to place a waterproof bandage over my stitches for extra protection.

"If you need anything, I'll be right outside the door. After you get undressed, be careful getting in the shower, and remember: sit on the shower seat. Don't try to stand in there. You might fall." I nodded, and he closed the door.

Alone at last—at least, aside from the mumbling of voices not quite audible through the door. I chose to ignore them and slipped off my robe, gown, and white cotton panties. I stepped slowly into the warm shower and sat on the cool metal seat.

The shower sprayer detached and I held it in one hand while the other lathered soap over my abused body.

I had to admit that by the time my hair was washed and body clean, I was exhausted. The only issue that bugged me was my back, which was in need of a good scrub from all the lying down I'd been doing over the last couple days. The sponge baths hadn't seemed to be enough, and it was the one place on my body that still felt oily and grimy.

With a grunt from the stab in my chest, I reached out and grabbed the towel, wrapping it around my front. After I was covered as much as possible, I turned around to call Jeffery in and see if he could help. It was his job, right? I had no clue, but I was desperate. Still, I wasn't going to show him more than necessary; he'd only see my back and a bit of my ass. It would be worth it to feel clean again.

Leaning back, I stretched my arm through the shower curtain and knocked on the door.

"Can you help me a moment, Jeffery?" I yelled.

Straightening myself back on the seat, it hit me: would Logan intervene yet again? Would he be that pigheaded? I should've told Jeffery to throw him out, but I didn't have it in me. I just wanted the sweat washed from my back—was that too much to ask?

I closed my eyes and begged for a little luck. *Please don't let Logan come in, please don't let Logan come in, please don't let Logan come—.*

The door opened, and when I peered over my shoulder, there he was—blocking the door.

"Get out!" I screamed, closing the curtain back all the way.

Jeffery was there on the other side of Logan, yet I couldn't see him. I could only hear him explaining how he was going to call security. Logan stood firm, his hands on each side of the door frame, back to me.

Was this a joke?

"What do you need?" Logan asked, craning his neck back.

What do I need? Ha, where to start that list? Aside from you getting out of my room and leaving me to finish putting myself together?

I was tired and ready for bed, so with a loud, drawn-out sigh expressing my annoyance, I conceded and held the washcloth out, keeping my back to him and eyes glued on the tiled wall ahead of me.

"Sir, security is on their way up," I heard Jeffery tell him.

My shoulders slumped forward.

"That's not necessary, but thank you. All right Logan, you want to help? Be my guest!"

Logan shut the door, grumbling something under his breath to Jeffery.

"I need help washing my back." I glanced over my shoulder with narrowed, threatening eyes. "If one single finger strays, I swear it will be gone!"

A single soft chuckle caught in his throat, and then I felt him move forward. His breath was on my skin, followed by the warm, soapy washcloth.

"Run the water down your back," he said, his voice strained.

Was I affecting him? I highly doubted it. He'd seen more naked backs than most men I knew.

I held the sprayer up over my shoulder and pulled my hair out of the way. Logan started at my neck, his fingers kneading the cloth against my skin, wiping away more than just grime. I closed my eyes and relaxed into the gentle feeling of the cloth over my tender back as he moved over my shoulder blades, taking his time not to miss a single spot.

"Does it hurt?" he asked after a few moments of silence.

"No."

It wasn't a lie—it really didn't. I'd caught a little glimpse in the mirror the day before of the superficial scratches across my back from the impact of the pavement, but there was little pain. Although that could've had something to do with the painkillers I was on, the more I thought about it.

The cloth cleaned the base of my back, and I could've sworn I heard him release a ragged breath.

"Cassandra—"

"Don't."

Once the cloth was gone, Logan leaned over and turned the water off, then wrapped my robe around me. He didn't speak a word and neither did I, but it didn't matter. I was hurt and angry, and all I wanted to do was heal my body before my heart.

We needed the silence; without it, he'd reel me back in. I knew that now. There was no doubt that my body was still attracted to him. I'd stand no chance, and that wasn't an option.

I swore right then as I stood from the shower seat, looking over at him, that I wouldn't let him charm me again. My heart was off limits, and it was time to prove that I was strong enough to put myself back together.

Logan left the room, and I dressed in a clean gown and

fresh panties from my small suitcase near the counter.

Logan was there to help me back to bed when I opened the door, dragging the IV pole behind me. Jeffery was standing in the doorway, and I wondered what Logan had said to him to put that look on his face.

I fixed a reassuring smile on my lips and watched him relax visibly.

"I'll leave you alone now, but if you need anything at all, just buzz," he said before leaving.

"Thank you," I said, slightly miffed he'd allowed Logan to help me in the bathroom.

Once I was tucked back into bed, Logan handed me a glass of ice water as though he could read my mind—my throat was parched. I sipped while he sat back in his chair, where he remained until the end of visiting hours. I didn't speak to him again, making it clear he was unwanted.

I hoped he'd leave me in peace and spare me the agony of enduring his beautiful eyes on me any longer. However, like before, he remained staring down at me thoughtfully the entire time until the nurse entered and informed him visiting hours were over.

"I'll see you in the morning, Cassandra," he said, standing and walking to claim his coat. "Sleep well."

"There's no reason to come back. I'm done, Logan. You can't change how I feel."

He slipped his watch back on and unrolled his sleeves before pulling on his coat.

"Good night."

That was all he said as he left the room, leaving me alone with my thoughts and resolute commitment to keep myself as guarded a possible to protect myself from him, no matter what I had to do. I wouldn't be that girl again.

The next morning, Logan was back by the time breakfast was served. He removed the cafeteria tray I'd been picking at and replaced it with a covered plate. He lifted the lid, revealing a beautiful omelet with all the fixings. Ignoring him, I dug in. It tasted as good as it looked.

Concentrating on the food, I smiled when I heard Logan leave the room. Was he really giving in—taking the hint that he was wasting his time? If so, then why would he show up to begin with? I held little hope.

As I assumed, he hadn't taken the hint. He was back less than a minute later, with a file box in his hands.

My brows knit together as he sat in the chair beside me and opened the lid. I watched, too curious to look away, when he set the box and lid on the floor and pulled out a stack of catalogs.

Was he really going to do some shopping here? I swallowed another bite, controlling the flurry of annoyance growing when he held up a Pottery Barn catalog and red marker, smiling.

"You don't have to talk to me, but I thought you might want to fight off some of your boredom by helping me finish the details of Julia's new place."

Julia's house—the house I bet him she would love and, if she did, he'd be my slave for a weekend. I grimaced at the thought of me being indebted to him.

"I was hoping to have it furnished by spring break and do the big reveal to her then," he continued, setting the items at my side on the bed when I made no move to take them from his hands. "She still doesn't know, and I'm sure you'll want to make it look perfect...unless you're calling off the bet?"

I wanted to say, "Yes—the bet is off, and you're crazy," and scream at him to get out of my room. But instead, I swallowed the bite of egg in my mouth and nodded. "A bet's a

35

bet."

After breakfast, I scoured the catalogs diligently, circling the most lavish, expensive items I found—ones I knew she'd love, but would impact Logan's bank account the most. The Restoration Hardware catalog was just the ticket for that.

It was in his hands, and I watched as he sat back in the chair, leg rested over his knee, flipping through pages. He circled something, then dog-eared a page. My attention was piqued—he'd been going through the same book for over an hour, and only pulled the marker from his ear a total of five times to note something he liked.

Curious, I dropped the catalog in my hand and snatched the one from his. The whole picture of him sitting there browsing for furniture was ridiculous, but still he sat there most of the morning. The page he'd been on had a bright-green circle around a beautiful leather sofa with silver-stud detail. The piece was gorgeous, but the fact that he'd picked it left me unsettled. With a quick hand, I pulled the cap of my marker free with my teeth, letting it protrude from my lips as I drew a giant X over his circle.

"And what's wrong with the sofa?" he asked, slightly miffed. He must've really liked it, which further pushed me to veto it.

"Too masculine."

He eyed me skeptically as I flipped through, starting over from page one until I landed on another item he'd circled: a stunning blue Moroccan area rug. I honestly would've chosen it, as well. With a shrewd smile in his direction, I crossed out the item and moved to the next page.

One after another, I crossed out his items and circled things I liked better. If I wanted to win the bet—and I did—I needed the house to be perfect: feminine and homey. I had it in the bag, especially since Logan had moved on from furniture catalogs to paint chips.

Before I could snatch the array of colors from his grip, he moved his hand back, shaking his head with a soft chuckle.

"Not so fast. You may be taking over decorating the place, but the color scheme is all mine. I'm not giving you the entire upper hand here."

My brows rose suggestively, and I feigned an exaggerated pout. "Oh, and here I thought you'd let a girl win. You know, so you could be my little slave for a couple days. All those possibilities..."

He was visibly affected by my seductive tone, but it didn't take long for his open mouth to shut into a boyish smirk. He leaned forward, handing over the color palette. "Do your worst, sweetheart," he whispered. "I'm already at your will."

I rolled my eyes in response. "On second thought, you can pick the paint. I'm confident enough without it to win this hands down."

He only grinned, watching me as I resumed my circling of knickknacks for the bookshelves I chose. Yeah, I was buying everything Julia would need and more.

———◆◆◆———

After lunch, my head began to throb, and I knew what that meant. I looked to the clock on the wall: after one. It was time for my daily exercise—the worst part of the day. I loved to work out, to run and stretch, but this was different—painful.

I closed my eyes and yawned to feign exhaustion, hoping he'd take the hint and leave me to rest so he wouldn't be around when Marilyn came to collect me.

It didn't work.

"Feel free to rest. I'm going to step out to call my assistant to come collect everything that needs to be ordered, then I'll be back." He stood and switched out the light.

Alone at last I smiled to myself as he walked to the door

just as Marilyn entered. *So close.*

"You know what time it is, Miss Cassandra." Marilyn's voice was soft and sweet but had an undertone of authority, and I'd seen it at work. No point in fighting the woman.

"You can go, Logan," I said, noticing him lingering at the doorway. *Please go.*

Marilyn was beside my bed in seconds, pulling back the blankets. I held them tightly, earning me a dubious look from the woman. I wasn't ready for Logan to see all my wounds.

"You have to do at least one lap, Cassandra. We can't have that leg stiffening up on you."

"I said go, Logan!" I didn't mean to yell as loudly as I did, but panic was setting in as she pulled the blanket from my grasp.

Logan stepped closer to me. I yanked on my gown to help cover the bandage, but I could tell by his stricken face that he saw.

"I think I'll stay," he said softly, now standing next to Marilyn with a frown.

Of course he would.

With a short breath, careful not to awaken the sleeping beast in my ribs, I shuffled both legs off the side of the bed. The bandage covered most of my thigh, and thankfully so did the hideous gown.

I sat there as Marilyn slid on the white robe to cover my backside and helped me to my feet. It took a moment to let my body stretch, willing myself to walk down the hall and back with no help. Marilyn was always there for support, but today I wanted to prove that I didn't need it. I was just fine, and ready to leave the hospital in the morning.

The moment I took my first step, I knew I was in trouble. My leg gave in and my knees wobbled, but I was able to catch myself on the railing of the bed. Not that I needed it—Logan's supportive arm was there, holding me up.

"I'm here. Let me help."

"It looks like I'm not needed today," Marilyn said with a smile, oblivious to the angry frown on my lips. "She needs to walk to the elevator and back on her own. Stay with her, though." And with that, she was gone.

"You ready?" he asked kindly.

"I guess." No way was I ready for him to see me in need of help. "You can let go now. You heard the woman: I need to do it on my own."

The warmth of his grip released my waist and I was standing freely, ready to get the walk over with.

To my complete satisfaction, I made it to the elevator without missing a beat—no stumbles or weaknesses—and with Logan behind me out of sight, I was able to truly enjoy the accomplishment. The doctors were right: my leg was healing. I finally believed them.

I turned to walk back, grinning to myself.

"I'm so sorry. You shouldn't be going through this." Logan looked at me, and it was then I noticed the forlorn expression from the previous day was back.

"Don't!" I snapped. "I just walked down a hall that I struggled with all week and still have the strength to walk back. You don't get to ruin that for me. You don't get to make me feel bad about the situation." I ambled on past him.

Damn it. I was in such a better place, and he squashed it. The walk back was eerily silent as I let the irritation pick at me.

When I landed back in bed, that nap sounded better than ever. I rolled to my side and closed my eyes.

"Goodbye, Logan."

I waited for him to reply—to say a thoughtful goodbye, or that he wasn't leaving. Instead, I heard him sit, and then he began to read aloud.

My eyes opened wide. He was reading to me—and not just any book, but the first classic novel I read as a young teen. Another tidbit my mother must've told him.

With a nearly silent sigh, I allowed my eyes to drift closed as Elizabeth Bennet prepared with her sisters for the dance that would lead her to making the acquaintance of Mr. Darcy.

The hum of Logan's sweet voice lulled me into my slumber, where he no longer awaited me in the alley. Rather, I found myself at home, standing in my backyard, watching Oliver chase Scout. But we weren't alone—Logan was there as well. Far off in the distance, the trees surrounding him stood miles away, yet his searing gaze was concentrated on me, searching my soul for answers I couldn't give.

Chapter Four

SCARS

"Rise and shine, sleepy head!"

My eyes fluttered open to meet the marvelous grin covering Hilary's cheerful face.

"Come on, the doctor's signing the papers for your release as we speak. Let's get you the hell out of this place."

I sat up, wiping the sleep from my eyes. Home, finally. A slow smile tugging on my lips lifted my spirits as her words settled over me.

"That's my girl. Now go get dressed." Hilary held out a pile of clothes and watched as I slipped my feet off the side of the bed but didn't make a move to stand.

"Can you just shut the curtain? I'll change here." I motioned my hand to the yellow drape behind her.

Hilary turned and rustled it closed without a word. After she helped me shuffle into a white shirt and pink sweats, I was feeling more eager than ever to get out of there.

———◆———

"Remember to continue taking the medication as needed for pain, and make sure you schedule an appointment next week to check your stitches. We want to make sure that leg keeps healing properly."

The doctor whom I'd seen since childhood stood across the room and rambled on and on as I sat at the edge of the bed, zoning out. Anxiety set my nerves on the fritz, my hands smoothing small circles over the mattress I'd be leaving for good as soon as he was done talking.

Hilary squatted in front of me and helped me slide on my comfy suede boots, though my attention was neither on her nor the doctor, but Logan. He'd come in sometime during my dressing, and was standing near the door, jotting down endless notes on a small black leather pad as the doctor listed off instructions.

He wasn't seriously going to visit me at home as much as he did here...was he?

Hilary smacked the bottom of my shoe when it was on and stood, a smile lighting her face when she turned to Logan, watching him asking the doctor a question. Of course he was.

It was his car that awaited me outside the hospital, since my mom was stuck with a shift she couldn't switch. After enough complaining, I managed to win a ride with Hilary.

I didn't say a word when he made it to my house before us. He stood in the driveway, waiting for her car to stop.

After opening the passenger-side door, he leaned down, encircling his arm around my waist, and helped me inside the house.

"It has to feel good to be home. I mean, we can finally see each other past seven," Hilary said with a laugh.

Visiting hours were no friend of hers. She'd tried to sneak in a couple times, but the nurses weren't having it. Not surprisingly, Logan was there after visiting hours, meeting nothing but giggles and blushing from the previously grouchy nurses once he explained why it was important he stayed. I was a lucky girl, they said. If only they knew.

Before I could respond, Logan reappeared from his jaunt

around the house, during which he'd surveyed every room for trip hazards and potential serial killers lurking in closets. He stood in the doorway to the living room, staring at me as I rested on the couch with a thin quilt covering my lap.

"Everything looks good in here, sweet—" He cut himself off.

Smart man. I pursed my lips, narrowing my eyes at the television, and he knew why. I'd made it clear I was not his sweetheart, and he was not to call me so.

Not bothering to look his way, I replied, "Of course it does. Now you can leave and not bother coming back."

"Cassandra!" Hilary gaped at me, appalled at my lack of appreciation.

Logan, however, seemed to have taken the jab in stride. "Right, well I'll bring dinner by tonight. Let her get some rest. She needs it," he said to Hilary, completely unaffected by my venomous tone.

I said nothing, expecting no less from him, since it was becoming our thing lately for him to hound me to no end. Being home reminded me of the last time I was there, dancing around, eager to wear my new party dress and confess my feelings to the man I was certain would be the last one I kissed on New Year's.

My nose scrunched. The image left a sour taste in my mouth.

Ignoring Hilary's pout, I picked up the remote and began flipping through the channels. Hilary, on the other hand, pushed off the couch with an exaggerated huff and walked Logan to the door, where they began talking in quiet voices.

"Thanks again," she said as he stepped outside, finally leaving us alone. The moment she shut the door and turned back to me, I knew I was in for a lecture.

"Look, I didn't want to press you in the hospital, but what the hell happened between you two?" She walked back to the armchair across from me.

I said nothing, eyes on the flickering screen.

"He just wants to help," she added, her voice raising a pitch.

"Mm-hmm."

She sat down and leaned forward, elbows resting on her thighs, waiting for me to explain myself. "He cares about you. You should have seen him the night of the accident. He was wrecked. I've never seen a grown man so broken. Maybe you should give him a chance."

I looked up at her, exasperated. "A chance to what? Completely incinerate what's left of my shattered heart? No thanks."

Her posture resigned, shoulders slumping forward. "Whatever happened between you guys, he's trying. He cares about you. He won't tell me or even Caleb what he did, but whatever it was, he hates himself for it. That has to be worth something."

No, it wasn't. I shot her a look that told her to drop it. If only she knew. As much as I wanted to tell her, I couldn't stomach the idea of repeating that night out loud.

I hit the channel button again and again before landing on a rerun of *Sex and the City*. Perfect—more women examining how much men sucked.

"Look, I'm not saying give him a chance romantically, Cassandra. Just maybe…I don't know, try being nice, or at least civil. What happened to my sweet best friend who never had a mean bone in her body?"

With my eyes trained on the television, I answered, "He broke her."

—◆◆◆—

It was just past four when I persuaded Hilary to leave, and I knew it would be at least another hour or two before Logan came back with dinner.

I was finally alone in my own house. All I wanted to do was crank up the stereo and dance around half naked, but I was stuck on the couch, drained from pain meds. There was, however, one thing I was dying to do so badly that I wasn't going to let anything stop me.

With a wholehearted grin in place, I wobbled around the house collecting candles, a lighter, and my cell phone, then stood in the opening to my small bathroom. The sun was shining brightly through the clouds, but with one tug of the blinds I was cast in a peaceful aura of darkness. I was absolutely giddy at the idea of taking a nice, relaxing bath…alone.

After easing down onto the linoleum beside the tub, taking gentle care when I bent forward to plug the drain and run the hot water, I began lighting the candles that lay scattered around me.

I positioned them around the room, my limbs growing heavier with each passing minute as the pain meds began to take full effect. The scent of lavender filled my nostrils, and with the flow of water filling the tub, a calmness settled over me.

Once I slinked out of my clothes, sealed a clear waterproof bandage over my thigh, and poured some sweet vanilla bubbles into the tub, I was ready to climb in.

With a nauseated groan, I nearly bit through my bottom lip as I maneuvered into the bath, being careful not to slip. I propped my foot up on the side; even with the bandage covering the stitches, the less water around it, the better. The last thing I needed was an infection. Once I was settled and comfortable, I rested my head against the cool porcelain.

For once, I could just lie back and let the warm water soothe my sore muscles. There was no rush to clean and go, or a nurse bathing me with basin of water and sponge, or my mother sitting on the toilet talking to me as I sat on the handicap chair in the shower.

I was home, in my bathtub, with no one to interrupt. It was the one thing I'd been secretly craving since I was released from ICU into a regular room. I sank further into the billowing bubbles, a smile on my face.

The fact that Logan was a constant in my life the past few days had been taking its toll. His image assaulted my dreams every sleeping moment. Even though dreams were better than nightmares, he was always there, waiting to torment me with the feelings for him I couldn't dispel. He'd charmed his way into my life, into my heart, as a dear friend. And by taking it to the next level, I'd lost that. I'd lost him. I knew the man he was when it came to women, and I was a fool, like always, to believe I was the one he'd change for.

A tear escaped from my eye and slid down my cheek. I didn't bother to wipe it away; instead, I allowed it to slide to my chin and fall into the water around me. With a deep breath, I closed my eyes, hoping to escape from the pressure of the outside world surrounding me.

———•◆•———

I awoke with a stir, splashing water around me, jerking up at the realization that I was sinking under the water. I was still in the tub. The muscles in my leg that had been resting on the edge were now rigid and sore. I choked back a yelp as I allowed it to fall into the water, aching from the discomfort it had endured during my little nap.

Oh crap!

Blood pounded in my ears, panic setting in as I realized a bath might not have been the best idea. As I attempted to sit up, my entire body cried out at the stiffness in my joints and distressing ache in my bruised ribs. My head throbbed and I dropped back against the tub, wanting to do nothing but cry. But no—that was the last thing I'd do.

I propped my shriveled hands on the edges of the tub, using all my strength to lift myself. The movements triggered a sharp, excruciating stab of pain that shot through the laceration down my thigh. A gurgling scream rose from my throat.

In a panic, I sought out my cell phone. I thought I'd brought it in with the candles, but as I looked around, I realized I'd left it on the hall table.

This is not good. My chest began to heave, and tears stung my eyes. What was I going to do?

To my relief, there was a knock on my front door only seconds later.

Logan? I wasn't positive, since he'd never knocked before. Worried it may be a stranger—or worse, a homicidal stranger—I tugged on the shower curtain until it fell free, the metal rod clanging to the floor.

"Cassandra!"

It was definitely Logan, and the knock from before was now a forceful pounding that could've easily busted down the door. I began pulling the clear vinyl curtain over me.

"Logan! I need you." *I did not just say that. Today is so not my day. I should've stayed at the hospital.*

I waited for another loud bang at my door or the crash from him breaking it down. Instead, I heard the sound of a key in the lock, then footsteps entering.

Logan had a key! How the hell did he get that? He'd returned the one from when I babysat Oliver before Christmas, so unless he'd made a copy…

"Where are you?"

The humiliation stung. What was it with Logan and bathrooms? I looked down at the clear plastic doing nothing to hide my sopping body and cringed. The fluffy towel on the rack against the far wall mocked me as I reached out in vain.

His voice grew closer, calling my name in a panic.

"In the bathroom," I croaked.

One hand covered my breasts over the sticky vinyl as I rolled slightly to my side, hiding my front as best as possible. I struggled against the tight space and cool water to press the curtain over my backside, attempting to shield the last shred of dignity I had.

I felt him approach before I saw him, goose bumps prickling my skin. With hesitant movements, I looked up, my breath catching. He was standing in the doorway, candlelight flickering around him. His dark, hooded eyes locked on mine, concern etched over his brow.

"How did you get in?" I asked more softly than I meant to, swallowing the lump in my throat. It was the only thing I could think to say to break the tension, and it seemed to work.

He tore his gaze away, stepping farther into the room and grabbing the fluffy white towel from the rack. With his back to me, I watched his shoulders rise and fall as he took a deep breath, then turned to face me. He seemed to have collected his thoughts, resuming the confident and smug Logan demeanor I remembered.

"Your mother gave me a key for situations..." His lip quirked up just the slightest bit. "Well, like this, I assume."

With a scoff, my eyes rolled back. He was overly amused with my situation.

"Just to clarify, this is not going to be a regular thing with us: you, me, bathrooms."

A familiar smirk grew over his lips shamelessly. "I have to admit, I quite like this being our thing." He kneeled down beside the tub, and I jerked back.

"Are you hurt?" The amused expression on his face was replaced with distressing concern.

"No, just sore."

"All right, let's get you out of here and into something other than a vinyl wrap. Not that I'm complaining, sweetheart." He frowned the instant the endearment slipped out. He looked away, eyes dipping with a sharp stare at the floor, then rising back to me. "Sorry. Force of habit around you."

"I've noticed," I breathed.

Our eyes locked, and it was who broke the stare. I wasn't going there again. It was done.

My chin jutted out and I kept my hands placed strategically as he positioned the towel over me, rubbing the soft cotton up and down my shivering arms. I kept my eyes downcast on the metal grommets punched into the curtain when he finally reached into the chilled water and pulled out the plug near my feet. I listened as the water drained, using it as a distraction.

"You know, I have to ask: why did you feel the necessity to bathe while home alone in your condition?"

"My condition?" I hissed, pursing my lips.

The water was draining quickly, the last of it circling the drain with a final loud gulp.

He recoiled, his eyes soft and rueful. "I didn't mean…" He sighed.

"Yeah, I get it. You know what? Just hand me my cell and you can go."

He stood and left the room. Was he really leaving that quickly?

He stepped back in a moment later with another towel he must've grabbed from the hall closet. His little house check earlier had him way too familiar with where things were.

"I'm not leaving you here like this. You'll freeze." He bent down, his face inches from mine. "Your lips are nearly blue."

His lips were perfection. I looked away. *No, not perfection—deceit.*

He held up the second towel but didn't lay it over me. Instead, he held it up, blocking my view of him.

What he doing? My brows pulled in.

"Let go of the curtain and use the towel I gave you to cover yourself," he explained.

Oh.

"No peeking!"

The towel shook in his hands as he chuckled. I released my clammy grip on the vinyl reluctantly and pushed it behind me, quickly wrapping the towel back over me.

"Okay," I said, nerves buzzing. Being naked that close to Logan began to stir the desire I feared I someday wouldn't be able to push back down.

Logan covered me with the towel in his hands and smiled. "I'm going to lift you out. Don't be stubborn—put all your weight on me."

I prepared for the closeness as he slid his hand under my damp, quivering legs and behind my back.

"Are you ready?" he asked, his rough voice barely above a whisper.

A shiver shot through me and I nodded, thankful for the candlelight that hid my terror as the pressure of his embrace seared into my skin. It felt so...right.

My teeth caught the inside of my bottom lip, determined to hide any revealing emotions. I interlocked my hands around his neck, his clean, familiar scent so close my head dropped of its own volition into the nook of his neck.

I'd never been more aware of my own body as I felt his brush against mine with every step he took as he clutched me in his arms. His scorching hands imprinted into my flesh as he carried me to my bedroom without a word and sat me on the corner of my bed.

The towel was clutched tightly in my grip against my chest as I turned away from him, desperate to hide both my nudity and the wound on my thigh. It hung open in the back, since it was draped over the front of me and my hands weren't flexible enough to keep it closed in the back. I rushed to bring the covers up in time to cover my behind.

Logan was standing at the edge of the bed directly behind

me, and the moment I grabbed the blanket was too late. I'd been too focused on my backside that I'd let down my guard and hadn't noticed the towel slipping away from my thigh, revealing my worst.

I couldn't look back up at him, feeling his intense gaze on the wound. The clear bandage I'd placed over it to protect the stitches from becoming saturated hid nothing.

My head dropped. I'd never felt uglier.

From the corner of my eye, I saw him hunch down and fall to his knees. I closed my eyes.

Yes, this is what you did to me.

It was wrong. He wasn't solely to blame. It wasn't him drinking and driving. It wasn't he who flew through the red light and nearly destroyed me. It was he, however, who caused me to lose my head and get in that car without a seatbelt. It was he who put me there with tears clouding my vision.

My thoughts were interrupted by the touch of his warm palm settling on my leg beside the bandage—inspecting it, from what I caught from my sidelong glance at him. My stomach flipped, heart pounding feverishly as the nerve endings in my leg jittered and buzzed to life. My eyelids snapped shut as Logan mimicked the skillful ease of a gifted surgeon to pull the bandage away slowly. To my disbelief, I didn't even wince; his touch was so gentle and slow.

My eyes opened gradually and cast down, unable to look at him as he placed the soiled bandage aside. I felt the pads of his fingertips trailing along the tender stitches that ran halfway down my outer thigh. Doctors said a scar was imminent, but that plastic surgery could make it near invisible in the future. I told them no. Not that I could afford the option, anyway, but this was me now. This was the mark on my body that reminded me I took a chance and lost.

My eyes fluttered as the pads of his fingertips continued their slow descent to where the stitches ended.

"Hideous, I know," I breathed finally, my body tense, embarrassment raw as his touch sent me spiraling.

Logan peered up at me, and I saw the swell of anguish in his eyes.

"You're beautiful, strong, and what every man could ever hope for. This," he said, his fingers continuing back up, gaze locked with mine, "proves you've lived life, but unfortunately trusted an unworthy man."

My eyelids shut tightly again, willing the tears not to spill forth from the way his soft voice faded into a broken whisper. A beat of silence was followed by my stomach exploding with butterflies when I felt his lips cover the top of the stitches. My hands clutched the towel more tightly, using it to control my urge to reach out to him as I sucked in a ragged breath.

With sensual tenderness surrounding his unexpected and gentle touch, I watched with half-lidded eyes as his lips pulled back, then placed another open-mouth kiss down a bit further. He kissed me over and over until his lips were halfway down my thigh and I was left with a tear-stained face and swollen heart.

Before I could speak, Logan tilted his head to the side and stared up at me, raising his thumb and wiping away my agony. A long, content moment settled between us until he was standing up and placing the blanket over my shoulders and around my legs, wrapping me in snugly.

Speechless, I watched as he strode over to my dresser and opened the top drawer.

I shuddered. *Not that drawer.*

With a boyish grin that lit a twinkle in his eye and a cocked, playful eyebrow, he looked back over his shoulder. He was holding a pair of yellow-and-white polka-dot panties.

"Interesting choices you have."

Any sexual tension between us was instantly squashed. I rolled my eyes, sniffing once, snipping away the final thread of intimacy we'd shared seconds earlier. I fought in vain to cover the smile threatening to break out.

Logan was trying to make it easier; I could see it in his posture as he turned back away for a moment, sifting through my unmentionables until he spoke to himself again.

"Perfect."

I waited anxiously, unsure what he'd found, when he stepped closer to the door and snagged the pale-pink robe from the hook beside it.

"Do you need help?" He set the robe beside me, holding my panties and a white lace bra as though he'd done so a thousand times before.

I shook my head once, too grateful for him breaking the tension that had been developing between us to be angry. Not a bit of me felt embarrassed when I held out my hand. My eyes narrowed into thin slits up at him, but not in the same way they had throughout the week. Logan had somehow managed to kiss away my anger—at least for the night.

"No, I'll be fine."

He placed the underwear in my hands with an easy smile. "I'll be right in the kitchen if you need me. I brought over Chinese tonight. Hope you like it."

He didn't already know? I wasn't expecting the way it lightened the heaviness inside me.

"Yeah, I do."

Chapter Five

HARD TRUTHS

I'd never have admitted it aloud, but my resolve toward Logan was already softening. Was that all it took—a few brief but incredibly intimate touches? A pleasant calmness over dinner that evening earned him an actual conversation as we sat at the table nearly an hour after the food was cleared from our plates.

This discovery should've made me happy or at least content, yet I awoke the next day feeling the exact opposite. I was falling for him again, and there would be no way to stop it if he kept up the perfect man-in-love spiel. I knew what he was doing, and as much as I wanted it to work, I was terrified.

Neighbors, I could live with, but even friends just seemed too difficult. As disheartening as it was, the notion of friendship seemed impossible with my irksome old feelings blurring the lines.

The week lurched by, and Logan never missed a beat. He sent a good-morning text first thing when I awoke and stopped by with both breakfast and dinner. I listened as he told me about Oliver, and even interacted with him over the designs of Julia's house.

However, I kept myself guarded so as not to step over the substantial line I'd drawn between us. I had to make it clear there was no chance for us. I couldn't let myself go down that road again only for him to walk away the moment things got rough—

or worse, once he grew bored. And the last thing I wanted to do was lead him on. I knew how that felt, and I wouldn't do that to him.

He didn't say a word or play the charming card when I switched to a clipped and guarded tone, but I knew he felt the change. His confident behavior slipped, and the sporadic words between us slowly grew into nothing more than civil, almost businesslike blurbs of 'Yes' or 'No' over the house project.

We exchanged a few small jokes here and there, with the occasional brush of his hand over mine. It stirred that familiar electric wave residing deep inside me, and yet he never showed a sign that he felt it. There was now an unspoken understanding that I had nothing left to give.

As the week drew to a close, I noticed his visits grew shorter. On Thursday, he brought dinner by, but didn't stay a minute after we finished eating.

He was finally taking the hint. I couldn't offer him more. I couldn't offer him anything. It wasn't until Friday, when I opened a door that should've remained closed, that everything changed.

Julia was standing on my porch, a shivery smile on her lips as she hurried inside to warm up.

"Hey, come in." I chuckled at her impatience.

"Thanks, its freezing out there!" She rubbed her gloved hands together and her body's stiffness from the bitterness of the blizzard began to wane. "Hope you're not busy. I needed to talk to you a minute."

"No, not busy. Just watching some trash TV." I sat back on the sofa, curious as to why she was visiting. It was a first—not that I minded.

"Sounds...fun."

Boring and mundane were more accurate. I hit the mute button and set the remote beside me. She sat on the other end of the couch.

"Listen, I know this is none of my business, but Logan's miserable."

I sat up further, brows rising at her brashness. "You're right. I don't mean to sound rude, but it isn't any of your business."

She sighed, tugging off her gloves. "I'm sorry. I don't normally get involved in any of my brothers' relationships. It's just that I've never seen him like this before. He's all mopey and grumpy, and besides hanging out with Oliver or coming to see you, he's checked out." Her words blew out in one long breath. She inhaled to fill her lungs and waited for me to respond.

Checked out? Logan? I couldn't picture it.

"I know he's your brother and I think it's sweet that you're trying to help, but there's nothing to be done. He can't expect me to come running into his arms when I can barely even walk."

She shook her head and groaned, irritated at my reply. "I'll be honest with you, Cassandra. I don't understand Logan most of the time when it comes to women. He's always so reserved, never wanting to even date."

A chuckle escaped and I sucked in my lips, containing my grin. "Sorry, it's just that Logan definitely *dates*…just not like most men," I said.

Julia relaxed into the sofa. "I know Logan, and I know that he…enjoys the company of many." Her words were so hesitant and forced I couldn't help but grin more widely.

"All right, fine! Logan's a slut! My fucked-up brother with commitment issues can't stand to even speak to a girl once he's screwed her. There, I said it, and I tried to warn you when we first met. But he already had his eye on you, and it was too late to try and stop it. God knows I tried! I knew this would happen. It always does."

She sighed, pulling off her thin designer hat and running her fingers through her hair. I swallowed hard, gaze fixed on the wall behind her now.

My cheeks heated, skin prickling with emotions I didn't recognize. *Always does?* Why did that send my gut roiling? My posture turned painfully stiff. *I'm one of many?*

Block it out. Block it out.

A shiver raced through me, awakening my senses that were slowly losing their grip on the fact that she was still there, watching me. Searching for all the strength I could muster, I pulled on an unaffected smile—so small I wondered whether it even looked like one—and found my voice.

"So if this always happens, why are you sitting here talking to me about it? You want me to screw your brother so he'll leave me alone?"

"No!" She looked appalled at first, and then her head ticked to the side. "Although that may work."

Now it was my turn to pull on a scrunched appalled and offended expression. She shook her head and cackled with frustration.

"All I'm trying to say is that when Logan sets his mind to something, he doesn't give up—ever. Right now, he wants you, and until you see that, you're fighting the inevitable. It's a game to him, and he *will* win. I know you're attracted to him, so why not just try and see what happens?"

"You just told me that he never even speaks to women when he's through with them, so why the hell would I take a chance with him?"

"Because I know you're different. He's only ever pursued one other woman." She paused, hesitant. "Oliver was almost three, and Logan met her on an airplane. Whoever she was, she played hard to get, and Logan flew out to see her every chance he had for about a month. He'd come back to the city frustrated, and we all thought it was hilarious. He'd found a woman who caught his attention, yet she wouldn't sleep with him. My other brothers and I thought she might be the one."

I released a breath, nearly suffocating from holding it in too long unknowingly. I couldn't hear this. It was too much. I was no different—another pursuit.

"I'm done," I breathed, heat stinging my eyes as tears glossed my vision.

"No, listen. It was a little over a month after he'd met her that he flew out one weekend and came back looking…satisfied. He went back one other time a few days later, and that was that."

There was a woman out there somewhere who'd endured the charm of Logan West and was left broken? Shocker. Bile began to rise inside me, and my head started spinning.

"He just walked away?" I managed.

"Yes, because she wanted more. She wanted to meet Oliver. He didn't even know how she found out he had a son. He doesn't talk to women about him."

"Julia, please just leave. As a woman yourself, how can you sit here and tell me this—sit here and ask me to give him a chance to humiliate me?"

"No, that's not what I'm doing. I want you to understand. You need to know this. When Logan was pursuing her, he never stopped sleeping around. Jax was staying with him at the time and said Logan had women over when Oliver visited my mother. He continued to have sex with other women." Her voice grew louder, hands working animatedly. "He never told her about Oliver! Don't you get it? Jax and I know for a fact that Logan hasn't slept with *anyone* since November. He went from getting caught screwing slutty women on balconies to showing no interest in the opposite sex. He's never been like this over a woman before—not even Natasha. You're different. He truly cares about you!"

"And if I'm just a conquest?"

"You're not. My brother is lost without you. He won't say it, but it's obvious it's destroying him. Can't you give him a chance—just one? I mean, at least try the friends thing again.

Please. He's a good guy, he's just… guarded."

I swallowed. My head was muddled and heavier than ever trying to process everything. It killed me that he was hurting, but so was I, and this new information only built an additional wall around the thick prison protecting my damaged heart.

"Julia, between you and me, I appreciate everything your brother has been doing. I really do, and it makes this so hard, but I can't go there again. I don't even know what to think about everything you've just told me." My voice lowered from the emotional exhaustion. "I need to focus on getting my life put back together before—"

"Why the hell are you here?" I looked up and found Logan standing in the doorway. Acid dripped from his tone.

"I was just visiting. Calm down."

"Oliver's with Jax. I told him you were going over to see him."

She narrowed her eyes as she stood. "I'm on my way. I just wanted to check in on Cassandra and see how she was feeling."

"You can see she's well," Logan scowled. It was obvious from his stance that he'd heard most of what she'd said to me. His jaw was set, eyes dark.

Julia walked to the door, glancing back to me with a pleading frown. I looked away, unable to take the pressure.

"I said I'm going. God, you need to relax!" Julia yelled, stomping past him and slamming the door behind her.

Silence hung between us for too long before he cleared his throat.

"I was stopping by to drop off the vitamins I told you about." Logan held out a bottle of pills. "Here."

"You need to apologize to her." I stood and grabbed the bottle, setting it on the coffee table.

"She needs to stay out of my personal life. Our relationship has nothing to do with her."

Relationship? Is that what he called this? I couldn't keep dragging him on when I knew it was going nowhere. Whether I was another conquest he needed to claim or there was even a small chance I meant more, I couldn't let anything happen.

I laid it out with a gentle tone. "Logan, I don't think you should keep coming by." My eyes locked with his, imploring him to hear me out once and for all. "I mean, this isn't going to go anywhere, and I don't want to see you get your hopes up or me broken all over again. So let's just end this…whatever this is…and both walk away."

"Why?"

My brows pulled in. "Why what? Logan, I can barely process what happened that night. It's still a painful mess in my head, and the last thing I can handle right now is trying to date someone I don't trust."

"No, why don't you want to see me get my hopes up?"

I don't know, because I'm not a complete bitch?

"Because I don't."

He stepped forward, standing inches from me. "Because you care."

"Logan." I sighed.

"Tell me you don't care."

"It's not enough," I murmured, his breath hot on my cheeks. I needed to step back, but the couch hit my legs, stopping me from moving. I couldn't think straight with him that close, so I just spoke quickly.

"I care about your feelings, just like I do Caleb's or Hilary's. That's not enough for what you want."

"You care as a friend."

Did I say that? No, he wasn't a friend. I wouldn't let him be—not again. I shook my head.

"You're lying, and we both know it, Cassandra. I know you care, and that's why I'm going to give you the space you need to make you see that I'm worth letting back in."

He leaned in and placed a chaste kiss to my temple, leaving

me breathless, and then turned to leave.

"I'll come by in a few days. If you need me, you know I'm only a call away."

The moment the door shut behind him, I slumped down on the couch. He wasn't going to make it easy on me, and a tiny piece of my heart swelled—a piece of hope that I fought to bury.

He was, however, offering me space and time—things I needed desperately without confusing emotions nauseating me or sexual tension so thick I could suffocate. I was handed a couple days off, and for that, I was grateful.

Chapter Six

HEAD GAMES

I spent the rest of the weekend hidden away inside, and by Tuesday night, I was beside myself with boredom. The sun had set over the trees as I rested on a chair on my back porch, staring out at the snow falling around me.

It was beautiful and peaceful, and after sitting for over an hour, watching the sunset, I was still in no rush to head inside. Activity in Logan's house appeared to be settling down for the night, the lights slowly flickering off one after another until only one was left glowing upstairs, at the very end of the hall, in the room closest to my house—his painting room.

I sighed, missing Oliver and Scout. I hoped they were having fun together. As much as I wanted to bring Scout home to keep me company, he was better over there for the time being. I'd planned to visit them multiple times, but it always fell through after I'd look at myself in the mirror. Even though Oliver had seen me at the hospital, I didn't want to go over until more of my bruises had healed.

For the time being, I needed to keep my distance from everyone and let my body fully recover. Tired, I allowed my heavy head to lean back against the headrest as I tightened the thick fleece blanket covering my coat and flannel pajamas around me.

My eyelids slid shut, the pain meds weighing me down, but

something caught my attention and I was drawn back to the Logan's window, where his curtain was now open. Through the darkness of the night, the light inside illuminated the room.

He was there, shirtless, facing away, staring at a canvas in front of him.

I sat up further, unable to remove my gaze as the muscles in his back bulged with every stroke of the brush. It was as though I was looking through a telescope the way I noticed every graceful movement his body made.

Any of my interest in what he was painting was lost when he stilled, lifting his head slightly and glancing over his shoulder. He'd seen me, and as hard as I tried, I couldn't peel my gaze away.

Ever so slowly, the corner of his lip curled up as his brow arched, with a tempting gleam in his eyes.

Clearing my throat, I dropped my head and shifted in my seat as I settled my gaze on the tree line ahead of me. I closed my eyes, clearing the image of him away. When I opened them again, he was there, standing directly in front of me, not only shirtless but wearing loose, light-wash jeans that hung low and were unbuttoned. They were covered in multiple streaks of dark paint.

"You like watching," he stated.

"Not tonight, Logan. I'm tired."

"So am I."

Instantly, I was pulled from the chair, my blanket falling to the ground as he tugged me into his arms.

"Of waiting?" His lips crashed over mine, demanding and forceful.

I was lost. His hands were everywhere, my shirt ripped away, followed by my red flannel pants. The freezing weather was nonexistent as his hand slid into my panties, sinking two fingers into me.

My breath rushed out, unsure what was happening. It was

too late to stop it; my body wouldn't allow it. Logan lifted me up, my legs wrapping around his waist, and it was then that I noticed his jeans were gone and his massive erection was pressing against me.

"So perfect," he murmured, his hand moving away, replaced by his manhood that in one swift movement plunged into me.

"Logan," I moaned, panting against his lips with each and every thrust.

My mouth traveled down the stubble of his jaw until it landed on his shoulder, where I kissed him over and over until my lips were swollen and tingling. His hands dug into my ass, holding me against him. Harder and harder he drove into my body, filling me with his need, until my entire body exploded, pulsating in his arms as he released inside me.

Catching my breath was impossible through the aftershock of the high. My brain had checked out. I drew back just enough to look into his eyes, and was met with that devilish smirk I hadn't seen in so long before he leaned in and ran his tongue up my cheek.

What?

I shook my head, unsure what to think when he did it again. Then I noticed his face starting to morph into that of an animal. I flew out of his arms and jerked up, opening my eyes to find me still in my chair with Scout, paws on my chest, licking my face.

Startled, I yelped, jumping up and tripping over the blanket still wrapped around my fully clothed body. There was no stopping the tumble that threw me to the ground, taking the chair and Scout down with me. Calming my breathing, I lay there in the snow, Scout barking beside me. I began laughing to myself.

"Are you all right?" Jax asked, standing over me.

"Yeah, just had a...dream."

"Oh, I noticed that." A grin grew over his lips.

Great! There had to be a way to get his brother out of my head.

Jax extended his hand down and helped me up. I set the blanket—now covered in snow—on the chair and scooped Scout into my arms, kissing the top of his head. I missed him more than I'd realized.

"What are you doing out here this late?" he asked, lifting the chair.

"I don't know. Getting tired sitting inside all the time."

He nodded. "Yeah, that's understandable. I'd go nuts without someone to keep me company." His brow arched and voice dropped. "Do you need some *company*, Cassie?"

I rolled my eyes. "No, I'm good, thanks." I chuckled.

"Well, the offer always stands, but you know you can always come over to our place. We have the game room, not to mention Oliver asks about you daily—hell, sometimes hourly." He laughed.

"I will soon." I gave Scout another tight squeeze, then placed him on the ground. Turning, I grabbed the blanket and began dusting off the snow.

"All right, I'm freezing, and this dog has some business to do so I can get some sleep. I'll see you around…and Cassie?"

I looked back and noticed his smile was replaced with an unfamiliar, almost strained expression.

"You still look good."

"Thanks." I snorted, shaking my head as my laughter followed.

"I'm just saying, don't hide away forever." His smile was back in place as he called for Scout to follow him back to his yard.

Smiling to myself, I folded the blanket over my arm and turned to walk inside when I noticed the window at Logan's house had the curtain open, just like in the dream. My smile dropped as I took him all in as he stood there, dressed in a plain white V-neck T-shirt covered in paint streaks, staring over at me.

With a slight nod, I offered a tight smile before turning away and heading inside.

—•◆•—

The rest of the week passed at the same sluggish rate, with Logan staying true to his word but the dreams constant. There was little to do, so I found myself in bed reading and staring up at nothing through the days, my thoughts wild during the nights.

My thoughts of him were distant, however, as I shoveled another spoonful of Hilary's mystery casserole into my mouth over Sunday dinner.

"You sure you're all right?" she asked, sipping her wine across the table from me.

"Perfect." I really was, but I knew what she was asking and I wasn't going there. "So, what's Caleb up to tonight? I'm sure you'd rather spend your Sunday with him over your dreary old friend."

"You're not dreary!" she sneered. "Although it would be nice to see you in something other than sweatpants."

I chuckled once at the disdain in her voice and crinkle of her upturned nose, then took another bite. I never knew what she put in the casserole, but was certain it was different each time.

"Caleb's stuck at Haven since he had a new guy up and quit on him last night," she explained.

"You poor thing."

"Yeah, but he said he'd stop by my place later and make it up to me." Her eyes brightened as she peered over the rim of her glass. "He's really good at the making-up-for-it part."

I swallowed and held up my hand, giggling. "All I need to know."

"So what about Logan? Did he stop by and annoy you today?"

"Not yet," I grumbled.

Hilary smiled, amused as her phone sang from her pocket. She pulled it out, scrolling her finger over it, and I watched as her smile melted into a bewildered frown.

"Hmmm," she said to herself, brows pinched.

"'Hmmm' what?"

"I don't know. It's... you know what, I'm sure it's nothing." The contrived half smile on her face and worried lines marring her forehead told me something was wrong.

"All right, what's up?" I asked directly, determined to get an answer.

She set the phone on the table. "That was Jennifer, the head waitress at Haven. Said I should come down and stake my claim."

A chuckle bubbled in my throat. "Stake your claim? To what?"

Her eyes searched her plate, and my understanding clicked.

"Caleb?" I nearly gasped. "Why? He wouldn't." I blinked twice, wiping the ridiculous thought away. Sitting further up in my seat, I spoke with nothing but sincerity. "Hilary, Caleb adores you. He'd never cheat."

"Neither would Mark. Isn't that what you always said?"

I hunched back, feeling like I'd just been slapped. "Ouch. That hurt," I mumbled.

She sighed. I'd never seen her so worried. It wasn't like her. "Sorry. I just...I can't lose him. I've never cared about anyone like this before. He's everything."

My heart ached for her. All too familiar was the feeling of falling for someone in a way that left you terrified by the powerful emotions it evoked.

"I know, but if he's cheating, he's not worth it. You have to trust that Caleb cares about you, loves you, and isn't stupid enough to screw that up."

Or would he? Were all men the same when it came to easy women?

I finished the final bite on my plate and pushed it forward. I'd eaten way too much of the mystery meal.

Hilary stood. "Will you come down there with me? Just to check in and say a quick hello?"

I nearly spit out the soda in my mouth as I stared at her, wide-eyed.

"Are you kidding? I just got of the hospital not even two weeks ago, and you want me to go to a bar with you—a bar that isn't exactly a place I'm eager to return to? You do realize what you're asking, right?"

She paled. "God." Her hands flew to her face, running over her forehead. "I'm sorry. I don't know what the hell I was thinking. Of course you can't go, and I know Caleb would never do anything like that. All right, moving on." She attempted to shake off her worry. "So what are you up for tonight: chick flick or zombies?"

Her phone chirped again, and I saw the struggle on her face as she tried to ignore it. Preoccupied in her head, she walked to the sink with her empty plate.

"I'm feeling a little zombie action myself," she said with an awkward chuckle.

How could I watch her sit beside me with anxious tremors all night? I wouldn't do that to her.

"Give me ten minutes and we'll go."

"What?" She whipped around, jaw dropped.

"I need to change, and then we'll go check in on your lover boy. However, when we get back, it's a chick flick—my choice." I stood up, plate in hand, and headed to the sink.

In a flash, she flung herself at me, wrapping me in a tight embrace. "Too tight!" I yelped, my chest screaming at her to release me. She dropped her arms instantly and pulled back, frowning.

"Shit, so sorry. How long did the doctor say your ribs were gonna be sore?"

"Another week or two, so no more bear hugs, got it?"

"Deal! Now you're sure you want to go? We don't have to. I'm a big girl, and I'll be all ri—"

"No, I don't want to go, but I'm not going to watch you worry yourself into a seizure either. I'm sure you'll find Caleb down there charming customers into buying more drinks, and not trying to get into their panties. And when you do, we're coming straight back here."

I walked toward my bedroom door as she called out, "You're the best!"

The thought of going out was one I dreaded. Still, I ran a brush through my knotted hair and tugged on a clean shirt and faded blue jeans. Sitting in her car on the icy roads and spending any time inside Haven so soon was not sitting well with me, but that's what friends were for, and I wasn't about to leave her hanging because of my own issues.

Chapter Seven

UNDERCOVER

Once Hilary was parked, she bolted from the car, slowing down and looking back once she was halfway out of the parking lot. She'd been a bundle of nerves the entire drive, which meant I was nearly wrecked. Her thumbs had kept a constant beating rhythm on the steering wheel. My anxiety had been lost in pleas with the universe that she was keeping her focus on the road and not the possibility of walking in and finding Caleb with another girl.

As we headed to the double doors of the swanky restaurant, I grimaced. It was time to face the music—literally. Even on a Sunday night after nine, Haven was alive with locals. My phone vibrated in my pocket and I pulled it out to catch the incoming text from my mother.

Just checking in. Love u.

"Logan?" Hilary interrupted my thoughts.

I shoved the phone back in my jeans and gave her a quick head shake. I still hadn't heard a word from him, although he'd made it clear I wouldn't. I just hated that I kept waiting for his call or unexpected text.

My body stiffened and I closed my eyes as we passed the infamous alley. Not even quickening my pace could stop the sizzling of my nerves and raging of my heart pounding against my ribcage.

"You sure you're okay being here?" Hilary asked, sensing my stiffness. "We can go. I don't mind. I shouldn't have even brought you here. I don't know what I was—"

"I promise, I'm fine," I said, swallowing the golf-ball-sized lump constricting my throat. "Now stop asking. I had to come back here eventually." I held a contrived smile as long as I could, but she wasn't buying it. The girl knew me better than anyone.

"Come on, let's get this over with so you can see how crazy you are," I added, snaking my arm around hers.

I'm fine, I repeated in my head. *We'll sneak in, and then right back out.* I just hoped it would be that quick. While I'd gotten dressed, Hilary had been talking to Jennifer on the phone. Turned out there was a mystery woman at the bar putting on a show, ready to pounce on Caleb any minute. Hilary was no pushover, nor was she shy when it came to defending what was hers. Whomever this woman was, she was about to have an eventful evening—and not the kind she'd been hoping for with Caleb.

The moment we stepped inside, I knew it wasn't going to be so simple. Jennifer saw us immediately, and diverted us to a corner in the back. Oh, the drama. My head was already throbbing.

"Where is this skank?" Hilary hissed, eyes scanning the dimly lit room.

The place was packed with diners laughing and soaking up the atmosphere. The bar was taken up by drinkers looking for company, the dance floor covered with sweaty bodies ready to move their nights to more private locations.

"Over there—dark hair, green dress," Jennifer answered, eyes fixed on the barstool across from Caleb.

The mystery woman wasn't hard to miss. Her long, shiny coat of dark wavy locks swung as her shoulders shook from laughter. The cut of her emerald-green dress let anyone interested know that she'd come out looking for more than just a drink. However, it wasn't she who held my attention or caused my anxiety to catapult.

With a heavy heart, I placed my hand on Hilary's shoulder. "I'm sure it's not what you think."

Did I really just say that? It was the same line she'd said to me over a year ago, and here we stood, watching Caleb leaning over the bar, inches from the woman, intrigued as if she'd said the most marvelous thing.

I waited for Hilary to say something—anything. Instead, she squared her shoulders and stomped toward them. I followed, ready as her backup for whatever she needed.

"Hey Caleb, how's work going?" Hilary's voice dripped with sarcasm and held a nasty bite.

"Hilary." Caleb straightened himself, his face losing color by the second.

The woman in the green dress twirled to meet our gaze, and my stomach churned. *Natasha.*

Hilary's face was plastered with an enormous contrite grin as she extended her hand to the woman she was ready to bitch slap across the room.

"Hi, I'm Hilary. You must be new in town."

Natasha only glanced impassively at the hand in front of her, then resumed sipping on her glass before answering. "I am, and Caleb here is doing a wonderful job keeping me company." Natasha set her sights on Caleb and never looked away, ignoring the threatening glare set on her.

"Is that so?" Hilary's narrowed eyes darted to Caleb's. "How sweet of him."

"I need to go check on something in the back. Hilary, would you mind helping me out?" Caleb asked, his wide eyes begging. I wanted to feel for the guy, seeing how nervous he was, but the flirty act between him and Natasha couldn't be denied.

Caleb stepped around the bar and reached for an arm

Hilary had crossed over her chest. She didn't budge it, but after a pause filled with menacing glares, she followed him reluctantly. She looked back at me and I nodded, letting her know I'd be there waiting.

"You look familiar. Have we met before?"

Great. Now I was stuck standing next to a curious-looking Natasha waiting for me to answer. The night was going down the drain quickly. I wasn't sure if she recognized me from New Year's, since she was only there a brief moment, but I wasn't about to help her out.

"I don't think so," I replied.

I walked a few stools down quickly, following the curve of the bar until Natasha was blocked from view, and took a seat. From there, I caught sight of Hilary and Caleb standing around the corner in the back. He was trying to explain himself—or so it looked like, from the constant movement of his lips and frantic arm motions—but she wasn't hearing it. Finally, his hands came down on her shoulders, and he crushed his mouth onto hers. She struggled under him for only a moment, and I shifted my uncomfortable gaze elsewhere.

"This was sent over by an admirer." The bartender smiled as he set a glass containing a frozen concoction in front of me.

Who would buy me a drink? "You have the wrong girl." I pushed it forward.

"Nope. It's for you."

I caught the guy's arm before he could walk farther down the bar.

"I can't drink it. Might as well take it back."

No mixing alcohol and pain meds—doctor's order, and one I wouldn't disobey. Not that I really needed them much anymore, but I'd taken one before I left the house.

He looked down at my drink and chuckled. "It's a virgin. Your mystery man demanded it so, and I made it myself."

My face screwed up as I lifted the drink and took a sip. It

was good, but it didn't answer who sent it.

"Turning down a free drink? You've always been too sweet for your own good," a familiar dull voice said as its owner slid down onto the stool beside me.

My eyes closed, shoulders painfully stiff until I inhaled a breath and let it out. No, this was one guy who'd never see me at anything but my best. He was nothing more than an annoyance. I turned, smiling cheekily at my ex-boyfriend, Mark.

I held the drink to my lips and took another sip, my eyes on him, then set it back down. "Obviously you don't me know as well as you think you do," I said with a contrived smile.

He chuckled, shaking his head down at his beer. "You're right, I probably don't know you as well as I should, considering our history. But I *do* know from the look on your face when you sat down that you'd rather be anywhere else."

"So you decided to buy me a drink?"

"Sorry, that's not from me, but I'll buy the next round," he said, smiling.

My phone vibrated against my leg and I pulled it out, thankful for the distraction, seeing the name I shouldn't have been expecting: Logan.

I'm in the back. Walk away from him now.

I rolled my eyes, not in the mood to be bossed around, and set my phone beside my drink.

"What do you want, Mark?" I drawled, narrowing my eyes at him.

"Julia told me about the accident. You look pretty good, considering."

I scoffed, staring down at my drink. I looked anything but good, and we both knew it.

"Was that all you wanted to say?" I asked, unimpressed.

"No." He sighed. "I saw you come in with Hilary and when she walked away, I figured I'd come say hi."

"Scared of Hilary, huh?" I snickered.

"The girl hates me."

"Can you blame her?" I . Yes, she definitely hated him.

"True. Look, Cassie, I never meant for things to happen the way they did with you. I mean, I loved you—hell, I still do."

"Don't!" I held up my hand, an angry frown on my lips.

"Relax, I'm just trying to say…I'm sorry." His tone softened. "Sorry for sleeping around, sorry for lying to you, and most of all, sorry for not treating you the way you deserved. You were always so good to me. Every time I screwed up, I swore I was going to come clean, but then you'd be waiting for me with your innocent smile full of love. I wanted it, I wanted you, it's just…I was young, and there were so many girls hanging around."

My gaze fell from him to my hands clutching my glass. An apology? I hadn't seen that coming.

My phone lit up with another text and, needing time to process my thoughts, I hit the screen to retrieve it.

U have 30 seconds to walk away.

I shook my head with a scoff, not sure which man was infuriating me the most.

"The day you caught me with Mackenzie woke me up. I felt like shit for hurting you."

"How many?" I asked after a long pause.

"What?"

I turned on the stool to face him fully. It was time for closure, once and for all.

"How many girls were there during the five years I spent as your lapdog, loving you blindly, planning my future around you?"

"Cassie—"

"How. Many?"

"I don't know."

"More than five?" I pressed.

"Look, it's not important," he replied, nerves evident in his expression.

"More than ten?" I hissed through clenched teeth.

"We don't need to rehash—"

"Answer my question, damn it!"

"I don't know...fifteen, twenty, maybe more," he confessed, unable to look me in the eye. "I lost track after the first few times."

"Twenty!?" I gasped as though I'd been slugged in the gut. I shouldn't have been surprised, but it was a huge number, and meant I probably knew most of the girls.

"Look," Mark said. He grabbed my hand, and I ripped it away. "I was a dumbass, and I should have told you, but—"

"Why did you even date me, then? What was the point when I obviously didn't make you happy or satisfy you?"

"I just...I don't fucking know, all right? It just kept happening, and you were always so sweet, and I didn't want to hurt your feelings."

My eyes grew wider. I was stunned. "You didn't want to hurt my feelings?" I all but yelled.

"I know it sounds a little messed up, but—"

"A little!?" I burst out laughing, my head falling back at how ridiculous his reasoning sounded. "Mark, do me a favor and listen to yourself the next time you try to apologize to someone."

My phone went off, and this time it was a call from Logan. Slowly, I hit 'Accept' and brought it to my ear.

"What?" I asked gently, my mind reeling, making a mental list of which of my friends in this small town would screw around with Mark.

"I'm going to fucking kill him if you don't tell him to leave!"

He wasn't serious. Before I could reply, I heard Caleb's muffled voice through the receiver.

"Calm down, Hilary's going now!" he told Logan.

"Get the hell off me!" Logan roared, and then there was a

loud scruff against the phone and a few grunts before Caleb's unaffected, clear voice was there.

"Hey, Cassie, you might want to tell Mark to head out for the night because I have three guys holding Logan back and I'm not sure how much longer they can manage."

With a puffed-out sigh, I shook my head. Logan needed to get a grip. I could talk to whomever I wanted.

I hung up and turned back to Mark, noticing Hilary rushing over.

"We need to go," she demanded, shooting a menacing glare at Mark.

"Everything all right?" he asked, ignoring her and taking a drink of his beer.

My shoulders lifted. "Give us a minute, Hilary."

An explosive crash in the back startled me. I shot a glance in that direction, then at Hilary.

"I don't think you have a minute," she answered, pulling me up from the stool. I grabbed my cell and plunged it into my pocket.

"I appreciate you apologizing, but it's a little late," I said to Mark. "You tore my world apart—a fake world that I obviously created in my head, but still my world. I can't forgive you for that, and I don't want to. I'm not sad or angry—I've just moved on. The fact that I can sit here and listen to you tell me you've been with half the girls in our high school and not break down crying proves that. So the next time you see me, don't come over. I'm not—"

Another massive crash of what sounded like pots and pans caused Hilary to drag me away and into the restroom.

"What the hell is going on back there!?" I asked the second the door closed behind us.

"Holy shit, you should have seen Logan! When he saw Mark walk over to you, he was about to run over there and rip into the guy. The only reason he stayed away so long was because Jax was there talking him down," she explained, fixing her hair in the mirror. "The guy has a temper, but what I want to know is why you were sitting there with Mark in the first place."

"It doesn't matter. What's going on with Caleb?" I asked, not wanting to think any more about either man from my past. "You don't seem brokenhearted."

"I've never been better. He was—" she began, but the interruption of the bathroom door opening revealing Natasha changed her grin into a more formal, friendly smile.

She strolled in, ignoring us as she went straight to the mirror and applied a new layer of deep-crimson lipstick. It did little for her olive complexion.

"Sorry about coming off a little harsh back there. It's been a long night," Hilary said in a way-too-friendly voice. "I hope you enjoy our small town."

"I'm sure I will. Caleb seems eager to show me around."

It took everything in me not to say something, but Hilary took the jab like a champ. I wasn't sure if Natasha had caught on to Caleb and Hilary's relationship status, and I knew from her seat she wouldn't have seen them kissing in the back, but anyone could've seen there was something between them from the way Hilary had stormed over originally.

"Yeah, Caleb's great. I'm sure you'll enjoy him." Hilary turned back to the mirror in front of her, smoothing a finger over her perfectly trimmed brow. We stood in silence until Natasha left a minute later.

"All right, spill! *You're sure she'll enjoy him?* What the hell, Hilary? Please don't tell me you guys have some weird open-relationship thing going on!"

"Hell no!" She turned away from the mirror, her face scrunched in disgust. "That is one man I'll never share."

"Good to know. So what's going on, then?"

"Caleb's doing a favor. He told me she's Logan's ex."

I nodded, confirming I already knew.

"She's pretty," Hilary said.

Yeah, she was. I sucked in my lips, averting my eyes that no doubt relayed the pang of jealousy I hated feeling.

"But you're gorgeous. She has nothing on you. Not to mention she looks like a slut."

A smile broke out over my face. "So what's the favor Caleb's doing?"

Her face lit up, ready to divulge, but first she danced over to the door and peeked out. All must've been clear, because she turned back and started talking.

"Logan asked if he'd try to get some information out of her—see why she was really back in town. You know, two guys working a scheme, playing out some James Bond fantasy. We would totally be the Bond girls!"

She looked pleased with the image, but I was more interested in hearing her continue. Catching the hint, she rolled her eyes at my insistent hand motion.

"Anyway, Logan told Natasha he'd meet her here, but when she arrived, he texted her that something came up and he couldn't make it. He said her drinks were on his tab for the night, then handed her off to Caleb, whose mission was to try and get her drunk and sweet talk her into spilling her guts." She said the last part with extra enthusiasm.

"Spilling her guts?" I laughed once. "So why is she back?"

"Turns out we interrupted before he got anything out of her—at least, anything other than the fact that she wants to take him back to her hotel and do things that would have me ripping her eyes out and send me to a life behind bars. Orange is *not* my color."

"Gotcha." I rubbed my hand over my chest, my brain nearing exhaustion. "Well, let's leave them to it, shall we?"

"Actually, Logan asked if I'd stay. He said he'd take you home, and I could cover his job."

My head began to pound. "His job?"

"Yeah, he's been in the back keeping an eye on her—you know, in case she really came back to try and take Oliver. He wants as much information as he can get on her, and from what I understand, she's not one to turn down a drink or five to loosen up. At least, he *was* keeping an eye on her till Mark decided to sit beside you. Now Caleb's trying to cool him down. Logan does not like Mark, by the way."

I only heard one thing. "Take Oliver? You mean she wants custody?"

The thought brought a tremble to my knees. Just the icy look in the woman's eyes told me she'd be no good for him, but maybe I was wrong. The fact that Logan was setting her up left me torn. What if all she really wanted was a fresh start?

"Logan didn't say. I only talked to him a moment in the kitchen—you know, in between his threats of killing the two cooks holding him down. Poor guys. One took a punch in the face."

"Oh my God!" I gasped. "Because he was trying to keep Logan from coming out and blowing some so-called scheme?"

"No, because the guy made a comment that he once heard Mark say you were terrible in bed."

I blanched. Mark had said that, and Logan had heard it.

"Ignore him. Mark just started rumors to keep other guys away from you because he knew you could do better."

"Right," I mumbled under my breath, my pulse racing. There were rumors? And to drive it home, they were about my performance in the bedroom? I wasn't sure how I felt, other than ready to get the hell out of there.

"Come on, let's get you home. I'm going to stay in the back with a camera, in case anything happens and Natasha does something he can use against her if she tries to go after Oliver."

Hilary walked with me across the restaurant, then gave me a small hug and a sympathetic smile. "It's gonna be all right. Logan should be waiting for you outside."

I slipped out my phone the second she was gone and sent a text.

At Haven. Need a ride home. Please get here fast.

It only took a minute to get a reply.

Be there in 5.

———◆◆◆———

I knew Logan was there the moment I opened the door and stepped outside, the cool night air filling my lungs and helping me keep myself strong. Logan paired with the Haven parking lot was not a friendly memory. He stood in a shadow beside the building.

"You're supposed to be at home resting." His hoarse voice was thick with underlying disdain.

I rolled my eyes, making sure he could see it. I knew where I was supposed to be, and it wasn't with some controlling nut. I started to continue making my way toward the sidewalk when his arm wrapped around my waist, steering me in the opposite direction.

"Cassandra, talk to me! Why did you sit there with him?" Logan yelled.

I flinched, not expecting harshness after the gentleness I'd experienced the past week from him.

"It's none of your business who I sit with!"

"He's no good! Don't let him sway you otherwise."

"You know what, Logan? Despite what you might think, I really can take care of myself. I know exactly who Mark is now, and I don't need you protecting me from him or anyone else!"

My head spun. Standing there with him again, so close and with such raw anger, caused the memory of New Year's to begin running wildly through my thoughts. Something in him seemed to notice, as his rage began to dissipate slowly.

"Fine. I'll go get the car. Wait here." Irritation riddled his voice.

Yeah, I was going to wait all right, but not for him. Just being in that parking lot left me raging inside, as memories of the last time we were there filled my thoughts. I closed my eyes, fighting to block out the haunting images with little success.

"Please hurry, please hurry," I whispered to myself, my hands shoved deep in my coat pockets, legs trembling. I needed my ride to arrive before he returned, and for once, my wish came true.

"I'm not even going to ask why you're here," Luke said, leaning over from the driver's seat to open the door.

"Good."

The moment I stepped forward, Logan's car pulled up, blocking the road from the traffic behind us. I hurried into Luke's truck and slammed the door just as Logan's door opened and he began jogging toward my side of the vehicle.

"Just go," I panted, my adrenaline spiking.

It was childish, but I needed Luke to put some distance between my past and me. Unfortunately, he wasn't moving, and instead staring at me like I was speaking a dead language. I shot him a puppy-eyed plea, but it was too late—his gaze was focused past me to my window, where Logan was lurking. He leaned down and tapped on it.

To my dismay, Luke hit the button to lower the window.

"I can take you home," Logan whispered, leaning against the truck.

"Already have a ride. Good night, Logan." I turned my gaze back out the windshield, staring at the snow-covered road and bright lampposts.

"I'm sorry, all right? I snapped seeing him there with you. Cassandra, I miss you."

I closed my eyes, his gentle words ripping through me and pounding on the walls surrounding my thumping but still broken heart.

"I'm tired," I murmured. "I just want to go home."

His thumb and forefinger caught my chin, turning my face back to him gently. "I'll stop by in the morning?"

The longing in his voice was thick and heavy, begging me to say yes. I needed to get away—from that place where my heart was destroyed, from him and his soul-searching gaze.

"Do what you want. We both know you will, anyway."

"It's too hard to stay away from you, Cassandra. It's killing me." He released my face, finding something in my eyes.

I looked away and took a breath, trying to stay strong. He always got to me. I couldn't hear anymore that night. I couldn't endure the agony in his voice.

"Good night, Logan. Let's go, Luke."

"Make sure she gets inside safely," Logan demanded.

"Of course. I'll take care of her."

Luke's words didn't appear to sit well with Logan. I caught his grip tightening on the windowpane of my door, and I turned to catch his hard stare at Luke. His jaw ticked, but my voice broke through and lightened the intensity.

"I'll be fine. You might as well stay and help Hilary." My own words fell out so evenly and calmly; I relaxed into them.

He stared at me in a long silence, then straightened himself and walked back to his car without another word.

"Take me home, Luke," I said, resting back in the seat.

———◆———

We drove in silence for only a few minutes before Luke asked, "So, you're not dating him, correct?"

"No," I said with a sigh. I didn't want to think about Logan or the darkness plaguing his deep-blue eyes tonight.

"Maybe you should clarify that with him. Or at least shoot him a text to get the hell off my bumper."

I whipped my head back and there, a few feet behind the

vehicle, was Logan's car, following us. I rolled my eyes and turned back around.

"Ignore him."

"Easier said than done. This truck's my baby. One scratch..."

I shook my head, laughing at the ridiculousness of that statement.

"Logan's a safe driver," I said, staring blankly out the window.

As we pulled up my driveway, Luke switched off the ignition, and the headlights of Logan's car pulled up on Luke's side.

"Thanks for the ride." I opened the truck door and looked back, catching Logan standing beside his car door, waiting—for what, I had no idea.

"You want me to walk you in and make sure he doesn't bother you?" Luke asked, his eyes on Logan's intimidating stance.

"No, go home and get some sleep. I owe you enough for making you drive all the way out here."

"It's not a problem, but between you and me, the guy has some serious boundary issues."

"You have no idea," I said with a small chuckle, and leaned across the seat to give him a warm hug and kiss on the cheek. "Thanks again, and good night."

As I climbed out, I noticed Logan's hard gaze was still fixed on Luke, who was now backing out of the driveway. With an irritated eye roll, I headed to the front door and pulled out my key.

"Cassandra—"

"Go home, Logan."

"I just wanted to make sure you got home safely."

I could feel him standing close behind me. Goose bumps flared over my neck and down my arms. Sweat beaded under my thick coat as my body reacted to his nearness, calling out for him to take what he wanted and put me out of my misery.

It was only a matter of time; we both knew it. The only thing I held out hope for was that when he was through with me, I'd someday find a man to put me back together.

The key turned in the lock and I opened the door, never once looking back until I stepped inside, doorknob in hand.

"Luke did a good job getting me home, so you can go," I said, and it wasn't a lie.

"I just wanted to make sure—"

"That I didn't screw him?"

Logan's head tilted slightly, his jaw set. "He wouldn't be that stupid," he said through gritted teeth.

With a sigh, I rolled my eyes. "Good night, Logan."

Logan lifted my chin, staring into my tired eyes. "This is killing me, Cassandra. I want you so badly, and to watch you push me further and further away..." He closed his eyes and shook his head once. "It's too much. I'm losing it."

"What do you want me to say?"

"Tell me you can forgive me...that you still want this." Logan dipped his head down, finger still under my chin, lifting my face as he crushed his lips down over mine.

The kiss was needy; Logan's hands slid over my cheeks and into my hair. His tongue ran over my lips and darted its way inside. I couldn't control myself; my body longed to be his, my thoughts cut off by the taste of his warm, minty breath.

My hands sneaked up and wrapped around his neck, drawing him closer. Every nerve ending in my body sputtered and roared when he pulled back just enough to see my face and gauge my conflicted expression.

"Stop," I breathed.

"No!"

"I can't, all right? I just...can't. I won't be another conquest. Another girl for you to pursue like the one you met on the airplane."

"What the fuck are you talking about? What girl? I haven't even looked at another woman!"

"Julia told me," I confessed, holding his steely gaze in mine. "About the woman you met a couple years ago and flew back and forth to see, doing to her what you're trying to do to me."

"My sister had no right to tell you anything. If you want to know about my past, then ask!" he all but roared, anger evident in his tight expression. "And as for this woman she told you about, my sister has spun that into something very different than it was. Have I ever met a woman on a plane before? Yes, I have—more than one. Not that I feel it's relevant, but if you feel the need to hear about my past, then I'll tell you. None of those women ever got more than a one-time trip to the airport hotel."

He was watching me as I stood there, hanging on every word.

"However, due to geographical issues and a bored mind, I found myself flying out to see one woman in particular who refused my advances. My attention was caught, which was what she'd set out to do. She started a game, trying to seduce me, and pulled back every time before I was satisfied.

"Did I want to date her, start a relationship? No! I wanted to fuck her, and made that perfectly clear. She was the one who thought she could persuade me otherwise—play me using sex so she could marry a man who would help boost her placement in society. There were no feelings involved—we played a *game*—and when I had my fill, I left. She knew exactly what it was. I never led her on, which was why she went snooping into my life and tried to meet my son."

I didn't know what to say. Of course he had a past—I knew that—but the fact that he'd been infatuated with someone before, even if he'd treated her differently, only fed my insecurities further.

"Don't keep pushing me away. You're not like her; you're

not like any of them. I feel this. I do. You're a part of me that I can't escape. I don't ever want to. I'll tell you whatever you need to hear, do whatever I have to. But you have to stop pushing me away," he pleaded, reaching out to grab my hands, but I stepped back farther into the house.

"You should go. I'm sorry, but you need to let me go. Don't keep doing this to me, to you. It's time to move on," I said, beginning to close the door.

He stood there, eyes dark and hard and jaw clenched until the door latched shut.

The moment I turned the lock, my back slumped against the closed door. The pain in my chest was gut-wrenching and tears pooled in my eyes, but the thought of giving in was more terrifying.

A loud spin of tires pulled me from my thoughts and I peeked out the front curtains to catch Logan peeling out of my driveway. But instead of pulling into his, he flew down the road, heading toward town.

Chapter Eight

POKER FACE

The next morning, I sat up, having spent too much of the night staring at the bronze ceiling light, my mind devoid of everything but him—the taste of his lips, feel of his hands. I wasted hours trying to decipher the oddity of my emotions and undeniable sensations in my body when he was near. The combination of his thick voice and deep, thoughtful eyes did something to me I couldn't comprehend. Worse was the knowledge that he left angry, heading someplace unknown to do God knew what.

With a scrunched face, I grimaced at the throb in my chest as I threw my legs off the side of the bed; it wasn't from my bruised ribs, but my angry heart. I didn't want to miss him. I didn't want to feel any of these complex and infuriating emotions tormenting me.

The rising sun shining through my bedroom curtains brought a frown to my lips. It was the time of morning I'd usually be out for a jog. Even in the coldest winters, I never skipped my morning exercise. But that wasn't an option now, and no amount of charming endearments, fancy flowers, or free meals would change that. Yet there was no denying Logan cared in a way that taunted me. But was it enough?

After watching him walk away, I was even more torn. I wished he could give me more time—allow me to come to him when I was ready.

With a tightening grip on the robe I'd flung on, I shuffled to the kitchen and poured myself a glass of orange juice. The plastic bottle of pain pills sat on the table, but the dull ache was manageable enough, so I decided to go without. A little pain was better than spending another day heavy headed from the side effect of fatigue they caused.

The sun was making its way up and the cool morning air leaked in from the old windows, further energizing my renewed spirit. It was a new day and the beginning of a new week, and I was ready to start taking advantage of a fresh start.

Enjoying the freedom of my own house so early in the morning, I heard a honk sound from outside. It was none of my business, but I couldn't help myself as I approached the front window and pulled back the curtain with one hand, holding my juice in the other. I beamed at the snow covering the ground, nearly a foot deep. My driveway sat empty. No car to warm up or scrape ice away from...no, my car sat in a junkyard somewhere, demolished.

The thought brought a sigh through my downturned lips, which grew deeper when I noticed movement in Logan's driveway. My attention was diverted back to why I was staring outside to begin with. I assumed he was heading to work, and part of me hoped he wouldn't stop over as he said he would. It was going to take more than a few days apart to flush him from my system.

What I wasn't expecting, however, was what I saw when I leaned in a little closer to the glass: he wasn't alone. Craning my neck every which way to get a better angle, I pressed my nose against the cold window, my breath fogging it up. I squinted to see beyond the snow-covered shrubs separating us and caught sight of a woman standing in front of him.

My stomach dropped, the death grip on my juice glass nearly bursting it into tiny shards as an unexpected surge of fury coursed through my veins. Logan stood beside a sleek black

SUV, laughing with the unfamiliar woman. Her short, dark hair was cut into a sloping bob, but that was about all I could make of her appearance other than the skintight jeans she wore with a form-fitting, snow-white coat.

My mouth lacked enough moisture due to my gaping, and thus swallowing proved futile. I stood there, unblinking, zoned out until the woman leaned in, embracing him in an all-too-comfortable and lingering hug followed by a kiss on his cheek.

I dropped the curtain and stepped back, struggling to control the jealousy festering in my heart and seeping into my wounds. I'd made it clear the previous night that he stood no chance, and he'd finally listened. That was that. Logan was the same guy he'd always been—quick to jump into bed with the first woman who looked his way. I knew it was bound to happen, but it still stung.

I wasn't worth fighting for, after all, and I was right to hold onto the fact that he wasn't going to change for some small-town kindergarten teacher.

The walk back to the kitchen was nothing more than a fog-induced trance. I dumped the remainder of my orange juice down the drain. Then something, most likely my self-preservation switch, clicked.

I was stronger than I ever thought possible—Logan had said so himself, though I didn't need to hear it from him to know it was true.

A soft knock rattled my front door as well as my thoughts, pulling me away from the melancholy breaking my spirit as quickly as it had recovered.

Through the peephole, I was met with the brilliant smile and scruff jaw of the infuriating neighbor I couldn't dismiss. I was sure he'd had a hell of good night with Miss Too Tall for Her Own Good, so what did he want with me?

I cringed. The fact that he was standing on my doorstep before eight in the morning after a tryst just further alluded to his disreputable nature.

Resolute to keep things civil, I cracked open the door just enough to see him. Cocking my head to the side, I outstretched a hand, holding it against the frame to block any chance he had at entering. If he so much as touched me after that bimbo had her claws on him, I was certain I'd either scream or knock him in the mouth; possibly both, with the way I was feeling—thoroughly disgusted.

"Good morning," he said with such tenderness that my backbone began to waver. "I hope you slept well. My night was…exhausting."

That definitely didn't help his case, and my heart took offense. It stiffened my body, reinforced my grip, and challenged my will to keep my reply civil. He must've seen the irritation in my set frown, because his brows lowered in thought before he spoke further. Was he going to pretend last night never happened?

"I shouldn't have left angry. I'm sorry. It's only been a week since you've been home." He ticked his head to the side, watching me stand there, giving nothing away before he sighed. "I know I have to give you more time…believe me, I'm trying, but it's just so damn hard. I'm not sure what to do anymore. This is all new to me, to…to feel this need for you." His voice strained with the weight of what he was trying to say. "I feel helpless…not being able to fix this. Make it right."

The walls surrounding my heart began to shudder and shake, and it took everything I had to keep it hidden.

"Mm-hmm," I replied, my lips clamped together tightly.

His pained eyes searched mine. "You have to give me something to hold onto, sweetheart…a reason to keep fighting when you repeatedly push me away."

I'm here! I wanted to shout out to the world. *Wait for me, please*, but I stood silent, terrified. How had I become so weak? Seeing him with that woman had pushed me over the edge. He'd want more than I could ever give him, so it was for the best if he walked away. Better to get out now before it was too late.

He nodded after a long, silent pause.

I hated him for bringing me so low, for creating a storm of brewing rage deep in my soul. I hated myself for wanting to take him in my arms and kiss him until I forgot. I had to fight through it to find a way to get him off my porch.

Finally, I opened my mouth and swallowed the rough lump that had formed, speaking in a soft voice. "I was about to take a shower, and though you seem to think that's our new thing, I prefer to do it alone. Goodbye."

"All right. I understand, and I can't say I blame you." His voice was a quiet rumble, his eyes downcast. "But I tried. I wanted you then, and I want you now....to love you and take care of you....but I can't keep waking up every day feeling like shit for something I didn't mean…something I can't take back." His eyes grew hard, staring straight through me now.

My teeth had dug so far into my bottom lip to silence the quivering forcing its way out that they nearly drew blood. He was hurting, but so was I, and it was exactly why this was for the best. We'd only hurt each other again. I didn't want to give him hope if there was none to take. He needed to move on.

I began to shut the door when his hand flew out, holding it open.

"I have to go out of town for a meeting. I tried to have it rescheduled, but it's important that I go."

"Then have a good day at work, Logan." My words were monotone, needing him to leave before I lost my resolve. I added a little smile to pull off the convincing performance…to let him leave not knowing my pain matched his.

The tension in his broad shoulders grew visibly stiffer. His jaw clenched, working under the skin until he spoke again, his eyes boring into mine.

"If I leave here right now with no word from you that we

ever have a chance…then I'm done. I won't come back. I'll move on, like you asked."

That was how much he cared? A week's worth of his time, and then he gives up? That wasn't love. Not to me.

The disturbing bite in his tone brought me back, and I released my sore bottom lip.

"*Goodbye*, Logan."

His expression hardened, a vein bulging in the side of his neck pulling my gaze from the tight frown marring his beautiful features as I held strong. It only took a brief moment until he turned on his heel and stalked down my front steps, cutting through the lawn to his house.

There was no stopping the waterworks that came when I slammed the door and fell to the floor, curling into a trembling ball. It was over. I wanted him out of my life, and now he was. If only I didn't feel like my entire world was falling further into pieces.

—◆◆◆—

By the time the clock struck ten that night, I'd called Hilary over to distract me from myself. We were sitting crossed-legged on my living-room floor, a deck of cards in hand and two empty wine bottles beside us. She was going to regret it in the morning, but the weatherman had called for an overnight snowstorm and she was convinced school would close down the next day.

"That is not a full house!" I exclaimed, bending forward to examine the cards she'd laid out. "Right? I mean…no, that's a…"

My head flew back as laughter broke out, followed by a sudden hiccup. My hand flew over my chest as I sucked in my lips, willing my giggling to cease.

"Yes it is! There is a—" She looked up from her cards she'd laid on the carpet, then quickly swooped them back into her hand. "Shit!"

"I'm out," I said, dropping the cards and rolling to my side, stretching out my legs. She did the same, her hand under her cheek propping her up, facing me. We officially sucked at poker.

"It's been over three weeks since the night of the accident. Eventually, you'll have to talk about what happened. You know that, right?"

Her voice was kind and gentle, but it still stung my heart. I was ashamed to tell her how Logan's feelings for me were so different from my own.

I mimicked her position and smiled, changing the subject. "So, did Caleb enjoy the Bond-girl look you had going on?"

With a slight pout to her lip, she conceded.

"Fine, we can talk about Caleb, but I'm not going to stop hounding you until I hear at least the Cliffs Notes version of New Year's. I need to know if I should be ashamed for being Team Logan." She tilted her head slightly, gauging my stoic emotions. "Should I? 'Cause I really like the guy, and it's obvious he genuinely cares about you."

Desperate for Logan's name to vanish from my ears, I asked the unthinkable that I knew she'd been waiting to gush about. "So, Caleb…what's he like in bed?"

She chuckled and dipped her head down, then looked back at me, grinning. "Amazing. Mind-blowing. Toe-curling. I have never screamed so loud in my life. And the way he's so eager to ensure I never leave bed unsatisfied…well, let's just say I'm madly in love with the man. It's better than I ever dreamed it could be."

I lay there resting my head on my arm and watching her talk, her eyes bright and face glowing as she filled me in on the little romantic gestures he did for her: the way he opened doors, held her hand, and never went to sleep without telling her he loved her. How did all that happen so soon? Logan and I met at the same time Caleb came back, and we were so far away from having any of that.

Hilary had it so easy. Caleb adored her, and anyone could see that. Logan, on the other hand, adored sex.

"We're out?" I asked, sitting up and shaking the empty bottles.

Hilary stood and reached for her phone on the coffee table. "Good thing Caleb has the hookup."

"The hookup?" I laughed.

"Yep, and he's going to make sure we have everything we need tonight." As she spoke, her fingers slid over the phone, texting. "Done. Reinforcements are on their way."

—◆◆◆—

"Tequila or the house special? Pick your poison. And if you so much as *hint* to Logan that I brought these over, I'll be sure no one in this town makes you a grilled cheese again," Caleb threatened with a half-serious smile as he stood at my door an hour later.

Giddy at seeing my favorite wine in his hand, I snatched the bottle, pulled him in for a quick hug, then grabbed the other bottle.

"Didn't realize you were a drinker." Luke appeared smiling beside Caleb, his eye flicking from me to the bottles I was clutching way too tightly.

"What can I say? I was feeling a celebration was in order. It's my first day off painkillers."

"Wow, already? I thought the doctor said it would be a few more days before you—"

"I'm fine, and right now, instead of feeling like my ribs are going to explode through my chest or my leg is being dug into, I only feel warm and fuzzy."

"Leave the girl be," Caleb interrupted, saving me from a big-brother speech as they walked inside.

"Finally!" Hilary was wrapped around Caleb before I even closed the door behind them.

"There's my girl," Caleb whispered into her lips as they kissed. Hilary's hands dipped to his waist and didn't stop until she had a firm grip on his ass.

"I would say get a room, but would prefer it not be in my house." I shook my head, sobering and not liking it.

"I'm a little drunk," Hilary giggled, holding up her thumb and pointer finger to show how much.

"I can see that." Caleb chuckled and placed a kiss on the tip of her nose.

Having seen too much, I headed to the kitchen for a glass.

"You do realize those lovebirds are not going to quit anytime soon, right?" Luke said, following me.

"Oh, well. I'm happy for them." I downed the glass I filled, then poured some more.

"Yeah, you look absolutely thrilled."

I glared at him but my lips betrayed me, pulling into a smile as I downed the second glass. I said nothing else, instead filling a glass for Hilary, and walked back out.

"No thanks. Caleb wants to take me for a ride in his car." She leaned in. "Actually, I'll be doing the riding," she whispered all too loudly.

I laughed. "Well, have fun, I guess."

Fantastic. Now I was going to be stuck home alone with no one to drink with. I barely drank in general, let alone by myself.

Her smile dropped, teeth tugging on her bottom lip. "No," she said, her eyes downcast. "That would make me a shitty friend. We'll stay. I can wait to get him alone."

I shook my head, smiling. "Go! Have fun. It's all right, really."

"You're sure? We can stay."

"Goodbye."

Hilary threw her arms around me, hugging me tightly. "I

promise I'll make it up to you," she whispered. I nodded and watched her flutter back to Caleb, her hands diving into his back pockets as her lips met his cheek.

"I'm not getting in that car," Luke stated from behind me.

Hilary stuck her tongue out at Luke playfully, then jumped up on Caleb's back.

"We won't do a thing till I get you home. Promise," Caleb said, looking back at his brother.

"Not falling for that again. My ass is not getting anywhere near that car while you two are in it," Luke said, making a face.

I swatted my hands at Caleb to go. Hilary waved with one hand, the other around his neck. As they walked out, I noticed his hands holding her ass to stabilize her on his back were already getting friskier by the second.

Yeah, they could leave. My night didn't need to include watching a make-out session. When I turned to walk to my couch, Luke was already comfortable on it, leg resting over his knee, drink in hand.

"I don't blame you. I wouldn't get in that car for a while if I were you." We both chuckled, and I slid down beside him. "You can crash here if you promise to be a good drinking buddy tonight."

He thought it over. "Fine, but I have two demands."

"Shoot."

"First, I have to say that for the record, I do not condone you drinking away your issues. And secondly, I want to hear what you know about Logan's sister."

I laughed, pretending I the one name I couldn't stand. "Deal."

Chapter Nine

SNOW ANGELS

Midnight had come and gone and still the music blared, rumbling through the house. Cards were scattered over my dining-room table, and the alcohol was gone. My plan to forget all about my troubles was going off without a hitch, aside from the maddening pang in the corner of my heart I had trouble ignoring.

Logan had already moved on. Why did that hurt so much? One minute I couldn't stand him, and the next, I needed him.

I lifted the bottle, staring at it as if I could will it to refill. No luck. Luke sat across from me with the last of the tequila in hand, staring out the window.

"Hey!" he complained when I snatched the bottle.

"Come on, let's build a snowman." I stood, wobbling to the back door.

"A snowman?" His eyes were glazed over when I looked back at him, grabbing a sweatshirt from the chair beside me. I giggled as he stared past me, confused and completely trashed.

"Uh-huh. You know, three balls and some twigs. Hmmm…carrots, and what else…" I pulled the hoodie over my thermal that I wore with dark-wash jeans and grabbed my boots.

He burst out laughing, head thrown back, but I was serious. I hadn't made a snowman since I was a child, and I was desperate to go outside and enjoy the snowfall.

My thick winter coat wasn't around, or at least within viewing distance to call out to me, and I was too far gone to process just how cold it would be that late at night in mid-January. Shoving my feet inside my tall suede boots, I was ready to go. He stood and pulled on his coat and gloves and ambled past me, holding open the door.

"Ladies first."

The snow on the ground was perfect. Soft and fresh, it continued to drift down over us. My hands stung from the thin gloves I grabbed walking outside and my ears throbbed from lack of a hat, but I was having too much fun to stop or even care.

Forming a small snowball, I rolled it on the ground. I watched mesmerized as it grew bigger and bigger, amazed at how easily it created the base.

Luke walked over carrying the belly for it, and I burst out laughing. The ball was more oval than round, and his expression changed from proud to insulted.

He dropped it in place on top of mine, and when he stepped back to admire our unfinished masterpiece, he slipped, stumbling over his own feet and landing on his back. He laughed so loudly I could've sworn it was coming through surround-sound speakers.

"Need a hand?" My eyes were filled with unshed tears from the endless laughter that poured out of me as I reached down. His face brightened and lips curled up, and before I had time to react, I saw the spark of mischief in his eye.

It was too late. He dragged me down beside him.

With a childlike giggle, I let out a deep breath, taking in the glorious view above. I didn't care that the cold was burning through my skin, my sweater buried in snow. The night sky was lit by the reflection in the snow of the bright stars above us. My eyes grew heavier the longer we lay there until I felt Luke sit up.

"I'm drunk," he grumbled, staring off at the woods.

"I didn't even think you knew what alcohol was," I admitted, giggling again. He was always so levelheaded—especially compared to Caleb.

"I'll have you know I've been to a few keggers in my day." He looked back, offended.

I raised an eyebrow, then blew out a deep, gurgled laugh.

"All right, one," he confessed. "But I dated a girl once who liked to party. She'd stop by my dorm after curfew and damn, was it always a night to remember."

"Luke!" I swatted him on the arm. I'd never heard him talk like that before. "I'm appalled, but relieved, to know you're not a virgin."

"A virgin!? Hey, Caleb isn't the only Townsend man who knows how to please a woman."

A light flickered on at Logan's house, drawing both our attention.

"Maybe Julia's there," I suggested, raising an eyebrow. "I would go see, but then I might run into you-know-who."

"Well, if you see the girl, maybe you'll tell her she's dating a douchebag." He stood and walked to my back porch, grabbing the tequila bottle and taking a long swig.

"Not my place," I sang out.

Luke must've sensed I didn't like where the conversation was heading because he called out, "Show me your wings, angel!"

I smiled. As if I could transport myself to the past as a child in my grandparents' backyard, I closed my eyes and moved my arms and legs, creating a beautiful angel.

My body was warm from the liquor, but the chill from the snow soaked through to the bone. The weight in my arms and legs took over, and slowly I began to drift into the night when the crunch of snow and an "Oh, shit!" from Luke brought me back.

"Get up!"

I opened my eyes, my carefree smile falling away, only to find a dark, familiar figure standing over me. My glossy eyes readjusted to the darkness, slowly revealing Logan's taut jaw and livid expression. I was too drunk to care, instead letting my gaze travel down his lean body, admiring the way his strong chest bulged from his dark wool coat.

His damp hair led my thoughts straight to him in the shower—an image I'd dreamed about multiple times before that fateful night—but even still, that thought alone held my attention. His hair was tousled just enough to help me visualize the way he must run his hands through it when he steps out of the shower. It was one of the sexiest things I'd ever seen.

Every inch of thrill inside me skyrocketed to life. I found myself becoming heated and aroused, and less frozen to the ground.

Why is he here? I thought he was gone for good. I guess that's the problem with being neighbors.

"So help me, God, Cassandra." He ran his hands over his face with an exasperated sigh. "You can either get up and walk back inside your house, or I'll carry your ass to mine." His voice was thick, serious, and surprisingly unpleasant, reminding me why I'd been trying to block him out all week to begin with.

Buzz kill.

I sat up on my elbows and scoffed. "No!" I exclaimed before falling back into my outline in the snow, grinning to myself.

Luke was there instantly when Logan reached down to me. "Hey, relax. I'll take her inside. She was just trying to have some fun."

Logan stood straight again to acknowledge him, shooting daggers, with his jaw clenched in a fury. "You're not taking her anywhere."

"What the hell is going on that you had to wake me at…oh, Cassandra's having a play date." Jax's chuckle rumbled through the night as he approached us. If I'd had half my wits, I would've been humiliated. "This is why you made me come out here to help you? 'Cause she's hooking up?"

Jax looked to me and winked. "Good for you, baby. Now carry on, and I'll get my big brother back to bed." Jax put his arm on Logan's shoulder, only to have it ripped away in the same instant.

"Take Luke back home to sleep it off in the guest room."

"I'm fine—"

Logan took two steps toward him, his jaw tight under the skin. "If you weren't Caleb's kid brother, I'd leave you to pass out here and fucking freeze."

"Logan!" I yelled. "What the hell is your problem!?"

I sat back up and attempted to pull myself to stand until the ground began to spin. Suddenly I was going down headfirst, so I used all my weight to throw myself back, falling on my ass. With my head hung low between my knees, buried in my hands, vomit began rising, too quickly to stop.

No, no, no!

I swallowed the burn back down, making a face at the acidic taste and rancid burn, then looked over at Luke. He gave a sympathetic shrug, and I could tell he was sobering up. I nodded, reassuring him I was all right, and watched him walk away with Jax.

"Come on." Logan's hand extended down to me. I slapped it away.

"Cassandra." He sighed. "You know I will carry you in there, sweet—" He stopped, unable to say it. His eyes dropped, and the guilt in them only fueled the fire burning inside me.

I wanted to laugh. I wasn't his sweetheart, and I was all too aware of that.

Taking a quick breath to find my balance, I scrambled to my feet, my body rocking side to side, head complaining. The stiffness in my joints and soreness in my chest were nothing

102

compared to the anger thundering though my entire system.

"That's right, I'm not your sweetheart, so you can't tell me what to do!"

"You're drunk. I'm putting you to bed," he demanded, and I snapped.

My body swayed forward and we were face to face, lips almost touching. "I'm sure your bed is already full of enough sluts to keep you busy tonight," I slurred venomously.

His hands clutched my shoulders, stabilizing me.

"Get off me, you ass!" I shoved him away.

His eyes darkened as he clutched me tighter, his back teeth grinding. "Cassandra," he warned, but I couldn't stop. I pushed against him with all my strength, and he released his hold on me.

"What!? What do you want from me!?" I yelled, stepping back, arms stretched out. Then it dawned on me. My eyes narrowed into menacing slits. "Oh, wait, I remember. You want to fuck me. Well, here I am! What are you waiting for, huh?"

He stood there, silently stoic.

"You want me? Come and get me." I yanked my freezing, wet hoodie over my head followed by the white thermal underneath, leaving me exposed in a pink cotton bra.

He stepped closer, intent on stopping my actions, but I continued backing away, nearly stumbling to the ground. By some luck, I managed to steady myself, rage controlling my moves.

My fingers worked quickly to undo the button of my jeans, but his hands were there, stopping me before I could tug the zipper down. I smacked his hand away and looked up to see his brows lowered over his glistening eyes, staring at my chest covered in deep-yellow bruises.

I snorted a half sob, half chuckle. "Oh, right, now you don't want me anymore—now that I'm damaged goods, now that you broke my heart and sent me off to get run down!" I poked my finger at his chest. "You should have stopped me from driving! Stopped me from leaving! Stopped me from ever falling in love with you!"

I slapped my hand over my mouth, breathless, speechless. *Love?* I gasped, staring dumbly at the ground, tears prickling my eyes.

"No." It spilled in a tiny whisper from my lips. *No no no.* I ached to take it back—not my confession to him, but from my own ears. *I never loved him, did I?* My head was spinning, and before I could figure it out, his rough, broken voice penetrated the silence.

"Cassandra."

I lifted my head slowly, meeting his glossy eyes that held so much tenderness I had to force myself to look away. It brought forth too many memories of the last few months I'd spent with him. I sucked in a chilly breath of air and released it again and again.

My hands trembled as I held them up to stop him from coming any closer when I heard his footsteps in the snow.

"No." I wiped away a stray tear. I needed to stay strong. I took another breath and met his gaze. "You don't get to be all nice now. You don't get to waltz back into my life as though nothing happened. I'm tired of this—tired of you playing games with me." My chin quivered, my teeth catching my bottom lip to calm it. I took another breath, closing my eyes as it refilled my lungs.

"You drive me insane. Do you understand that? Do you realize what you've done to me?" My hands flew up, gripping the sides of my head, pulling at my hair. "You made me feel all those things. Why?" My voice grew louder as the war raged inside me, and my arms dropped to my sides. "Why did you do this to me? Why did you make me care about you? Why? Answer me!"

He said nothing.

Unable to control myself any longer, I barreled forward and smacked him hard against the chest. "Answer me, God damn it!"

It felt good, but I knew it wasn't right. It wasn't me. I didn't know who I was anymore.

Logan didn't even stumble back. His strong body took each blow with ease as he let me unload on him.

"Why? Please, tell me why!" I screamed, shoving him again and again. "I wanted you, all of you, and it was just a game! Why? Do you like seeing me suffering—dying inside every time you're near? Because even after what you did, what you said to me, I still feel you there, in my broken heart. You're a part of me, and I hate you for that! So tell me why! Please!" I continued, tears raining down my face, my palms banging against his chest over and over until my head dropped forward and rested there.

"I thought you were different, but it was all a game," I finished, panting.

My voice was not my own. Defeated, my knees gave out, causing me to slump down. He caught me before I hit the ground and pulled me up, cradling me in his arms, where I cried. It hurt everywhere as he carried me inside.

Blood pounded in my ears and nausea settled over me as my anger washed away, and I was left with my raw, vulnerable pain, laid out for him to see. With my head buried in his neck, tears covering my face, I let it all out in a shattered whisper.

"You terrify me. I fight so...so hard to keep my guard up, to push you away... even if that means you'll hate me. Everyone can hate me for pushing you away...but they don't know. They don't feel it. It hurts. Everything hurts, 'cause I miss you. I miss us." I shook my head violently. "I can't. I can't."

"Shhh, you need rest right now." We were in my bedroom, and he laid me down on the mattress gently.

"I know what you're doing, and I know that it's working. But I can't...I can't, Logan, please..." My eyelids were heavy, a fog setting in as they drifted shut. I wasn't sure whether I said it aloud, but I longed for him to hear me as I repeated "Don't hurt me" until I was taken away into the darkness.

Chapter Ten

NAKED

Bright, glaring light assaulted my eyelids, causing my face to scrunch, squeezing them tightly. With a zombie-like groan, I pulled away from my liquor-fueled slumber. In one swift motion, I whipped my pounding head around, burying it under my pillow. The movement was too quick and my head too heavy; nausea hit instantly. I choked down the rising bile and grabbed my head.

"Oh, God," I croaked.

"Good morning, sweetheart."

My eyes flew open, my body painfully rigid.

What is he doing here?

"On the side table. Drink *all* of it."

I lifted my head, hair wild around my face, just enough to see the tall glass of water with two oval pills sitting beside it. As much as I wanted to tell him to get the hell out, my throat was too parched.

First things first: with a trembling hand, I lifted the water slowly and savored the coolness breaking through, hydrating me back to the living. I popped the pills a second later, then lay back with a sigh, twisting around to stare at the ceiling. I wasn't in the mood to deal with him right then, and the memory of the previous night was still nothing but a blur.

A sharp burn tore through my stomach, followed by a low

growl. *Definitely should've eaten more last night.* I rubbed my hand over my abs under the blanket and froze.

What the hell!?

With my heart rate picking up as my thought process jolted back to life, blood rushed to my cheeks, pushing me faster through the fog. I sat up on my elbows, clutching the blanket to my chest, and narrowed my eyes at the infuriatingly beautiful man staring back at me, unaffected.

"Where the hell are my clothes!?"

Logan sat in the armchair across from my bed, his leg slung over his knee, giving nothing away in his expression.

"You were soaked to the bone."

"So you stripped me down?"

"To be honest, you did most of the work for me."

What? What happened last night?

Unable to support myself any longer, I fell back onto the pillows and closed my eyes, begging the memories to return. Logan remained silent, as if waiting for it all to come back to me. It wasn't long before I was watching a slow-moving picture in my foggy mind, reliving the events of the past night. It was all there: the memory of me screaming at him, telling him to screw me, and then attacking him until I could stand no longer. I had no clear recollection of what all I'd said to him, only remembering the image of him standing there, stoic, taking each blow I delivered to his hard chest.

I groaned for at least the third time that morning, holding my head and rolling to my side, feeling worse about myself.

"Can you leave now, please?" My voice was hollow, and nothing more than a defeated whisper. I was too tired to fight with him.

"Not yet. We need to talk first."

"I have nothing to say." I couldn't look at him now. I hated even talking to him—not because I was angry about New Year's or embarrassed by my actions; no, it was worse. I couldn't bear to be around him because seeing him there for that one small moment in my bedroom, so gorgeous in a plain white tee and black pajama pants, caused my entire existence to still call out to him.

"I have plenty to say, and I need for you to listen. Understand?" His voice grew darker, and my anger brewed.

With a huff, I gripped the covers that were half hiding my face, resisting the urge to peer over at him. "I'm not a child!"

"Considering your actions last night, I may beg to differ."

That was it. I wanted him out. I didn't care that his mere presence left me strangely aroused, or that despite everything, I still longed to be in his arms. He needed to get out.

I tore the blanket off my body—which was covered only in pink lace panties—and climbed out of bed. Swallowing down the nausea the fast movement brought up and with one hand covering my breasts, I pointed to my bedroom door with the other.

"Get the hell out of my house, Logan!"

He stood, eyes on mine and not once straying down my body. He must've had a good-enough look while undressing me already.

"No. Now lie back down before you hurt yourself."

I only saw red. "What is your problem? Why are you still here? Take a hint already!" I balled my free hand into a fist, calming myself. "You know what? Ah! Never mind. I already know why you're here." I tilted my head to the side. "It's called guilt. Well, don't sweat it—I survived."

He stalked toward me, standing a few feet directly in front of me with a tight jaw and hard eyes.

"I fucked up with you. It's the biggest regret I've ever had, and I endure it every second of every damn day. But I will not stand by and watch you act out like you did last night, getting drunk and nearly passing out in the shitty ten-degree weather. No, that's not happening, because whether you want to believe it or not, I care about you. I have ever since that damned carnival, and I'm not going to let you hurt yourself because you can't deal with how you feel about me."

"Feel about you?" I hissed. "You are such an egotistical ass! I thought you were done—walking away for good!"

"Turns out no matter how hard I try, I can't get you out of my head. That leaves only one choice: you will get over yourself and let me in!"

"Let you in?" I barked, laughing manically. "I did, and you treated me like dirt the moment it got rough!"

"Fuck!" he roared. "You will forgive me, God damn it! You can't stay mad at me forever. I won't allow it."

"And I won't let you make a fool of me twice!"

"I won't! Don't you get it!? I can't get you out of my head, Cassandra. Just give me a chance. Tell me you're mine."

I inhaled through my nostrils, wanting him to see, to understand.

"Listen to yourself. Two weeks! It's been two weeks. So you tell me—is that all you think it takes to earn my forgiveness, my trust, and my love? I was with Mark for *five* years, loyal to a fault, and yet I'm unable to forgive him, so why should I forgive you?"

His eyes darkened as he stepped closer, his hand reaching out, palm cradling my cheek. "Because unlike Mark, I know how precious you are."

"Yet you walked away yesterday morning," I interrupted.

His shoulders fell, hand dropping away. "I…"

His expression was pained, his words hesitant. "I came back. That's what matters." Everything in him shifted back to the confident man I knew as he continued.

"No! You still walked away because I'm not ready. And I'll never be ready. I know I've been hard on you, doing everything I can to force you to see that I'm nothing special, not worth your time. But it's because I can't go back to where we were that night. It should never have happened. We should have stayed friends and never tried—"

"No! I'll regret that night for the rest of my life, but not us taking a chance. That was the best thing we did. I want to know everything about you, hear your voice every morning and every night. I will never risk losing you again. I can't sleep thinking of you alone in this house, so close yet so far away. I know you're scared, and I know it's only been a couple weeks. I don't expect you to crawl into bed with me and let me claim you as mine. I'm only asking that you stop pushing me away."

My eyes closed. "Logan, I don't know who I am right now," I managed, my breath ragged. "My head's all screwed up, and I don't want to hurt you, but seeing you tears me up. I don't know what I feel for you anymore, or if I even feel anything at all."

"Don't lie to me. It's easy to see the effect I have on you."

I attempted to push back, furious at myself that he was right, that I was so weak. But he grabbed my forearms and ran his hands back up my cheeks, cradling my face in his hands again.

"As well as the incredible effect you have on me. I can't even describe it, the way you make me feel...so alive...so hungry for life, for you, for love. It's all so new to me, but I don't want to lose it. I don't want to lose you. It fucking kills me every night, thinking about what I said to you."

Logan dropped his hands away and stepped back, standing in silence for a long moment, his brows drawn low in thought. I didn't speak either as I watched him, my rage dying down as my heart broke all over again. We were shattered—both of us.

With soft eyes and a strained hoarse voice, he continued. "I'll never forgive myself for what I did to you." His voice was lost in his throat. He swallowed, his face torn, and placed his hands on my forearms, which I took comfort in against all rational thought. "Cassandra, I want a chance to make this right.

Not because of guilt, but because I lo—"

"Don't." I spoke quickly, surprising myself, but I couldn't hear it. "Don't you dare say those words to me." I sat back on my bed with a slow grace.

Logan dipped down in front of my knees and pulled the blanket up from behind me. Tiny goose bumps flared over my body. His thumb caressed my bare back for the briefest moment when he pulled it over my shoulders, and I leaned into it. It felt so good, but the pain associated with his touch seared my heart. Tears sprung from my eyes, and I dropped my head into my hands.

"Shhh, please…don't cry, sweetheart."

I sobbed harder. His arm wrapped around me, the bed shifting with his weight beside me. I didn't fight him when he pulled me to his chest. I couldn't fight it, and in that moment, I didn't want to. The world around me faded away, leaving me with only my tears and his closeness.

I didn't know how much time passed—seconds, minutes, perhaps hours—before my tears slowed and my breathing finally came easier. His hand ran through my hair, providing comfort only he could offer. His sweet voice soothed me, assuring me that I'd be all right—that we'd be all right.

I lay there numb in his arms, snuggling in his lap, my head tucked into the nape of his neck. His skin was so warm and inviting, I couldn't resist inhaling his intoxicating masculinity. Before I could tell myself to stop and that it was dangerous to go there, my lips were on him. Defenseless to his body speaking to mine, they brushed lightly across his neck and back again, where I placed a small lingering kiss under his chin.

He didn't move or say a word, but from the way his hand stilled mid-caress on my back, I knew he felt it—felt the hope I held onto that one day I could forgive him, that there might still be a possibility for us to share a love so powerful it could erase my pain, insecurities, and distrust; a love that could wipe away the past. But for now, it wasn't there. A shred of hope was all I had to give.

With a small sniffle, I wiped my nose, not wanting the moment to end and reality to crash back down over us. I felt his body stiffen when I began to sit up, holding me in place.

Did he feel it, too? Did it torture him to let me go as much as it did me?

If I allowed myself a moment of honesty, I'd admit I never wanted to be apart from him, my Logan, the man I thought I knew. But the truth was there was more to Logan than I'd realized. He was more than just the guy I fell for, and I couldn't trust him anymore.

I braced myself against his chest, sneaking another greedy touch as I sat up. Before I let go fully, his hands went to the sides of my face, cupping my cheeks, the pads of his thumbs wiping away final stray tears.

"I'm sorry. Out of everyone, I never wanted to hurt you. I'm...I'm thoughtless and careless. I'd never allowed anyone in after Natasha left, yet I couldn't keep you away. I'm drawn to you, Cassandra—I have been ever since that morning I jogged behind you, admiring your body, wanting to reach out and snatch you up to have my way with you. I'll never forget the image of you in those little shorts you were wearing." He smiled at the memory he must've been recollecting while my cheeks flushed.

"I have never been more aroused at the break of dawn running down a back country road, but then you went and leapt over that damn puddle, so carefree and full of life. Something inside me cracked open, and I knew you could be so much more than another frivolous night tryst. It terrified me how quickly I wanted to know more about you."

My eyes fell to my lap as he released my face, moving his thumb and forefinger to take my chin gently, lifting my head up to meet his eyes. They were glossy with unshed tears.

"I tried to fight it, Cassandra. I thought if I could charm you, convince you to give me one night, that it would make you no different than any other woman. But you are so headstrong. I loved that about you."

There was that word again—a word I couldn't hear from his perfect lips. He loved that about me.

Wait, *loved*? As in past tense? Did it even matter anymore?

It must have, because I couldn't stop myself from leaning in and touching my lips to his very gently. His hold fell from my chin, and with calculated ease, as though he afraid he'd scare me away, his hand slid to my cheek.

His lips never moved, his fingertips stroking my flushed cheek as my mouth pressed to his. There was nothing else; I just stayed there, inhaling the moment, wishing I could forget all the reasons why I couldn't let him back in.

With a soft peck, I rested my forehead against his and swallowed the lump swelling in my throat.

"I can't," I murmured, breathless. "I'm so…scared. Please…"

He cupped my face and pulled me back to see it clearly. "I know, and I'm well aware that I don't deserve you. But I need you to know I never meant what I said that night. I wanted to give you everything, and I still do. You're the only woman I've ever felt this way about."

His thumb ran over my chin, eyes flickering to my lips that longed to connect with his once more. Yet I knew I wasn't ready, and didn't believe I ever would be. For forgiveness, perhaps, but I'd never be able to forget all the red flags that had been in my face, now scolding me for thinking he'd change—for me.

"I can't walk away. Not from you. It nearly killed me waiting for any information from the doctors in the hospital. I wouldn't have survived had I lost you, and now you're here, in my arms, and I'll never let you go again."

"Logan, I—"

"It's okay to be frightened; hell, I've never been more terrified in my life. I know how I made you feel, and you have every right to hate me right now."

"I don't hate you. I hate myself for still wanting you."

His voice deepened, taking on a firm authority. "I'll prove to you that I can be everything you need—everything you always wanted. My heart and soul belong to you, and I'll wait as long as it takes."

His hands released my face and ran teasingly down my arms, then clasped my own hands. He lifted them to his lips, placed a soft lingering kiss on my knuckles, then looked up at me.

"I'll wait till my dying breath to hold you again—to see you look at me and want me the way you did that night. Till then, I'll be here. Whatever you need, I'll be here for you."

With my broken heart bulging in my chest, I reached out to wipe away the tear that fell from his watery blue eyes.

His lips pulled into the faintest smile before he stood from the bed, looking down at me. I wanted to jump into his arms while begging the universe to take away our pain; it drove me near insanity. Yet I continued to sit there, tears stinging my eyes and blurring my vision. With all the willpower I had, they never slid free.

I finally managed to find a sliver of my normal voice. "You should go."

He nodded again, leaning down to place the tiniest kiss on my cheek. I closed my eyes, never wanting the moment to end, knowing that my guard would go back up once he walked out the door. My resolve to remain still nearly faltered in that instant, but his sweet, sensual touch was quick; before I knew it, he was walking to the bedroom door.

He grabbed his coat from the chair and put it on, shoved his hands deep into his loose pajama-pant pockets, and looked back.

"If you need anything—anything at all—call me. I'm always here. Don't ever be stubborn with me, Cassandra." His voice was stern with an underlying tenderness, warming me from the inside out.

"Thank you," I replied softly.

"Anytime, sweetheart."

I watched as he turned and left me alone in the house to deal with the aftermath of the emotions roiling inside me.

Chapter Eleven

NEIGHBORS

With one knock, the door opened to a beaming Oliver. I was early, but he didn't seem to notice. That was the beauty with kids.

Oliver had called earlier that week to invite me over for lunch, and I couldn't refuse him. Whatever was or wasn't happening between Logan and me, it changed nothing about my friendship with Oliver. He always made me smile, and lately I needed that more than anything.

"Cassie!" His grin faltered a beat as he appraised me with a nervous eye, but upon realizing I was nearly good as new, his expression perked back up.

"How you been, buddy?" I asked, hating that he looked sad for even the briefest moment.

I was knocked back slightly when he threw himself forward, wrapping his arms around my waist, hugging me. A bark sounded from behind him, and he pulled away to lift Scout in his arms.

"See, I told you she was okay," Oliver whispered to the pup.

I smiled. How could I not? I was okay, and things were finally getting back to normal—or as normal as they could.

Oliver held the door for me and scolded Scout for standing in my way as I entered. I followed him to the living room and relaxed down into the sleek brown leather armchair. The memories of my last time here, at Christmas, fell over me.

The house was no longer decorated with wreaths and garland. The Christmas tree was gone—nothing but a faded memory that, after everything, I still cherished. My hand flew to my wrist that no longer bore the charm bracelet Logan had given me. It was gone—thrown on the pavement in that alley, hurled viciously to the ground with the condom he'd chucked at me moments before.

I blanched at the painful memory. *Here in this room, we were once happy…and even felt almost like a famil—*.

No. I shook the thought from my head. My issues with Logan didn't matter today. I was here to see Oliver.

"Are you listening to yourself? You know she'll only hurt him!"

My head twisted back toward the entryway of the room as Julia's voice filtered in. She sounded furious, and the stomping heading in my direction confirmed it.

"It's my decision to make, Julia, not yours."

My posture stiffened. *Logan.*

Focusing on Oliver, who was on the floor in front of me playing with Scout, I frowned. His head dropped low, and it was painfully obvious his little ears were perked.

"I'm sure everything's fine," I tried to reassure him with a soft smile. "Grown-ups sometimes forget it's not nice to yell."

He shrugged. "Aunt Julia's mad at Daddy. They yell a lot now."

My heart broke for him. "I'm sure it's nothing. Julia loves your daddy very much."

He looked up at me, then glanced warily to the doorway, listening. The air around us quieted as the muffled voices moved deeper into the house.

Thank God. Oliver didn't need to hear them fighting, especially if my instincts were spot on and it was about Natasha.

"Can I tell you a secret?" Oliver asked quietly, looking back at me with bright eyes.

"Of course."

He jumped to his feet, and in a flash was sitting on the arm of the chair beside me. He leaned his tiny frame in, cupping my ear, and whispered, "Mommy came back for me."

He knew. I wanted to be happy for him. Perhaps Natasha was ready to be a mother; she was so young when she had him. I didn't know the woman, so maybe I was wrong, but my stomach still clenched—not at the thought of Oliver having his mother back in his life, but at the concern that Natasha wouldn't be the mother he was hoping for.

I hoped I was wrong.

"Have you seen her?" I asked, concern heavy in my voice. I tried to hide it beneath my smile. Just the thought of Natasha prancing back into their lives to fill the role of mother…or more…left me weary. But maybe it would be good for Logan and Oliver, and maybe it would help me move on. I only wanted to see them both happy.

"No, but they talk about her all the time now. I hear them." He frowned. "They want her to go away. She won't, right?"

What could I say? How could I ease his worry? I rubbed my hand down his arm and squeezed his hand. "I don't know, but no matter what, your daddy's here."

I couldn't lie to him. I knew what it felt like to be young and out of the loop from when my father left. It was sometimes worse than the truth.

His head shook and he pulled his hand away before running across the room to catch Scout. When he finally caught the pup, I heard him tell him in a hushed confidence, "She won't leave. I know it."

Before I could offer him some words of comfort, our attention was pulled to the heavy sigh heaved in our direction. I glanced up to see Julia standing in the entryway.

"Hey, we didn't hear you come in, sorry." She walked into the room and slouched down on the couch across from me.

"It's all right, Oliver let me in. I told Logan noon, and—"

"Ugh! I hope you can talk some sense into him!"

I looked down at Oliver, who was lying on his stomach a few feet away, his tiny bare feet kicking the air as he played tug of war using a toy Scout held in his mouth.

Julia noticed and ran her hands down her face, then rested them under her chin. "You need to try and talk some sense into Logan, please. He has to understand why it's a bad idea to let you-know-who back in."

Julia must not have known that Oliver was well aware of whom she was speaking about. I wanted to grab his hand and take him outside, away from it all, but I couldn't. He'd have to face it someday.

"I'm sure Logan will make the right decision," I replied in a hushed voice.

She scoffed. "In case you haven't noticed yet, Logan rarely makes the right decision."

"I thought you were leaving." Logan entered the room, and I couldn't find the strength to look up at him. His rough voice vibrated through my chest, sending chills up my spine.

"I am!" Julia pushed off from her spot on the couch and strolled over to Oliver, then bent down to whisper something in his ear. He nodded, smiling.

"I love you, little guy." Julia placed a kiss on top of his wavy hair. She stood, scowling at Logan, and then turned to me. "Talk to him."

What was I supposed to say to Logan? Oliver was his son.

With that, she walked away, and I was left with a perplexed Logan searching my expression. His hair was disheveled, and I wondered how many times he'd run his hands through it that morning.

The loose, light-wash jeans he'd matched with a thin black

T-shirt were casual and easy. They'd been thrown on with no thought; his sex appeal didn't take work. The muscles in his chest tightened when he reached down and ran his hand over Oliver's head, sharing a loving smile with his son.

"Sorry, I came early. I didn't mean to interrupt."

"Never apologize, Cassandra." He sat in the same spot Julia had occupied, his attention trained on his son, laughing as Scout yapped when Oliver overpowered him and held up the toy. "We're just honored you came over, right Oliver?"

"We missed you," Oliver answered, not looking at either of us.

"I missed you too, so thank you for having me over." I smiled. "Now, you haven't told me: how's school going? Must be nice to be back after Christmas break."

I wished I was able to go back myself, but I was out until March. I hated it, but had agreed it was for the best. Attempting to keep up with a group of five-year-olds wouldn't help me heal any faster.

"Fine." His tone dropped. That didn't sound good. Last I remembered, he couldn't stop talking about school.

"Did something happen?"

Oliver sat petting Scout, a contemplative stare in his eyes, before opening up. "Brody said he was Leo's friend, but Leo don't like me. He never talks to me."

"Ahh, I see." I smiled over at Logan, who was relaxing back in the sofa, listening. "You know, some kids are shy and don't talk a lot. Maybe you can try talking to him and then you can be his friend too."

Oliver looked up, thinking it over. "He does have a really cool dinosaur T-shirt." His face brightened. "I like dinosaurs too."

Logan and I both laughed.

"See, so it sounds like you just need to try and talk to him."

"Okay."

I laughed again at his easy agreement. Ah, to be a kid again.

"Why don't you go get cleaned up for lunch, Oliver?" Logan spoke up after a few comfortable minutes of silence.

Oliver smiled at me. "I'll be right back. Daddy made mac and cheese, 'cause you love it just like me!" He grabbed Scout and ran out of the room.

Logan sat up on the sofa, his hands kneading the back of his neck. He sighed, then looked over at me with a thin smile. "Thanks for coming. He's been so worried, and I've been—"

"It's no problem," I cut in, and we shared an awkward chuckle. "Sorry, didn't mean to interrupt. Go on."

He shook his head, smiling softly. "I was just going to say that I've tried convincing him you were fine, but seeing you himself helps."

I nodded in agreement, with no other words to say. A long pause stood between us.

"So, she's really here to stay, then?" I asked, purposely not speaking Natasha's name. I shouldn't have even asked, but curiosity got the best of me.

"It appears so." He looked down at the arm of the couch.

"What does that mean for Oliver? Aren't you worried she may leave him again?"

The nerves in my system were gone when he looked up at me with wary eyes, and I could see he was torn over her return. I leaned forward as best I could. "She's his mother, but you're his daddy," I whispered. "I know you'll make the right call for him."

"She says she misses him, and I know he wants to see her. I just don't know if...if I can trust her. I can't let him get hurt."

"Yeah, I noticed your trust issue with the whole James Bond setup."

His brows rose, lips curling up. "James Bond? Is this some fantasy of yours I should know about?"

My head fell, cheeks flushed. We needed to get back on topic—quickly.

I looked back up, serious. "All you can do is be there for Oliver if he wants to see her. If you try and keep her away, he'll blame you. He knows she's here."

Logan sighed, his hand running through his hair.

"Of course he does. How could he not, with the way Julia and Jax carry on about it? Obviously, they are not happy with things. They're not exactly fans of Natasha. My mother seems to be the only person who believes I'd be doing the right thing if I let her see him."

It was absurd, but for some reason, that hurt. Logan's mother liked Natasha.

"You can only do what *you* think is right."

The conversation seemed to exhaust him, but he didn't change the subject. Instead, he spoke softly, for my ears only. "Natasha threatened to tell him I kept them apart if I didn't let her see him. I can't have my son hating me—not now, not later. He needs to see her. I just hope she's grown up."

Oh, she looked *pretty grown up, all right.* A flash of her double Ds spilling out of that emerald dress left my stomach in knots. I may not have officially met her, but I already wasn't a fan.

"Didn't she want you, as well, on New Year's?"

Why did I ask that? I blamed the striking image of her in my head, ogling him that night. It still wasn't right to ask. I wasn't thinking. We weren't friends. I was out of line, but I couldn't help myself.

"Sorry, don't answer that. It's not my business," I added quickly, rubbing my suddenly clammy hands together.

His eyes locked with mine, his stare heavy and thick with that familiar tension I only ever experienced from him.

"I don't want Natasha. There is only woman I will ever want. I've told you this."

My breathing grew more labored the longer he searched my eyes, seeking entrance to my soul. I blinked, shutting him out.

"And the woman here the other morning?" Why was I still

talking?

He looked confused, and it only further added to the fury I felt at the mental image of her wrapping him in her arms and kissing his cheek. It was so intimate, and less like the other women I was used to seeing leave his house.

I needed to get up and go find Oliver, but instead I was sucked in by the side of me that still held onto a tiny shred of hope for us—the senseless side.

"You saw me with Katherine?" His brows rose, surprised.

"Yeah, Katherine, you know—gorgeous brunette wearing mile-high pumps with a tweed blazer and skintight jeans. I'm sure you remember her." I guess I'd gotten a good-enough view of the woman. I hated to admit how much that image of her with him had haunted me.

To my disbelief, his eyes lit up and lips pulled into a broad grin, and suddenly he was laughing. I had half the nerve to get up and stomp straight out.

"Oh, it's funny? You know what?" I shook my head, infuriated. "Screw you, Logan! I couldn't care less how many sluts you go through." I stood up, wanting to enjoy lunch with Oliver then hightail it out of there.

He grabbed my wrist and stood beside me, still grinning like a schoolboy. He had to have seen my anger brewing, because his lips pulled in as he shook his head once, attempting to stifle his chuckle and control his amusement at my expense.

How dare he laugh at me—and only a couple days after spewing all that nonsense about waiting for me.

"Katherine's never really been my type."

At least, not his type once he was through with her. "Right, I'm sure." Sarcasm was heavy in my tone. "Whatever, it doesn't matter. Honestly, I was just surprised to see you gave her the courtesy of walking her to her car."

Something in him switched, and the light in his eyes dimmed considerably. Was he angry? Did I insult him? A part of me hoped so, since he'd had the audacity to laugh at me.

"She isn't my type, and never has been. I especially think my older brother would highly disapprove."

What? I scrunched my face in confusion, but before I could answer, Oliver was bouncing back into the room.

"Come on, aren't you hungry?" he asked, lifting the dark cloud forming above us.

"We'll be right there. I was just telling Cassandra about Katherine." The side of his mouth pulled up and I stiffened. Katherine could not have been some random hookup if she knew Oliver and his brother...and then it hit me.

"Aunt Katie is the best. She makes pancakes that look like Mickey Mouse!"

I swallowed, nodding away my embarrassment. "She's your brother's wife," I grumbled under my breath.

Logan simply raised his brows and watched me shift uncomfortably from foot to foot.

"Why don't you go get the pictures you colored for Cassandra and meet us in the dining room? We'll be right there," Logan said, and Oliver left the room, excited to show me his artwork.

My thoughts of why I made such a scene and acted so childish were interrupted when he wrapped his arms fully around me and held me in place.

"You're jealous." His fingers delicately moved the strand of hair that had fallen over my eyes in my rush to leave the room.

"Why would I be? Whatever we had, I'm over it. I came over to have lunch with Oliver, so if you'll excuse me." My tone was laced in ice as I yanked myself out of his grip, but I didn't care. I was humiliated that he was seeing through my defenses.

His intoxicating breath tickled my lips as he held me close. "I dislike Luke."

Where did that come from?

"What?"

"Luke, Caleb's kid brother. The guy who's been hounding you, waiting for the right time to pounce."

The confusion on my face slipped into a grin matching his previous one, and like him, I began to laugh.

"Pounce? Luke?" I laughed harder, dipping my head back. Luke was so not interested like that.

Logan raked his fingers over the waistband of my jeans. His fingers brushed my skin, cutting off my giggles in an instant.

My pulse accelerated, and heat coursed up from my toes, surging to the deepest part of me. He'd never touched me there before. I closed my eyes as he spoke.

"He wants you, but the question is: do you want him?"

I was about to tell him how ridiculous he was, but then realized he was jealous. The flash of insecurity I saw in his eyes drove me to say my next words.

"Maybe. He's sweet, honest, and…" I leaned into his ear, his hand still pressing on my stomach. "…he's quite sexy."

I pulled away with a smirk.

"Interesting. I'll accept that challenge, sweetheart—not that the boy presents one."

Boy? Luke was only a few years younger than Logan. His arrogance knew no bounds.

"Are you coming?" Oliver called out.

I stepped away from Logan, feeling even more confused about what was evolving between us, yet with a calmness settling over my heart.

Chapter Twelve

HAUNTED

The grin on my face was bigger than I remembered it being in ages; it felt like my first full day back to my old self. The snow was a thick blanket covering the earth, but it didn't stand a chance at deterring me. The moment I finished stretching, I was out the door.

Starting off light and easy, I hit the pavement, snow crunching under my feet. The cold morning air rushed through me as I increased my speed down the back road, my face nothing but a carefree grin.

It was invigorating—the pull of my tight muscles and the chance to put everything behind me. It was only a month earlier that I was lying in that hospital bed, dreaming of the moment I'd be back out there. My eyes slid shut for a moment and my mouth opened just enough to suck in a deep breath. With my ribs healed, I could finally enjoy the fresh, snowy breeze knocking into me.

When I returned home an hour later, out of breath and loving it, I was met with the cheerful grin of Oliver standing beside Julia on my front porch.

"Hey, what are you guys doing up so early?" I asked as I came to a stop in front of them, wiping the cold sweat from my brow.

"Oliver saw you out on the road and wanted to come over

to see you before I took him to school," Julia explained with a wary tone I didn't understand.

"Well, I like hearing that." I smiled his way.

"How are you feeling? Must be doing pretty good to go out for a run in this weather."

I shrugged. I enjoyed the winter air. "Better. Things are getting better."

"You got a car, finally, huh?" I followed her glance to the aged black Honda sitting in my driveway.

"No, just borrowing my mom's."

She was only loaning it to me while I waited for my appointment at the bank. The loan officer had a busy schedule, but was able to squeeze me in the following week. My mother, however, was under the impression that I was waiting to speak to Logan about writing a new check after I'd convinced her to let me talk to him. And since her boyfriend was more than happy to shuttle her around until I got my own vehicle, she was officially off my back about it.

Julia nodded with a sympathetic smile and looked down to Oliver. He took a step forward when I opened the door for them to enter, but Julia's hand landed on his shoulder, stopping him in his tracks.

"We can't stay. Don't want him to be late, sorry," Julia said, standing in place, and I noticed the tiredness in her tone.

"Oh, okay. Is everything all right?" I asked, watching as Scout ran up and Oliver squatted down to scoop him up. It was nice to finally be able to handle having a puppy in the house again. Bringing him home after my lunch with Oliver had been hard to watch. You'd have thought they were parting for a cross-country voyage until I reminded Oliver he could come over anytime he wanted to visit.

Giggling at the pup licking his tiny face, Oliver looked up to Julia. "Can I ask now?"

She nodded and then looked to me, an irritated scowl

settling between her brows.

Before I could question it, Oliver burst out, "My mom came to see me! She said she'd take me out soon, too." He was practically stuttering with excitement.

I kept my thin smile fixed in place, glancing up at the now-understandable gloomy expression on Julia. She made a face.

"That's great. I'm so happy for you, Oliver."

He looked pleased, and set Scout back on the ground. "I told her 'bout the tree house, but Daddy said she's not allowed to see it. Said I had to ask you first. Can I show her when she comes back?"

Natasha—Logan's ex—in my tree house? Not a chance, and I didn't even want to analyze why that bothered me so much. But she was Oliver's mother…how could I say no?

"Sure, of course," I replied with a nod, attempting to cover the hesitation in my voice.

"I told Daddy you'd say yes!" He ran into me, hugging me around the waist until Julia told him it was time to go. He looked up, and added, "She'll love it as much as we do!"

"I'm sure she will." A broken and awkward laugh fell from my lips as he hopped down from the porch steps.

"See you Saturday, Cassie!" Julia called back as they cut through the lawn back to Logan's.

I gave a nod, then quickly realized I had no clue why I was seeing her this weekend.

"Saturday?"

She turned back, her brows pinched together. "Yeah, Logan's birthday."

Birthday? "Oh, I didn't know."

She rolled her eyes and scoffed. "Of course he didn't tell you. He's not big on celebrating it, but we force him to sit down and open a few presents and eat cake. We do the big party next month; since Oliver's birthday is exactly one month to the day of Logan's, my mother goes all out for that one. So it's just Jax,

Oliver, and me for Logan's, but it's nice." She hesitated for a brief moment before adding, "Mark has to work late, so he won't be there."

This was news to me, as well as her nervousness at bringing up Mark. Did she know more about our past? It didn't matter, and the party was way too family-oriented for me to be included in it.

"Thanks, but I don't think I should come. Like you said, it's just you and Jax—family."

"And my mom," Oliver chimed in. "I invited her too."

"You what?" Julia snapped.

"Daddy said I could," he defended with a pouting lip.

With a huff, Julia looked back to me. She was definitely not okay with Oliver's last-minute invite.

"Like I said, it's Saturday at six, and I know Logan would love for you to be there. Just think about it."

I nodded, unsure why I didn't clarify right away that I wouldn't be attending. Instead, I grabbed Scout and headed inside, eager to clear my head with a cool shower.

Logan was back to work, which meant I had a lot of free alone time on my hands. I spent most of the week sitting in my freezing attic, rummaging through the last of my grandparents' treasures. After sliding the last box down the ladder and watching it smack on the hall floor below, I stood looking around at the empty space.

As a kid, I was never allowed in the small room. I'd always wondered what I'd find if I pulled down the ladder and snuck up. Grandma swore it was nothing more than a dusty dropping zone with stacks of boxes and old furniture, but seeing it empty aside from an old sofa and antique dresser which were too heavy to move, I realized 'small' was not the word to describe it—

dusty, yes, but it was larger than I'd expected.

Two stained-glass windows filtered in light on each side of the room, highlighting the dark wooden floors. Years of neglect and wear magnified the floor's true age, but there was something comforting in it. I sat with my back against the bare brick wall, losing myself in a daydream of turning it into my own private office—or secret library.

I sat beside the sofa that was covered in a drop cloth and closed my eyes. Color schemes and furniture layouts played through my mind, just as they had for Julia's house. I could dream at least.

The instant the phone vibrated beside me, I was pulled back to the empty room covered in cobwebs and layers of dust, as well as the somber reality of my empty bank account. No lavish makeover happening there.

I knew without looking whom the text was from. It'd been over two hours since I'd received one from Logan, with my last to him explaining I was getting my hands dirty and didn't wish to be bothered.

With a smile, I read.

Still cleaning?

How did he know getting my hands dirty meant cleaning? He knew me better than I cared to admit. I replied.

Just finished.

Logan was careful not to hover too closely after my lunch with Oliver, but that didn't mean he wasn't blowing up my phone at least a dozen times a day—all texts, never once a call. I guess if we didn't hear each other's voices, it didn't count as actually talking—at least, not to him.

Can I see you tonight?

It was the same request every night, and my reply was always the same.

No.

Instantly, he answered back.

I'll bring dinner. Grilled cheese. Oliver can supervise

Lol. I'll pass but tell Oliver I miss him

I will. Have a good night Cassandra.

You too.

I tucked my phone in my pocket, but the moment I went to stand, it vibrated again. He normally accepted my refusal and wouldn't text again until after eight or nine to say good night.

The screen flashed and my finger swiped over it to show a text from Julia.

U still coming tonight?

I groaned, shoulders slouching. Logan's birthday. I'd been so focused on sorting years of baggage that I'd completely forgotten.

Sorry can't. Tell Oliver I said hi :)

Don't leave me with a depressed brother and his ex-bitch. U sure I can't convince u?

That certainly didn't help her case. If she wanted to convince me, she shouldn't have reminded me what I'd be walking in on.

Sorry. Have fun though!

Yeah right! Thanks!

My head rested against the cool wall, glad to have gotten out of the party so easily, and it was then that I noticed the purple hat box stashed behind the sofa. Grandma hadn't been a very fashionable woman, so I wasn't sure what I'd find inside as I pulled it out and placed it on the floor in front of my crossed legs. Confused by what I was looking down at, I removed a letter that had my mother's name written on it in my grandmother's hand from atop a pile of envelopes.

The letter inside was short and to the point:

Felicia,

Please see to it that Cassandra receives these when you're ready. I'm sorry I couldn't tell you. I've always loved

*you like a daughter, but he's my son. I hope you
understand.*

I swallowed. My father? I should've closed the lid and
thrown out the box, or taken it to my mother, whom my
grandmother seemed to have had expected to find it. However, I
found myself pulling out the first envelope, postmarked two
years after he left. Whatever grandma was hiding, I needed to
know.

Mom,

*I'm sorry this hurts you so much, but I told you, I can't
come back. I can't face them. I won't write again. I don't
want to further upset you. I can't explain my love for her,
but it's unlike anything I've ever felt before. She's my
everything. If you gave Nina a chance, you'd see…*

"Nina?" I gasped, dropping the letter.

Nina? My babysitter who went off to college the same time
my father left Nina? No, it was too much to assume. There had
to be thousands of women in the world with that same name.

I didn't need to know any more. Whatever the letters said
didn't mean anything other than further damage to my faith in
men. I stuffed the letter back in the envelope and saw the
photograph peeking out from under the stack. I couldn't stop
myself from pulling it out to reveal a smiling picture of my
father, his arm wrapped around the same Nina who played
Barbies with me almost every Saturday for an entire year.

Irate, I shoved it back inside and placed the lid on the box
before standing and releasing a deep breath, wishing I'd never
looked behind the couch to begin with.

Once I climbed down from the attic and closed up the
ladder carefully, tucking it back into the ceiling, I took a quick
shower, resigned to forget what I'd read.

An hour later, I plopped down on my couch, phone in hand, and sent the text to Logan that should've gone out after Julia's reminder text, had I not gotten distracted. Logan and I weren't friends anymore, but I liked things being civil between us. I wasn't going to overthink it; just a simple text, nothing special.

Happy birthday!

There, a neighborly deed done well. He'd never even told me it was his birthday, so maybe he didn't want me to know. I rarely knew what he was thinking.

I waited for a reply, but it never came. I figured he was busy at work or on his way home, where he'd be bombarded with his family—his family that included Natasha. I wondered what that would be like for him after all this time...to have her back and celebrating his birthday.

It wasn't my business, and I wasn't going to dwell.

Chapter Thirteen

BIRTHDAY ULTIMATUMS

Ringing shook through my head. I swatted my arm at nothing and rolled my head to the other side, but it didn't stop. Instead, it seemed to only grow louder and clearer as my eyes flickered open, adjusting to the darkness. The only light was from the glow illuminating my nightstand. The ringing stopped and I closed my eyes again, relaxing back into the mattress, when the annoying chirping started again.

"Hello?" I croaked, pressing the phone to my ear, still in a sleepy daze.

"About time!"

"Hilary?" My voice cracked, riddled with exhaustion. "What time is it?"

"Nine thirty. Did I wake you?"

I swallowed, clearing the dryness in my throat. "Mm-hmm." My hand wiped away the sleep in my eyes.

"The fact that you're sleeping at this hour on a Saturday night is another issue we need to discuss, but right now you need to come down to Haven."

The nerves in her voice crawled under my skin. I made a face, pulling myself up and resting against the headboard. "Why, is everything all right?"

"No, now hurry up and get down here!"

The line went dead, and I knew if I didn't get dressed and

drag myself down there, she'd only keep calling.

—•◆•—

"This better be important!" I complained the moment I stepped inside the bustling restaurant, with Hilary waiting at the door.

She looked nervous.

"I didn't know who else to call, and Caleb agreed you were the best person."

Best person for what? I gave her a pointed look.

"Don't be mad, please." She stepped aside with a tense shrug, revealing the view of the bar and the back of a hard body I recognized instantly.

Logan.

This had to be a joke. Was it some ridiculous attempt to lure me out on a Saturday night? The fact that it was his birthday, as well, didn't go unnoticed. Whatever he was playing at tonight wasn't working.

"You have thirty seconds to explain why you called me."

"He's been drinking, and…" Hilary sighed, her hopeful eyes imploring me to care. "And he needs a friend."

"Great, glad Caleb's here." I turned on my heel to leave.

Hilary grabbed my arm. "What am I supposed to do? He won't talk to Caleb or me. He's just been sitting there knocking back drinks, looking miserable with a busted hand."

"Busted hand?"

"Yeah, I gave him a clean rag, but he wouldn't let me near it. Said he deserved worse."

Deserved worse? For crying out loud, it was his birthday. Why the hell was he down at the bar drinking himself into a self-deprecating hangover?

"Fine, but next time, call Julia or Jax."

"I did. Julia told me to call you."

I huffed out a half chuckle, half sigh. Of course she did.

When was that girl going to realize I wasn't dating her brother, and therefore wasn't responsible for him?

The moment I slipped off my coat, Hilary relaxed. I handed it to her, straightening my shoulders as I headed over.

"What are you up to, birthday boy?" I asked with sarcasm heavy in my tone, slinging my leg over the stool beside him.

He didn't bother to spare me a glance. "Having a drink. What about you?"

I noticed his hand resting on the bar, knuckles splintered and raw, dried blood covering the wounds.

"Well, I *was* enjoying a pleasant night's rest till I was called down here to talk you out of drinking yourself into a stupor. Come on, I'll drive you home."

"You shouldn't be here, driving at this hour with the weather outside. It was a waste of your time, and you could have gotten hurt...again. Go home. I'll have someone escort you to make sure you make it there safely."

"I don't need an *escort* anywhere!" I snapped.

Still looking ahead, he sighed. "Good night, Cassandra. Go back to your warm bed."

Logan lifted his finger to the bartender for another drink, but the moment the old man set down the filled shot glass, I shook my head slowly, spelling it out with my menacing scowl that Logan would be having no more. He took the hint, backing up with a single nod.

"I'm cutting you off and taking you home."

The deep, throaty chuckle he let out washed over me, further alerting me to what I was dealing with—especially when he angled his dropped head just enough to catch my gaze.

After a long pause, he spoke. "You look stunning tonight...but then again, you always do."

I rolled my eyes. The oversized pale-pink button-down I wore had been my pajamas for the night, and was matched with a pair of jeans I'd tugged out of my dresser drawer in the dark and hopped into. Nothing stunning about it.

Before I could scoff in his face, his body leaned into mine, nose nuzzling my hair.

"And you smell so…sweet."

My breath caught. I was going to need a drink. I threw up my hand to the bartender and when he looked my way, I called out, "I'll have what he had."

The bartender nodded, and I looked back at Logan.

"Not exactly sure you can handle that, sweetheart."

"You have no idea what I can handle."

His gaze bore into mine, searching the double meaning in my words. I was the first to break the stare, reaching out and grabbing his bloodied hand.

"What happened?"

"Life happened. My life," he answered, staring down at the wound cradled in my palm.

"You might need stitches."

"I won't. It's not that deep."

"You should at least clean it up. A few bandages will help."

He pulled his hand away, irritation heavy in his posture. I rolled my eyes and the rag sitting on the other side of him. It must've been the one Hilary brought. I pushed off the stool and stretched over the bar in front of him. His breath tickled my ear as I snatched the towel quickly and fell back in my seat.

"We need to at least clean the blood off."

The bartender set down a shot glass and filled it with an amber liquid. "A water too—no ice," I said, examining Logan's busted knuckles.

I picked up the glass with my free hand and tipped it back. My tongue shot out as the liquor burned its way down my throat and warmed my stomach. My face pinched, and I tried to shake it off.

"I warned you. Not your type of drink." Logan chuckled.

My mouth was still complaining when Logan took the shot

glass and downed the remainder of the liquor. With a smug grin, he set it back down. The bartender interrupted our challenging stare when he set a mug filled with tap water in front of me.

I didn't say a word, and instead dunked a side of the towel into it and let the water drip over Logan's wounds before carefully wiping away the traces of his obviously unpleasant night. He sat there watching me, with eyes I couldn't look up at as I tended to his care.

"So, seriously, what happened?" I prompted, finding the knuckles nearly shredded. "It's your birthday. You were supposed to be celebrating."

"Why didn't you come? Julia told me she invited you."

"Answer my question first." I peered up for just a moment and watched his frown deepen.

"Oliver wanted Natasha to come, and I didn't want to disappoint him." He stopped, gazing down at the bar.

"And…"

"And she came. Oliver was happy, hooked onto her every word, following her around the entire time. She even read him a story and tucked him into bed."

Wow, not how I pictured Natasha at all. Maybe I really misjudged her.

"So what's the problem?"

"She then made her way into my bedroom, undressed, and climbed into bed."

I blanched, gripping his hand more tightly than I realized, gaping at him.

"O-oh," I mumbled. Why was I suddenly feeling shell-shocked?

The wince on his face caught my attention, and I released his hand from my death grip. "Shit, sorry."

He chuckled to himself. "You know, I think that's the first swear word I've heard slip from your lovely mouth."

Flushed, I focused back on his hand attentively, wiping the

cloth over it one final time.

"All cleaned up. You sure you don't want me to ask Caleb for the first-aid kit? It's not a problem, and you really need to keep the cuts—"

His pointer finger shot out and landed on my lips, silencing me.

"I didn't sleep with her."

I nodded, unable to speak over the jealous wave crushing my chest. His finger trailed over my bottom lip until it reached the corner of my mouth and dropped away.

"I came in, found her there, and demanded that she get out. Unfortunately, she refused, and then informed me that she was moving in. Explained how she already told Oliver the wonderful news, and unless I wanted him to hate me for kicking her out on the streets, I had to give her a chance and come to bed." His words turned into an angry hiss, his back teeth grinding together.

Wow, Natasha had some gall. He slowly craned his neck back to face me.

"I don't respond well to threats, and I especially don't allow someone I despise to tell me what to do," he continued, jaw clenched. "The moment my fist went through the wall, Natasha was out of bed and already threatening to yell for Oliver, so I left. Called Julia to come stay the night there and came down here for a drink."

Holy hell, the woman was crazy.

"So what now? She's really moving in?"

I thought about Natasha living in the same house as Logan, using Oliver. *But for what? What was she up to?*

"Let's not talk about her again. Not tonight," he said.

I was staring down at his hand in thought when he interrupted my troubled mind.

"I think a kiss will help more than a bandage."

"You wish!" I laughed and slapped his forearm playfully, earning me a wry chuckle and lightening the direction the mood was heading in. I propped my elbow on top of the bar, resting my cheek on my hand.

I was no longer his friend, and even though I felt for his situation and for Oliver, it wasn't any of my business. As a friendly neighbor, I didn't owe him anything except perhaps one more offer to drive him home, and then I'd be gone.

"I thought a good nurse was eager to please her patient," he teased.

I scoffed and glanced down at the bar before looking back up seconds later.

"Seriously, do you want a ride home or not? You're drunk, and I'm not really in the mood for games."

"Games," he mimicked with a thick, disheartening snicker. Something in his mood shifted back to that dark place I'd walked in on originally as he repeated the word again to himself. "Games. I've always loved a good game." His head dipped to the side, tired, hooded eyes locking with mine. "You were the best and worst game I ever played."

My heart pounded against my chest; the pain was unbearable. Finally, he could admit it. I was nothing but a game. A challenge.

He looked straight ahead again, staring blankly at the rows of bottles perched on the wall ahead of us. His voice came out a rough murmur.

"But then I lost. Not the first time I've lost something, but you…" He looked back at me, voice growing, eyes searching mine. "You took more than anyone before. You took a piece of me I can't get back—I don't want back. I only want you, and you…you can hardly even look at me anymore."

What could I say to that? I couldn't find the words, and it took all my strength to break our shared gaze.

He chuckled again. "I'm not drunk, Cassandra. There's not enough alcohol in the world to get me drunk enough to forget what I had with you. What we almost had together." His lips molded into an angry frown. I watched as he spoke, heat rising through me as he laid his deepest fears on the table.

"I almost killed you. I let that bitch get in my head, and it was you who suffered for it. I'm such a piece of shit—an unworthy bastard—and yet I still tried to win you back, wanting to convince you that I could be better, be what you need. But I can't. I'm no good for anyone, and especially not you. You're an angel, and you deserve so much more."

Logan gripped the shot glass that sat untouched in front of him and tipped it back, closing his eyes as the liquid worked its way into his system, then slammed it back down.

"Logan, you're a good guy. I never would have gotten close to you to begin with if you weren't. I wish things had been different between us, I'm not going to lie—you know what you meant to me, you had to have seen how much I wanted you—but I can't forget what happened. The way you made me feel in that alley...I've never felt so cheap." I sighed, twisting my palm over my chin to rub my tired eyes. "Maybe this is for the best. You would have grown bored with me and eventually wanted to move back to the city once Julia graduated. We never would have lasted."

His jaw clenched. "You really believe that?"

"You can't expect me to believe that you'd all of a sudden go from sleeping with more women than I can count to just little ole me." A soft, insecure laugh crept out.

He stared at me silently, his eyes taking in my expression, reading me. I shifted on the stool, uncomfortable under his penetrating gaze. What the hell was he thinking?

"Why don't you see it? You're so fucking beautiful, and you don't even see it!" A spark of anger flashed in his eyes. "There was a time I wanted to feel you pressed under me, that sharp tongue of yours put to work in ways you could only imagine. But then somehow I lost myself—forgot about how much I wanted just your body at my control. It was deeper than even I realized.

"It was you, Cassandra—your heart, your kindness—and before I knew what was happening or had a chance to stop it, I found myself lying in bed at night wanting to hold only you. To kiss you, worship you, and finally discover what it was like to make love to a woman."

I sat there, the lost butterflies that'd been hidden for the past month buzzing to life throughout my clenched gut. My heart raced, and I watched with soft eyes as his hand reached out, the pad of his thumb caressing my cheek and catching the single revealing tear that slid out of my unsuspecting eye.

He placed his thumb in his mouth, sucking it clean before whispering, "Tell me to walk away. Tell me to leave and let you go. Tell me I have no chance, and that you'll never love me, and I'll listen. I'll never bother you again. If you want me to move away, I'll put my house on the market tomorrow and be gone. I just need you to be honest and tell me. I can't see you in pain anymore, and I know it's me that's hurting you."

Harsh tears stung my cloudy eyes, his words cutting deep. My eyes never strayed from his. My heart screamed out to him, beating against my ribcage, fighting with everything it had to reach him and beg him to stay. But all I could hear was the voice in my head telling me, "This is it. Your next words will forever change your life, one way or another."

Could I really let him leave? Could I walk away from the one man who awoke something so pure and raw inside me? What if he was the one—the one I was waiting for?

Can I really live without him? I—

It happened in a flash: my body thrust forward, crushing my lips onto his. There was no thought behind it—only need.

Logan reacted instantly, pulling me closer with his hands in my hair, kissing me with a ferocious need. My tongue ran along his bottom lip, searching for entrance, but he pulled back, resting his forehead on mine. "I adore you."

With a ragged breath, I opened my mouth just enough to

slide my tongue into his.

Chapter Fourteen

BOMBSHELLS

Heat was all I felt—a scorching wave of warmth prickling my skin, flooding my system, and fueling the arousal building within me as Logan's tongue parted my lips and dived in, exploring and dancing with mine.

My legs were between his, his hands in my hair. It felt so good, yet my brain was flickering back to life despite my will to block it out.

What am I doing?

No, I wasn't going to think—not now—just feel. It was amazing and perfect, sating my angry nerves that had been restless for far too long. I kissed him harder, as though there was nothing else in the world I should be doing, as his hands traveled down my back and settled on my hips.

My head was spinning, focusing on only one thing: his unrelenting and demanding kiss. It matched mine with every move, every prod of his tongue.

"Logan?"

I pulled back, panting, head dropped.

What?

Blinking once, twice, three times slammed me back to reality. I straightened, letting my hair fall down to block my flushed face from the room—the bar full of patrons getting a free show.

"Excuse us, ladies, we were in the middle of something," Logan said to the female voice that had interrupted us.

I didn't dare look back, though her voice was much too squeaky to belong to Natasha.

"Wow, forgotten already," another girl chimed in as I held up my hand to the bartender for another shot.

The weight of Logan's stare boring into my side grew unbearable as I sat in silence. I blocked him out and downed the shot that was in front of me instantly.

When his fingers slid through my hair, tucking it behind my ears and revealing my hidden emotions, I stiffened.

"Let's get you home, sweetheart," he whispered, leaning in and placing a soft kiss on the corner of my jaw. I bit my bottom lip and closed my eyes, struggling to collect my thoughts.

"Come on, there's no way you could forget about us. The fun on the airplane? Come on, it was just the other week."

The other week? My eyes closed, gut churning.

I felt Logan move back from me. "Leave!" he demanded, his voice taking on a stern edge.

The girl scoffed. "Really?" She giggled, then lowered her voice to a seductive purr. "Since when do you like privacy?"

I swallowed hard, my icy veins flooding with rage, chilling me to the bone and extinguishing the fire Logan had lit seconds earlier. I wouldn't let this break me. I was going to sit right there and hold it together. Logan was a free man who could do whatever or whomever he wanted. As much as it hurt, I feigned indifference. My eyes were set on the bartender as he walked past with a bottle in hand. I threw up my hand, requesting one more.

"We're leaving," Logan snarled, yet the girls didn't seem to hear him. One of them leaned in behind me, snickering.

"Word of advice: the man likes it rough and he prefers two at once, so why don't you let us take over and you can go find yourself some nice boy next door to take home?"

I heard and felt Logan stand, but I was already out of my seat. That was too much.

"He's all yours," I shot back, walking out.

There it was—yet another item on the endless list of reasons Logan was off limits. Why men sucked. Why he was nothing more than a man I was attracted to. I had to get out of my head. I wouldn't let it happen. Not again.

He likes it rough. Two at once.

The words replayed through my thoughts as I pushed open the front door, heading to the parking lot. My day was bad enough discovering my dad had run off with my nineteen-year-old babysitter, and now this?

"Cassandra! Stop!"

"You should go back in, Logan. I'd hate for you to miss out on a sure thing tonight!" I yelled.

"Cassandra!" he threatened.

"Go! They know what you like, and for the record, I could never share a man, so why waste your time?"

"Stop!" Logan grabbed my arm and whirled me around. "I'm not that man anymore! Now listen to me!"

I yanked my arm free, standing off the sidewalk in the freezing night air, snow flurrying down over us.

"But you were that man a week ago for them?"

His expression softened. "Sweetheart—"

"When? When were you with them?"

"I'm sorry."

"No, tell me when. That night Luke drove me home? I saw you head back into town."

Logan's eyes never strayed from mine as he spoke. "I did come back to Haven that night. Natasha had left the bar and I needed a drink. I was angry, and those girls approached me. I told them I wasn't interested, but they still gave me their numbers."

"And you kept them?"

"I put them in my coat pocket and didn't think about it again until the next morning after our conversation at your house. When I left for my business trip, my head was a mess. I thought I just needed to give up and go back to my old life—let you go so you could find someone to make you happy."

"I don't understand. When did you call them?"

His head ticked slightly to the side, reluctant to say more.

My eyes closed, and I inhaled a breath as realization sunk in. "You took them with you."

"I wanted to move on. Not for me, but for you. To leave you alone, and I thought—"

"You took two women on a business trip for sex minutes after you left my door."

"They didn't mean anything. I regretted it the moment it happened, but it was too late. I just wanted to get you out of my head. You were never going to give me a chance. "

"You're right. It's better this way. You've solidified my belief that there is no future for us."

"No, you didn't want me, and I just needed to see if—"

"If you could forget me by having sex with strangers? I got it, loud and clear!"

"I know how it sounds, and I wish it'd never happened, but it did. I had a moment of weakness because the woman I love wouldn't even allow me to drive her home! I haven't wanted to sleep with anyone but you for months, and those girls were no different. I hated myself every second I was with them."

"Yet you still gave them a time to remember."

His expression lost its remorseful softness. "I'm through talking about them. This is about us!"

"Don't you get it yet!?" I shouted with a ridiculous cackle as he regarded me with a tight expression. "There is no 'us'! We won't work, Logan—ever! We're different people. I want a completely different life than you." I nearly screamed it out, not only for him to understand once and for all, but for myself as well.

I turned and began walking again. It felt good—

liberating—to release it from my body. We would never have a happily ever after. It wasn't in the cards for us.

It took only a second or two until he was there, jogging over and stepping in front of me.

"You don't know what I want because you won't give me a chance to—"

"A chance to what, Logan? Even if I forgot about those girls, you'd be miserable with me after the first week. You're not exactly the monogamous type, so why are you pushing this?"

He opened his mouth to speak, but I beat him to it.

"I'm not into women," I said with unwavering confidence. It was time he saw exactly what he was working so hard to obtain. "Never been with one, and never plan to. So you and me?" My finger flipped between us. "This is just some irrational attraction that has gone on for too long. I'm done feeling like this—enduring this connection based purely on lust. That's it. Bottom line: we have no future together. Why can't you see that?"

"You don't know me as well as you think you do, sweetheart." His jaw was clenched, hard eyes on me.

"I know you spent weeks trying to be my friend just so you could sleep with me!" I blurted out. "And I know the longer you keep reeling me in, the harder it's going to be to put myself back together when you toss me aside like all the rest. Like the girls in there. I can't." My head dropped, eyes slamming shut. "I can't be one of those women, Logan. It would destroy me."

He said nothing, lifting my hands in his. I tugged them away and looked up at him, determined to keep the upper hand as long as possible. He was winning, and there was no way I could stop it.

I spoke with newfound determination and strength. "So let's just get this over with—right where we started, exactly where you wanted it!"

I reached out and gripped the fabric of his dark wool coat

around his forearms and crushed my lips to his before he had a chance to reply. The pounding music blaring from the bar set the tone of our pained kiss. This was it. I was giving him what he wanted—what my body needed.

On my terms.

Clutching onto Logan for dear life, I ambled backward, his hands now tight around my waist. He kissed me with equal force.

There we were—ready, wanting. Quick and hard in the parking lot of Haven. The thought broke the last shred of hope I'd held onto as his hands roamed freely over my back and down to my ass, squeezing me against him.

When I hit the wall, stopping my steps, my hands worked quickly, making its way down his broad chest and pushing his unbuttoned coat open. The width of it hung around me, sucking me into the warmth and heady scent I'd forever crave, despite myself.

"Cassandra." My name on his lips sounded almost like a plea.

A plea for more?

With one hand holding him close around his neck, the other traveled to the waist of his trousers and, in a brazen move, stroked his growing erection. Tonight I'd be the woman who took what she wanted, then walked away before he had a chance to.

A groan poured from his lips and vibrated through mine. He pulled me closer, his manhood pressed tight against the fabric covering my body, begging to be released. With angry hands and skillful fingers needing to make a point and show him exactly what was behind his fascination with me, I tugged open his belt.

I caught his bottom lip in my teeth, tugging and nipping, leaving kisses over his five o'clock shadow. I made my way up to his ear, where I ran my tongue over his lobe.

"Sweetheart…"

Pleased I was able to take control so easily, I ran my tongue over his earlobe and whispered, "It's time we got this over with." Not missing a beat, my lips descended to his neck as my fingers snapped open the button on his fly.

The zipper was in my hand, and with one look up under my long lashes to Logan's dark, tense eyes, I dropped down to my knees—a first for me—taking his zipper down with me.

This was what he wanted, and this is what it would take to show him I was no different from any other girl. I was nothing he'd consider special for long.

My hand dipped inside his open pants, grabbing his hard, impressive length. The strong, hefty girth filled my palm; he was larger than I'd dreamt, and oh, how I'd experienced hours and hours of fantasies about the moment I'd finally have him like this. None of them even came close to reality.

When I closed my palm around him, I gave a firm squeeze, relishing the sight of his head falling back as he grunted an inaudible mumble. I pulled his erection completely free of the prohibiting fabric to take control over his body.

I wasn't prepared for his reaction. He stepped back with a loud huff.

"Damn it!" Logan grunted as he tucked himself back in and zipped his pants. "Not like this," he said to himself, but I caught it.

Snowflakes floated down around him as he turned his back to me, and I watched the rise and fall of his shoulders as he took a deep breath and then ran his hands through his hair.

Slowly, he turned back and looked down at me, still on my knees, muddled with chaotic thoughts and arousal, desperate to be sated.

"Get. Up!" he growled, his face set with rage.

"Why? This is what you want—your words, I believe, were that you wanted to 'fuck me in the alley'! So what's the problem?

You want to move down a few more feet to be in that exact spot?"

"Get. The fuck. Off your knees!"

It was irrational, but I wasn't moving. "Get the fuck out of my head!" I screamed.

He stood over me, eyes wide with fury, and ripped me from the ground, holding me up by my forearms.

"Why?" he hissed through gritted teeth, nostrils flared. "Are you that scared of me—of the possibility of us?"

"Shut up!" I struggled in his arms and beat my hands against his chest, but his grip never wavered.

"I'm not the same man I was then."

"A week ago?" I scoffed.

"You didn't want me!" he protested, but I was too lost in my anger to process anything at that moment. "You changed me, Cassandra—showed me what was possible. What do I have to do? Tell me anything, and I'll do it!"

I let out a heavy breath and sunk into his hold on me.

"I never wanted a relationship with any woman after Natasha. Do you hear me? Never. I foolishly convinced myself that what I had with her was as good as love could get, so I gave up and never thought about the possibility of it again." He crooked his finger under my chin, lifting my face to him.

"I hate that you saw my past indiscretions, and worse, what you saw of them tonight. I have no excuse, but a man has needs, Cassandra, and I was never one to refrain from activities I found enjoyable. So for the past four years, I've taken what I wanted— what desperate women threw so easily at me. You should have never had to listen to those girls in there who meant nothing to me—women I never spared another thought about after I'd left them."

I tried to look away—it was too much to hear—but he held my chin firmly.

"I was miserable, Cassandra, for years—young, and unsure

how to raise Oliver on my own. So I did things that I regret—things at the time to…to help me feel. Regain the control that Natasha stole. It was nothing more than a means to an end for lonely nights. I can't deny that I had more than a man's fair share, but I never felt like this. Not until you."

"Don't say that," I all but pleaded under my breath.

"What do you want me to say, then? What can I do?"

The liquor was fueling my actions—at least, that was how I justified what I said next, because it was as shocking to me as it was to him.

I held his gaze in mine and murmured, "Show me."

Chapter Fifteen

REALITY CRASHES

The kiss he bestowed upon my lips was anything but forgettable, soft yet demanding. His hands reached behind me and lifted me up into his arms, and I didn't fight him.

I went with it, my body needing to feel the connection, if only once. I never stopped kissing him, my tongue exploring the hidden caverns of his warm mouth laced with the taste of liquor and mint. Even as I felt him walking, carrying me away, I never broke the contact.

The steps he took were up metal stairs. When he stopped at the top, he released one hand and dug it into his pocket, but I only held him tighter around the neck, not wanting to break the moment. My brain switched back off happily, going with what felt right.

A door creaked open and he carried me farther, my hands fisting his dark hair. Uncontrollable, my hips began grinding against his strong abs, ready for what I knew would be a night to remember—even if it meant spending the rest of my life trying to forget it.

This wasn't love. Love shouldn't be this hard…this painful.

Blissfully lost in the lust consuming me, I wasn't prepared for the drop that landed me on an unfamiliar bed in a dark room. My skin tingled, blood pounding in my ears, urging me to continue what I'd started.

"Where are we?" I breathed, releasing my lips from his and sitting up beside him. He stood at the end of the bed, regarding me with a focused eye.

Why did I have to speak? Why did I care where we were? I needed more of him. I sat up on my knees and ran my fingers over his open fly that he'd never re-buttoned.

"Alone." His voice was delicious and raspy, eyes glowing in the darkness. He caught my hand and brought it to his lips, kissing the pad of my thumb and working his way to each finger until he reached my pinky.

I looked around, unsure of my next move, doubt beginning to creep in when Logan released my hand and sat beside me on the bed. He caught my face, caressing my cheeks, successful at regaining my full attention.

"I promise we're alone. I own the building and we rent out these rooms ...well, all but this one."

"Okay," I replied dumbly. My hand lifted to his jaw, fingers tracing his lower lip, eyes searching his. With nothing but want, I swung my leg over his lap, straddling him.

"Kiss me, damn it."

And he did, ruthlessly. His hands gripped my hips, bringing me as close to him as possible, but it didn't last. The moment I slid my hands over the swells of his chest, he hesitated. His hands loosened, stroking my jean-covered thighs at a deliberately slow pace.

I sat back just enough to trail my hands down his strong arms, tracing the ripples of his muscles with my finger, then dipped my head down to place a wet kiss on the side of his neck. A relaxed, pleased moan greeted me, building my confidence and urging me on.

"We should get some sleep," he said out of the blue, placing a tender kiss to the tip of my nose. He lifted me up, set me back on the bed, and stood up, walking across the room and flicking a switch by the door.

My hand went up over my squinting eyes, struggling to adjust to the cruel light glowing from the lamp on the nightstand directly to my left.

What the hell was he doing? Where was the action, the passion? The I've-got-to-have-you-now in the heat of the moment?

Instead, his hands were digging in his pockets as he stood in front of a tall dresser. He pulled out his cell phone, keys, and wallet, setting them on top of it.

This was definitely not how I thought things were going to be. Not that I'd planned this or even had a shred of conscience while he carried me to some hole in the wall, but now, sitting there watching him take his time across the room, the moment was officially gone.

Or was it? Logan pulled off his shirt and unzipped his trousers, sliding them down and off his frame. Body-hugging black boxer briefs clung to his solid legs. I swallowed, staring at the package they contained until I felt a prickle flare over my skin.

Slowly, I glanced up to find him watching me, staring at him until his mouth turned up in a crooked grin. My head turned to the side with an eye roll. This wasn't how I'd expected things to go.

Actually, I hadn't expected anything. I hadn't been thinking—only acting—but now I couldn't stop chastising myself for being so damn weak. I wanted it to be quick and to the point—have him like the girls in the bar had. Not like this. Not with him staring at me, searching me for a sign I couldn't give.

"I don't mind you watching, sweetheart."

Why am I still here?

Logan was gorgeous in an unbelievable I'll-probably-never-see-a-man-like-him-again way, but still, my thoughts were no longer lost in the fog of passion. My brain was full steam ahead, telling me to ignore the tingling arousal pooling in my stomach and run—run fast, and run far.

"I've got to go." I pushed off the bed, failing to collect my thoughts and ease my screaming libido that was begging me to stay.

Logan was behind me the moment I reached the door, my clammy hand gripping the knob.

His fingertips caressed the sensitive skin on the back of my neck and trailed down my spine as he slipped my coat down my arms and spoke in a rough whisper. "I didn't bring you up here for sex, Cassandra. You want me to show you? Then I will."

Slowly, he turned me around. His arms stretched out and rested on the door behind me, blocking me in. "I want you to see me, know me, and forget the past."

I let my head fall forward against the door and closed my eyes. "You should go home, Logan. It's your birthday. You should be with your family. I should be anywhere but here."

I wasn't even sure what I was saying. I just opened my mouth, and the words fell out in my desperate attempt to get away before his tenderness penetrated the piece of my heart he'd cracked open and only just begun repairing.

"You can't drive, and neither can I."

"What?" My eyes flew open, and I whipped around to meet his soft gaze. "Yes, I can," I defended, nearly breathless at his bare rippled chest pressed against me.

"Besides the fact that you had shots downstairs, you're flustered. I won't let you drive yourself home tonight, and I've had more than the legal limit. So you might as well stay with me."

Stay with him? Not now. Not after he gave me time to think and said all the right things, splitting a crack down the side of the stone fortress surrounding my battered heart. No, I needed to get out of there.

With a deep breath in and back out, my eyes closed for a moment while I collected myself. Then I was back—strong.

Chin up, shoulders straight.

"Believe me when I tell you, Logan, that your birthday will be a lot more fun if I leave." I ducked under his arm, putting distance between us.

He remained unaffected, turning with an easy smile, as if I'd said nothing but sweet sentiments. "My birthday is nearly over, and I never got my wish."

He looked so beautiful staring at me with such tenderness. Why had I kissed him? Why did the thought of him walking away, disappearing from my life, send such a panic tearing through me, propelling me straight into his arms?

"Well, nobody said it had to come true the same day." My voice shook at the thoughtful look crossing his face. What was wrong with me? Why did he have to look so vulnerable?

He stepped closer, eyes pleading. "Don't leave. Please."

My eyes fluttered shut, a ragged breath slipping out as his words danced over me. This was so hard. So unbearable.

"Logan, I—"

His hand flipped the light switch back off, casting us once again in darkness lit only by the bright moon shining off the snow outside and filtering in.

"My wish was to hold you for one night. No sex, I swear, just you sleeping safely in my arms. Please, let me show you what you need to see…how good it can be."

The man needed to stop with the *please*s. They washed over me, taking my breath and leaving me with nothing more than an open heart and nodding head.

I followed his lead when he took my hand, guiding me back to the bed. Peeling back the covers with the sweetest smile, he asked me with the gentlest voice, "Would you like to undress?"

Snapped out of my trance did not even come close to how I felt. It was as though someone woke me from my dreams of heaven with a douse of ice water.

"What?" I snapped, outraged. *Undress? I thought he said no sex.*

His head tilted to the side. "You need to work on that trust in me. I simply meant your jeans might not be the most comfortable."

I glanced over to his trousers across the room on a chair and blanched. Could I really sleep beside a half-naked Logan while I was half naked myself?

No. No I couldn't.

"Jeans are staying on," I answered.

What was I saying? How did this happen? How did he talk me into spending the night with him? I'd kissed him, wanted him. It was hot and could've led to sex, but he ruined that when he switched on the damn light—and my moral self-worth.

"Logan, I'm sorry, but I can't do this," I whispered, trying to keep the calmness in the room.

"Take off your jeans and lie down. Your shirt is long enough to cover you."

I stepped back from the bed. I needed to run before it was too late.

Logan was there in an instant. "Trust me, just once. We were friends once, Cassandra. Please just give it back until morning."

Moving to the farthest corner of the room, I turned around and unbuttoned my pants. My oversized shirt hid my ass as I slid free from my jeans, a confident smile growing on my face. I wasn't going to be the only one uncomfortable in that bed.

When I turned back around, I was faced with an observing Logan. He didn't even try to hide the fact that he'd been caught.

I rolled my eyes, sauntered quickly across the room, and climbed into the bed, pulling the blanket to my chin.

"I'm only staying because I did have a drink tonight, but this doesn't mean we're friends again."

Logan let out a real laugh that lightened my worry. "Of course, but just so I can keep up, what are we, sweetheart?"

I thought it over for a moment as he slid into bed beside

me, his legs brushing over mine.

Should've kept the jeans on.

"Neighbors," I answered finally. Tonight wasn't going to change that. I couldn't let it.

"That's all?"

I looked over at him, his head flat on the soft down pillow. "For the record, you've come a long way from the bastard I wanted to stab in the eye when he carried me to the bathroom that day in the hospital."

"I can imagine." He chuckled louder.

The charge in the air between us dispersed the longer we lay there, me staring at the ceiling, him staring at me.

The image of Logan stripped down to his briefs filled my thoughts. His chest was a hard wall of rippling muscles. His arms were tantalizingly strong, and built to do more than work behind a desk. Lying beside him, it was hard not to appreciate the care he put into his body.

I needed a distraction.

Glancing around the room, I got more than that. We were above Haven—I was positive of that, since he'd carried me up stairs and the music from the bar filtered in through the vents with the heat. I remembered hearing there used to be a couple apartments up here, but this was just a room with a door that looked like it led to a bathroom. What the hell was this place?

"So you rent these rooms? Not, like…by the hour?" I asked with a cocked brow.

"It's not my business how long they rent as long as they pay up. It was Caleb's idea to turn the crumbling apartments into a few rooms when he renovated. Figured it could bring in some extra revenue from customers who had too much to drink below, or simply leasing them out like any other hotel, since the only other place to stay in town is so rundown it should be condemned."

He was talking with ease until he caught the expression on

my conflicted face.

"To clarify, this room has never been occupied by anyone other than me. I use it as a place to stay on long nights I don't want to go home to an empty house when Oliver is visiting in the city. "

I stiffened, looking away. *Is this his...sex den?*

Lifting my head, I looked to the window and noticed the balcony that stared right back at me. Julia's words from the day she'd opened up about Logan's past ran through my head. She'd said he was caught on a balcony with a woman.

How had I not noticed it before then? I couldn't stay there any longer.

"Oh God." I cringed as I sat up, wide-eyed at the realization.

Logan's arm came down over my waist, locking me down, then his body rolled, leaning over me. His eyes searched mine as he hovered above me, both arms stretched out on either side of me, caging me in.

"No," he stated firmly.

No? He must've seen my confusion, because he continued.

"Calm those gears in that hectic head of yours, sweetheart. I've never brought anyone in here before. I, myself, have only slept here twice."

I sucked in a deep breath as my eyes wandered down to his bare chest. The man definitely knew how to take care of his body, and it was suddenly getting a little warm in the room.

"The balcony...your sister once said..." I let my words hang, swallowing to find my voice.

"That wasn't here, or even in this building, I swear. I've only used this place to rest."

Relief was heavy in my body, and a soft smile turned up the corner of his lips.

"A little faith in me from time to time would be appreciated. Is that a possibility?"

I shrugged my shoulders into the pillow under my head, and in doing so my elbows moved out, knocking into his arms. His muscles bulged as he lowered himself down as if doing a push up, his breath mixing with mine.

"Are you going to make me beg?"

Oh God, he was too close. My legs tightened together in need, and I was thankful they were already squeezed between his strong limbs.

"I'm waiting," he prompted, his nose nearly touching mine. "You asked me to show you. You should know better than to take back a request so...enticing."

"Logan..." I wasn't even sure I said it aloud until he replied with his lips on my cheek, gliding over my scorching skin and down over my chin, following the curve of my neck.

"I can't...think." I swallowed, desperate for space. "Get up. Off!"

"No."

His nose stroked my neck, followed by his wet lips over my clavicle.

"Log—"

His tongue dipped into the hollow of my clavicle. "You feel this. I know you do."

There was no denying and no stopping it when he pulled back to grip the hem of my shirt and yanked it up, over my head. My weight was unable to stop him, unable to hold it on, with my body following his lead.

"What about this?" His tongue ran down between my breasts, which were covered by a white lace bra. "Do you feel that?"

Logan spoke so deeply to my body that I clutched a handful of the comforter pooled at my waist. His tongue swirled below my right breast just under the lace, then to the left. I waited for him to rip the bra to shreds or move it to display my breasts, but they remained covered.

"Yes, I feel it," I murmured, my voice strained and broken as I kicked the blanket away and raised my legs to circle his waist, desperate to bridge the connection I craved like nothing else. "Please, I need you," I begged, grinding against him, begging for him to finally take me.

"You need me?" He repeated my plea.

"Yes."

"You want me?" His lips were tickling my stomach relentlessly, further fanning the fire building at my core.

"Logan…" I moaned when his mouth covered my breast over the lace and, after a hard suck, released it with a devious smirk.

"You want me to show you—show you how good it can be?" His voice was thick and rough, and it thundered right through me.

"Yes. Show me," I begged with a longing I couldn't control.

His eyes darkened and his body slid down, rubbing over mine in the process. His palm rested on my abdomen, holding me still as his mouth moved down and landed over my hip.

I moaned a deep, needy hum. His tongue swirled across my abs again and again, circling my bellybutton and causing my hips to lift off the bed. He held me down and rolled to the side, lying half over me, half on the mattress.

He had me panting with desire, and there was no coming back from it.

With bated breath, I was locked on watching his every move. His lips kissed farther down to the hem of my panties and then back up, teasing me.

"Show you like this?" He words were nothing but a clipped rumble as he hooked a finger under my panties and tugged the thin lace fabric between his fingers.

My heart thundered, stomach turning, until he spoke again.

"Yes," I moaned, squirming with desire.

His tongue dipped into my bellybutton, one hand kneading my breast. The other slid fully into my panties, stroking my needy sex. My head fell back onto the pillow, my body nothing but shudders and pleas.

"Oh, God, Logan!"

My toes curled. It was unlike anything I'd ever felt before— completely unexpected—as he massaged my breasts, then leaned up and placed his lips over mine, kissing my lips with a confident ease, aware of what he was doing to me, while his other hand caressed between my legs.

"I know you feel this. You feel me giving you this pleasure—no one else but me. You want more?" he asked, his lips sliding to my cheek, where he placed the sweetest peck.

His thumb ravaged my pleasure point and my hands wrapped around him, nails digging into his back. It had been so long. The massive spring inside me tightened to a point that was nearly painful. I couldn't handle it. My clammy hands tore up his back and buried themselves in his hair.

"Yes! Logan, please!"

I was lost to something primal and foreign—something I thought I'd experienced so many times before, but it was never like this.

"Let it go. I'm here…trust me. I'll always be the one to give you what you need."

My body began pulsating, stomach tight and hard, until my breath caught and my body exploded over his hand. It was unlike anything I'd ever felt before, and the screams that rang out of me weren't my own.

They couldn't be. It wasn't like me to feel…that.

Bucking my hips forward one last time, I lay there breathless, covered in a sheen of sweat, gasping for air to replenish my winded lungs.

The grin on my face brought a sweet, boyish laugh from the man who'd quite literally my mind. He rolled over to his side and propped himself up on one elbow, watching me.

"You're so beautiful, sleepy, and satisfied," he said, raking his hand up from my sex and running his thumb over his bottom lip before depositing it into his mouth.

I flushed, struggling for breath. "Not completely satisfied."

"You need more?" he asked, head tilted to the side, observing me carefully. "So do I. I need your trust, your heart, and your soul. I want you to be mine completely."

"Then take me."

He rolled back over me, putting us in the same position we were earlier, his nose brushing back and forth over mine. "Tell me you believe I'll never want another—nobody ever but you."

I swallowed, unsure how to answer in my aroused state.

"I want you. Nothing else matters. Not now. Take me. Take what you want."

His head fell forward, my nostrils hit with the intoxicating scent of a beachy day. Whatever shampoo he used, I would never forget that smell. It was so unique and clean.

When he looked back up with an unexpected grin, I couldn't help but smile in return, unsure what had brought it on.

"You sure know how to work a determined man, sweetheart." His thoughtful features softened, his grin melting into a soft, easy smile. "Don't ever lose that strength. I adore you for it."

Slowly, his lips lowered over mine, and after one lingering peck, he rolled back to his side.

"And you once called me a tease," I said with a head shake and soft breath of laughter, staring at the darkness above us.

"You were never a tease—merely a goddess I was unworthy of."

He really needed to stop with the sweet talk.

Silence hung over us while I found my breath and closed my eyes, my arousal fading as quickly as it had materialized. My thoughts erupted with the uncontrollable desire to lick my lips, taste him, and savor it. Yet with his eyes on me, my mind sunk into the depths of a reality I could no longer deny. What had happened? Was it real? Did I imagine him giving me so much pleasure?

My mind raced with images of rolling over onto him and forcing him to give me what I wanted—to finish it. Force him to take what I knew he wanted. But I didn't. I knew that look on his face. The ball was in his court, and for the night, we'd keep it there. He looked relaxed—happy—and I didn't want to change that. His happiness lightened my entire body.

I needed to either change gears quickly or get up and leave, and the second option was unbearable to think about. My body was already half asleep—or, more accurately, coming down from a high and not willing to move.

"I thought Caleb owned the building," I said, thankful for something to talk about.

"We're partners in it," he replied casually.

"Partners?" I rolled my head to the side, brows knit together, staring at him looking at me with an easy smile.

"Is that so hard to believe?"

"Yes. I thought you met him after you moved here."

Logan chuckled and shook his head once. "No."

My curiosity was now fully piqued.

"Three years ago."

Three years ago? What?

Then it clicked.

"You've known Caleb for three years?" Interesting…someone who might have a clue what the elusive Caleb had been doing while he was away.

He nodded with that same sweet smile that begged for me to return one, and I did.

"Why didn't I know this?" I asked, rolling further to my side to better face him, eager to hear what he had to say.

"You never asked."

"I just assumed that—"

"Well, you know what they say about assuming."

"Ha ha." I rolled my eyes, but my smile never faded. "So how did you guys meet?"

"I kicked his ass."

My eyes widened, my body shaking with laughter.

"You kicked his ass?" I said through the images in my thoughts. With another chuckle, I covered my mouth with my hand. "Why?"

"I love seeing you laugh. I didn't realize how much I missed that."

With my eyes locked on his, I swallowed and found my words. "Why did you feel the need to harm Caleb?" I asked, changing the subject.

Logan tucked his arm under his pillow, his gaze never leaving mine. "He was out on a date with Julia."

"Julia? Three years ago?"

My face scrunched up as I did the math in my head.

"Exactly. When you catch your sixteen-year-old sister on a date with a grown man when she's supposed to be home sound asleep, you tend to throw a few swings."

"But you two seem to get along now."

"That's because he was smart enough not to swing back. I got in one good blow, my sister hanging off my back screaming for me to stop, and I could tell by the way he stared up at her he didn't know she was underage. My sister was a spoiled brat back then, and with one stomp of her foot, she showed her maturity and he apologized. Even offered to buy me a round."

I listened, impressed how easily men could get over things.

"Julia wasn't too happy about it, but he and I became fast friends."

"So when he moved back to Harmony…"

"Julia wanted to move here first, which I later found out had to do with Mark. Caleb saw the diner as a place to invest, and the paper all but fell in my lap. Funny how things work out."

I couldn't believe what I was hearing—or worse, that there was so much about Logan I didn't really know. The time we'd spent together over the fall was great, but aside from a few conversations about Natasha, he'd rarely opened up about his past.

"So I have to ask…" I smiled to myself, catching my bottom lip between my teeth, knowing this was none of my business but wanting the information nonetheless. "Did Caleb ever talk about Hilary after he moved back?"

A chuckle rumbled in his chest. "That's such a girl thing to ask, sweetheart." He shook his head, grinning. "And here I thought you had a little more class than that."

I reached over and smacked his chest. "Just curious."

Logan caught my arm, and with bated breath, I watched him place it to his lips and kiss my palm before holding it against him, over his beating heart. I didn't move—not even when he laid his hand over mine, all but trapping it.

I couldn't look away from where my hand lay, but his eyes on me pulled my attention up his chest slowly to meet his soft . With a release of breath, I relaxed, my hand comfortable on his warm chest. The thump of each beat of his heart soothed something deep within me.

"The guy had it bad," Logan said, puncturing our silence. "Something about remembering Hilary always hanging around your place as kids. He said he never thought about her one way or another back then, but the night of the open house, he was hooked. Wouldn't shut up about how much she grew up."

I couldn't stop smiling, relieved to know Caleb was in it as much as Hilary was. We lay there a while longer, enjoying the closeness—at least for the night.

"My father left my mom and me for my babysitter," I said, unsure why I was opening up. It was just so easy with him.

"I'm sorry."

I didn't need to say more. It just felt good to get it out.

Minutes passed in a silent, enjoyable calm.

"Thank you…for this," he said as my body began to relax and mold into the mattress, my hand still on him. The easiness between us weighed on my conscience as I pulled my hand free from under him slowly. The thump of his heart began to quicken, but I knew it was for the best.

Staring up into nothing again, I struggled to control my emotions. It felt good to be there with each other—too good, too comfortable. Like when we were friends.

"I forgive you." My voice was as weak as my pulse, and I was stunned I was able to speak those words aloud. I hadn't even known it was true until it fell out of my lips.

The intensity in the gaze he set on me was too heavy for me to look his way.

"Cassandra, I wasn't trying to push you to—"

Hearing the nerves evident in his voice, I rolled to face him, smiling softly.

"I know, and that's not why I'm saying it. I just want you to know I understand that Natasha coming back that night was a shock to you."

"It doesn't make up for—" I placed my pointer finger over his lips.

"We were friends—amazing friends—and I know you were hurting that night when you saw her. I should have gotten Caleb to take you home, or…I don't know." My finger fell away, and we both lay there on our sides, gazes locked on each other.

"I just wish I could forget. I wish it never happened, but it did, and it left me with all these insecurities I can't get past." I paused briefly. "Logan, I want to be your friend…I do…but this thing between us, it's not love. I don't know what it is, but until we work it out, I can't be around you like this. It's too painful."

Logan lay there, his eyes glistening in the darkness, and nodded slowly. "I won't give up. Love's not supposed to be easy, and this is love, Cassandra. You'll never convince me otherwise. I know you're scared to believe in me again, but I'm not that guy anymore. Not with you."

"How can you say that? How can you go from having sex with multiple women to just…me?"

"It's not even a thought that's crossed my mind. I told you—they never meant a thing to me. It's only you, Cassandra."

My eyes prickled with unshed tears. "What if I'm not enough?" I breathed out in a nearly silent whisper. My darkest fear lay out before us.

"How can you ask that?"

"Logan," I sighed. "I've been with one guy my entire life—a guy who cheated on me God knows how many times. There's only one reason he would have done that: I wasn't en—"

"Enough!"

Exactly, I thought, rolling onto my back. Logan reached an arm under me, pulling me over to his side. My head rested over his naked chest, where my hand had been minutes earlier.

With a gentle kiss to my forehead, he whispered, "I'll do whatever it takes to prove to you how remarkable you are, and that what we have is more than lust."

"You don't know that. What if it isn't?"

"I've experienced lust enough times before to know it's never felt like this. If that's all I wanted, I would have had you in every position imaginable on this mattress tonight, burying myself in you."

I closed my eyes, wishing that were a possibility. Maybe friends with benefits? Logan had brought that up once when we first became friends, and the thought had appalled me. But now it didn't sound so bad. Anything more was too much. He'd slept with those two women hours after saying he wanted only me. I couldn't trust him—not with my heart.

"We'll see," I said, my eyelids growing heavy.

I could spend every night lying there, my head twisting up

170

to the nook of his neck when he tugged me closer.

"I can offer friends, Logan. That's all," I whispered into the darkness.

"No. I won't settle for that."

"So it's all or nothing?" I asked, my chin quivering.

Would this be the one and only time he held me in his arms?

"Yes. I won't pretend that we're nothing more than friendly neighbors. You can't ask for that—anything but that."

I sighed, a single tear escaping my closed eyes. He'd see this was only lust, and maybe then, after these feelings were squashed, we could find our way back to friends—or, if he wanted, nothing at all.

"Good night, Logan. Happy birthday," I murmured into the darkness.

"Good night, Cassandra." His voice was barely audible when he added, "Sleep well, sweetheart."

My heart clenched, swelling in my chest and bulging against my ribcage as I lay there the entire night, unable to sleep. Tears beckoned, but I refused to shed more. I wouldn't let him see what the thought of losing him for good would do to me.

He'd made it clear: he didn't want to be friends, so now it was time to move on…one way or another.

Chapter Sixteen

REVEALING

Hilary and I walked down Main Street, spending the afternoon shopping. I hadn't told her what happened only a few days earlier with the man I refused to think about. I had a feeling the spa day she insisted dragging me to on her dime was to get me spilling.

"What you thinking about over there?"

I opened my eyes, head down in the face rest of the massage table. What did she *think* I was ? The kneading and massaging to my back were exactly what the doctor ordered.

"Nothing. Completely relaxed," I murmured, then closed my eyes and allowed my conscience to drift into a peaceful tranquility.

"I'm glad."

That was all? No inquisition on where Logan and I disappeared to that night, or how Caleb saw me sneaking out at the break of dawn?

The massage continued without another word spoken from her table, which was situated next to mine. My mind clicked off, and I drifted to heaven.

"You awake?"

"Hmmm."

"Come on, massage is over," Hilary giggled.

I didn't want to get up. I wanted to remain glued to that

table for as long as possible.

"Oh, hi Logan!"

What the hell!?

I jumped up, grasping my towel to my body, whipping my head around the room. I found only one person, and that was Hilary and Hilary alone. She sucked in her lips, restraining her cheeky grin.

"Sorry, had to get you up before they kicked us out." She shrugged a shoulder innocently.

"Low, very low." I climbed down and followed her back to the changing room, my head still spinning from the lack of oxygen, my reserves depleted by her joke.

———◆◆◆———

"Hey, how you feeling?"

When is everyone going to stop asking me that? My answer was always the same, no matter how often everyone asked: fine. I was always fine.

But instead of replaying my usual response, I switched it up for the concerned guy treating us to yet another meal on the house.

"Peachy." I smiled widely and brightly.

Caleb chuckled. "Glad to hear it. And what about you, baby? Are you feeling peachy this afternoon? 'Cause if not…" He let his words hang and dipped down, ensnaring Hilary's lips with his.

My menu went up in my hands, and I looked it over as though I didn't already know what I was about to order. The moan Hilary let out when he pulled away made me smile. The girl was deliriously happy.

"So, we gonna get some waters over here or should I give up now?" I teased.

"Water? You sure?" Caleb pressed, glancing between Hilary

and me.

"Yep. It's supposed to cleanse the soul or, at least, that's what we've spent the day hearing. The more water the better, so keep it coming. I've got serious demons that need to be flushed out."

He eyed me a moment longer, then nodded with a thin, knowing smile.

Yeah, I had a demon, all right. One in particular latched on tight.

Immediately, Caleb sent the waiter over with two tall glasses of water, with lemons attached to the rims.

"A demon, huh? Does he have a name?" Hilary asked, an entertained smile playing on her lips as she squeezed a lemon into her water.

I took a breath and readied myself for what I was about to say. It had been over a month since the accident, and it was time to talk it out with my best friend to help sort out my feelings.

"I was going to sleep with him," I confessed, looking up hesitantly.

Her posture relaxed, and she dropped her straw in the cup. "New Year's?"

I nodded. "Yeah, but then Natasha showed up, and…" I shook my head and stared down into my glass, twirling my straw. "…he changed. Something happened to him. He was cold, and…harsh."

She waited patiently for me to find the right words.

"We were in the alley here, and I thought if I could just get him back home, I could talk to him. Get him to open up and let me in." I closed my eyes tightly as I continued, attempting to block the images of that night. "We were kissing, really going at it, and I stopped him."

"Oh my God! Did he—"

"No!" I cut off her thought. The look of horror on her face pushed me to spit out the rest.

"He didn't do anything. I told him he needed to go home and get some sleep, and he snapped. Said all he wanted was…" I lowered my voice in shame and embarrassment. "…to fuck me."

The sigh she released crashed over me, weighing me down. I tried to brush it off and continued.

"Anyway, long story short, I left a crying mess, which is why I wasn't wearing my seatbelt or why, when that car blew through the red light, I didn't even see it coming."

Hilary was quiet for a long while, waiting, it seemed, in case I had more to say, but I was done.

"What he said to you was cruel, and you can be damn sure I'm going to knock him in the nuts the next time I see the bastard."

At the awkward clearing of a throat, we both looked up to see the paled waiter standing at our table, and from the look on his face and squirm in his hips, he'd definitely caught her statement. I flushed with embarrassment as Hilary dug into her meal happily, oblivious.

There was no reason to reply to that statement after the waiter left. Hilary could be my guest. I took a sip of the cool water and relaxed into the booth.

"So now you know why I wasn't thrilled about his constant visiting, or the fact that he offered to pay my hospital bills."

Her gaze shifted side to side—her usual nervous tick.

"What?" I prompted.

"Nothing." Head down, she focused on digging her fork around the salad in front of her, searching for another black olive.

"Tell me!"

"He didn't *offer* to pay your hospital bills—he did pay them. Handed over his credit card and demanded every bill be charged to him."

I rolled my eyes. I'd assumed him paying was to come out of the check I tore up. Of course I was wrong. That explained why I had yet to receive any bills. Fine—I'd do things my way.

"I'll speak to the hospital first thing in the morning. Find out how much it was and pay him back."

She gave me a skeptical stare. "With what? You sent your mom on that cruise with the rest of your inheritance."

"I'm refinancing the house. Don't worry about it. And if you speak a word of this to my mother, I'll tell Caleb all about your little Winnie the Pooh phobia!"

"Pipe down, girl! Shit, I wasn't going to tell her, but you better keep your mouth shut. You swore on it! Last thing I need is Caleb waking me up with that creepy bear!" Her entire body shuddered.

"You're crazy, you know that?" I laughed, then took a bite of my sandwich.

We ate quietly for a while, watching the people around us shuffle in over their lunch breaks, until she looked over at me, her expression clouded with hesitation.

"What happened the other night? We saw you and Logan kissing, and then those girls. What did they say?"

"They were looking to go another round with him."

"Ugh, I thought that might have been the case from the way you stormed out. I tried to go after you, but Logan was already out the door by the time I got up."

I nodded, taking another bite.

"Caleb said he thought he saw you the next morning," she said, pretending to be less investigative then she really was.

Might was well get it all out and hope she can help me sort through the mud in my brain.

"We slept together." I worded it that way just so I could see her reaction.

Her hand flew to her mouth, covering her burst of laughter. Through it, she managed a babbling, "Oh my God! Really!? I mean…I would say it's about damn time, but after learning about New Year's…how are you feeling about it?"

I laughed and took a sip of water. "It wasn't like that. I mean… sort of, but…I'm not sure what it was. He took me upstairs and then asked me to stay the night in his arms. Said it was his birthday wish." I raised my brows, watching the grin she tried in vain to control. "Cheesy, right?"

It was cheesy, but it sure hadn't felt that way in the moment. Not even close.

"I don't know. It's kind of sweet…romantic. The guy really is crazy about you, even if he acted like an ass. Plus, he looks like the type who can pull off a corny line and wet your panties while doing so." She smirked, arching a brow.

I tried to bite back my laughter. "It doesn't matter. Nothing else is going to happen with Logan—not in the way he wants, at least. My only goal is to get him out of my head and out of my dreams; hell, he's a constant there that I can't much longer. Irrational or not, after everything he's done for me, I'm not interested in a relationship with Logan."

I planted my elbows on the table, cradling my chin.

"You're both so damn headstrong I'm not sure what to say. I mean, Caleb says Logan's a good guy and that he's never seen him act like this over another girl before. That has to count for something."

I sighed, head down, staring at my half-eaten sandwich with an appetite that suddenly abandoned me.

"It does, which is why I wish we could get over this attraction and try to go back to being friends. If only he could just see that it's better that way."

"All right, we'll figure this out, and help you come to a place where he no longer affects you. But first, clarify…did he round any bases?"

I made a face. "Oh, he rounded a few. I've never felt anything like it before—I mean, Mark was always in such a rush to jump to the main event. He never…" I looked around, reminding myself I was in a room full of diners. "He never did that. Logan wanted to give me pleasure, while Mark was all about taking it for himself."

"So it was good?" She lifted her fork and stabbed a piece of lettuce, grinning cheekily.

"More like phenomenal—better than any fantasy I could ever imagine. That is, until he refused to go further and then told me we couldn't be friends."

Hilary nearly choked on her mouthful of salad. "Why friends? I mean, you just said…"

"It's what I want, all right? And if we can get over this attraction, I think we could have that again. Last night when we were talking, just talking…I missed that."

"So what are you going to do?"

"I need to have sex with him," I stated with resolve.

"Um…why, exactly?" Her words came out as confused as the look on her face.

"It's not as crazy as you make it sound! I think one night of sex would answer all my questions, once and for all. And then afterward, one of two things will happen: he'll either leave satisfied, feeling like he conquered me the same as he has others and leave me alone for good, or he'll see the only thing between us was lust—that I have hardly any experience in the bedroom to hold his attention, and that we're better off as friends. As long as I keep my heart out of it, then it will be nothing more than a good time. One we both want."

"And if he enjoys you in the bedroom and never wants to let you go?"

"This is Logan West we're talking about. I know you don't know him that well, but ask your boyfriend. Turns out he and Caleb have a history. He'll tell you Logan is not one to settle down."

"I know, he already has, constantly. Caleb was not thrilled about Logan pursuing you in the beginning; they actually had a few blowups over it. But since the hospital, Caleb's convinced that Logan's really in it for the right reasons. He cares about you. Listen, you're my best friend, so just tell me what I can do to help."

I shrugged, watching her pop the fork into her mouth. "I have a few ideas. I just have to play it right—make him think he's winning, that he's the one calling the shots. And then when I have him alone again, I'll seduce him to the point that he can't refuse."

"Good luck," she said, unconvinced. "Caleb says he's a control freak."

"That's an understatement. Last night, he made it clear he thought he was in charge."

"And obviously it wasn't all bad." Her face brightened and brows wiggled, her closed mouth turning up into a suggestive grin as she chewed.

"He has some talents to be applauded, but then again he *has* spent plenty of time learning. A man with that much experience should never disappoint."

"Did you guys sleep naked? I mean, honestly, that seems impossible with the sexual tension you have going on."

"He wore boxer briefs."

"Very nice," she said with a hint of laughter.

After finishing our food, I pushed my plate forward and pulled some money out of my wallet to tip the waiter. "All right, we ready now?"

"Can I be honest without you hating me?" she asked, stirring her empty glass of ice with her straw, peering up at me under her lashes.

I nodded hesitantly.

"I don't think you should run out and forgive Logan right away, but I was with you that night. I saw how excited you were to meet him there. I know you were in love with him then."

"I wasn—"

She held up her hand, cutting me off. "Listen, give it time, but don't go screwing it up by trying to use sex to push him away so far that you'll lose him. Natasha coming back that night had to have been a shock for both of you. He was hurting and acted out, but he wasn't driving the car that hit you."

"How he made me feel hurt ten times worse than that car."

"I know."

"No you don't! What if Caleb said those things to you? Your worst fear thrown in your face, along with a cheap condom." My voice was hushed and shattered, but conveyed the anger I felt. I was about to tell her about the two women he'd slept with, but I didn't have it in me to bring it up. I never wanted to think about it again. I'd told him to move on, and he had—at least for the day.

"I get that you're scared, and—"

"I'm terrified beyond words—freaking petrified!" I propped my elbows on the table, cradling my cheeks in my palms. "I can't sleep at night without a sick need to call him or text him...beg him to come over and make it all go away. But I'm absolutely frightened that he'll only hurt me again, and I can't handle that. I've offered friendship, and I want to make that work if he sticks around after I give him what he really wants, but I'm not stupid enough to fall again."

"Okay, just be careful." She smiled gently, doing her best to be the loyal best friend I needed.

Finally, she seemed to understand. It wasn't that I didn't want Logan—I did, more than anything—I just couldn't let go enough to risk another chance with him. I wasn't sure I'd survive it, and I hated how weak it made me feel.

Chapter Seventeen
BEST-LAID PLANS

"Caleb!"

I heard rather than saw Oliver when he walked in. My head shot up, staring at the door where he stood, with Logan directly behind him.

My stomach tightened at the sight of him. His dark wool coat hung open, with his dark work suit underneath it. He looked good, but then again, he always did.

No. I needed to remain unaffected, no matter how much my brain replayed our last interaction—our first, but not last, rendezvous in bed.

"Hey, little buddy!" Caleb replied, bending down and holding up his hand for a high five.

"Are you going to go and say hi?" Hilary's voice broke my stare.

I knew I shouldn't, considering I'd been ignoring Logan's texts since that night while I worked out my thoughts, but I didn't want that to stop me from speaking to Oliver. Not to mention I needed to stick to the plan and get it over with.

"Yeah, a quick hello. I'll be right back."

As I walked over, smiling at how happy Oliver appeared, I stopped abruptly when I saw who entered behind Logan. Her head was down as she placed her phone back in her purse, but I recognized her immediately: Natasha.

Slowly, I began to turn around, but it was too late. Logan saw me first and I couldn't bring myself to look like a fool, so instead of turning back, I began to detour to the ladies' room when Oliver called out, "Cassie!"

Damn it. Natasha being there forced my confidence out the window. I'd been trying to forget she even existed. I released a breath, ran my tongue over my dry lips, plastered a surprised smile on my face, then turned around.

"Hey! What are you up to?" I asked, strolling back over, eyes focused entirely on Oliver.

I could feel Logan's piercing gaze boring into me. I had no doubt Natasha was staring as well, but I continued over, smiling at the young tot beaming as he wrapped his hand around the slender hand beside him. I followed it up the arm of his mother. My smile held firm, stinging my cheeks.

"This is my mom!" Oliver's voice was proud, and full of genuine admiration for the woman. "This is Cassie!"

I nodded, taking her all in once again. The woman really was everything I would expect Logan to want. Her long legs rocked a pair of dark skinny jeans and she wore a pair of patent-leather knee-high boots with a black fitted jacket, an expensive scarf wrapped twice around her neck.

"Hi, it's a pleasure to officially meet you, Cassie." From the way she bit out my name, I knew we'd never be friends.

I noticed her glance from me to Logan and back again. It was then that I finally allowed myself to look over at him. He was watching with keen interest as I swallowed the lump in my throat.

"You too," I replied as kindly as possible through my uncomfortable smile.

What else was I supposed to say? "Glad to see you're back after abandoning your family" Honestly, I wanted to lean forward and let her know what would happen if she broke Oliver's fragile heart. The thought caused me to wince.

"So, Oliver tells me you're a teacher. Sounds like an interesting job. All those kids running around." She laughed once, and my dislike for her was cemented. It wasn't fair to her, and it wasn't like me, but my protectiveness for Oliver knew no bounds.

"Sorry, if you would excuse me for just a moment, I need to use the restroom." I caught the knitted brow on Logan's stern expression as I turned and ambled straight to the ladies' room. I didn't stop until I was in front of the small sink, hands gripping it on either side, face down, trying to collect my thoughts.

What was wrong with me? Was I always going to be this weak, now that I gave in just a little? No, soon enough this would be over.

Get it together!

I needed to prove to Logan, to myself, that I could hold my own and keep my heart protected after the war that withered it.

I'd tried to ignore her existence, even after I'd seen her leaving Logan's house the day before. She was living with him, as far as I knew, and I couldn't push past the worry that if she was living under the same roof as him, something might happen. They had a history, and it was obvious she wanted him. The fact that he allowed her to live there only helped me stick to my determination that he and I would never be a couple.

With a deep breath, I twisted on the cold water and splashed my hands in it. I ran it up my arms, cooling the heat flashes he'd set upon me. I wiped the wetness over my forehead, lost in how I was going to go back out there and play it cool. I felt antsy, my nerves skittering through my veins.

I sighed. *Why did she have to be so beautiful?*

"She's nothing compared to you."

I jumped, whipping around, splashing water on the floor in the process of turning to see Logan standing just inside the door.

Crap, did I say that out loud?

"What are you doing in here?" I gasped.

I looked around. Was I in the guys' restroom? I cringed inwardly, my cheeks searing. My luck was always crap.

No urinals in sight—that was a good sign. I tilted my head just enough to sneak a quick peek under the few stalls for feet.

All alone. *Phew.*

The relieved feeling only lasted until I looked back at Logan and saw that intense look in his eyes—one that reminded me he'd slept with me, half naked, rubbing against him and looked forward to doing so again…soon.

This was it—the moment I needed him to play into my hand.

I took two long strides toward the door, but he blocked my path and, to my body's uproar, reached back and twisted the lock.

"What are you doing?" I hissed, standing tall.

I needed to play hard to get or he'd see right through me, but his perfect five o'clock shadow and alluring lips were almost too much to endure.

"Unlock the door. Someone may need to come in! Someone, as in the woman living with you now."

"I don't care. And the only reason I haven't kicked her out of my house is because I don't want her using Oliver against me. I need to know why she came back, and I need to keep an eye on her when she's around my son. But for the record, she's sleeping in the guest house in the back. And nothing, I mean *nothing*, will ever happen between me and her again. It's been over for years, Cassandra."

"That's none of my business." I jutted out my chin, holding my own, protecting my heart swelling in my chest. "I'm leaving. Goodbye Logan."

I went right and he mimicked my movement, so I stepped left and he did the same, dancing to block my every maneuver. I huffed a heavy sigh—not because I wanted to escape, but because I wanted to wrap myself around him and beg him to have me right there. Instead, I stepped back.

"Fine, what do you want?" I crossed my arms over my chest, big-girl panties on tight, putting on my show.

"To see you smile, always." His words were so sweet and sincere, and they mirrored the soft gaze in his eyes.

I pulled on the most contrived smile I could muster, my eyes squinting in the process. "Happy now?"

He shook his head. "Not yet. Have lunch with me."

"Already ate."

"A drink."

"Not thirsty."

"A kiss."

"Never again." With that, I was feeling proud, and moved to brush past him.

No such luck. He twirled me around to face him, then stepped into me. I stepped back, and he continued until my heel was pressed into the tile wall and my back was firmly against it. His hands rested against the wall on either side of my head, palms flat.

"Logan," I breathed. His clean scent, with a hint of lime, filled my senses.

"Cassandra." His voice was so soft, so tender and delicious, that my insides caved. "One date—that's all I want. A real date."

No reply left my mouth as I looked up into his piercing blue eyes. His thumb trailed across the back of my hand, which hung stiffly at my side.

"I won't take no for an answer," he added.

It had only been three days since the night he claimed a part of me. The heat pooling in my center agreed that was too long. I was a strong, empowered woman; I told myself to keep the performance going. This was a man who would bring me to my knees and abandon me there if I wasn't careful. That thought alone helped hide my arousal.

But when the tip of his tongue darted out and glossed a

thin line across his bottom lip, I forgot everything except my desire to taste his flawless lips hovering so close to mine.

I saw it in his eyes when I finally looked up. I stared too long and obliviously, and he knew it.

"Forgive me."

What?

Before I could ask, his lips were on mine, hard and demanding. I fought not to give in to it, balling my hands into fists and locking them at my side.

Hard to get. That was my role now, but damn, was it difficult.

I wasn't going to touch him. If I kept my hands to myself and focused on something—anything—other than how amazing he felt and tasted, then maybe he'd take a hint and release me. Give me a chance to regroup.

He pulled back just enough to murmur, "Please."

Everything inside me exploded, with his need devouring both of us. I stood my ground and opened my mouth to protest, but Logan used it to his advantage and slid his tongue inside.

I was done. My hands flew up to his neck, tugging and grasping his hair, losing myself in his embrace. One arm was wrapped around my waist with his other hand on my cheek, holding me near. I couldn't describe the emotions flurrying inside me—everything from passion, to need, to lust. I wanted to erase our past, making our lives easier.

It was I who finally found the strength to break the kiss. "Stop."

He did so instantly.

Panting, I breathed out, "Your son is waiting with your ex."

Thank God I could even think to speak, let alone find a valid excuse with the way my head was clouded from the passion that sparked between us.

He smiled and leaned back in, placing a tiny kiss on the tip of my nose, then stepped away, giving me breathing room.

"Natasha wanted to take him out for lunch. I agreed only on the condition that I'd bring him and wait here while they ate."

"I thought she lived with you."

"I allow her to stay in the guest house in the back with a few ground rules. We came to a compromise that she'd be able to stay there and see Oliver under supervision, as long as she understood that I was off limits completely. Until I figure out her game, I'd prefer to keep my eye on her, anyway."

"Just your eye?" I scoffed.

"Don't ever be jealous of her. I'm not interested, and that will never change."

He stood in front of me, watching my every breath, waiting for my reply that never came. Instead, I focused on the other part of his statement—one that was equally surprising.

"Since when do you compromise, anyway?" I laughed.

"I've done so on rare occasion," he replied, searching me. "Do you have anything in particular you'd like to compromise on?"

My brows pulled in. "Like what? You leaving me alone and me not kneeing you in the balls the next time you try to touch me?"

The corner of his lip curled up. "I was thinking more like you go on a date with me and I'll stop pressing you into walls and beds—at least, until you're ready." I caught the gleam in his eye, testing me.

I hated to admit how much I liked him pressing me into things. I bit my lip, not pleased with my thoughts. I was going to have to deal with Logan in a new way if I wanted to keep my heart out of it and protected. A light flicked on in my head and I stepped forward, standing toe to toe with Logan, who stared down at me, intrigued.

"One date." My pointer finger jabbed his chest. "My house, my rules. Tomorrow night. Deal?"

The excitement in his eyes couldn't be matched. He held out his hand for me to shake.

"Deal."

He didn't shake my hand when I held it out; instead, he brought it to his lips and placed a lingering, open-mouth kiss on my palm.

My eyelids closed on a sigh that stung my very center as his lips moved ever so slightly. I yanked my hand free, goose bumps flaring over every inch of my heated skin.

"Six sharp. If you're late, don't bother knocking."

With a devilishly triumphant grin firmly in place over his lips, he stepped out of the way for me to walk past him, heading back to meet Hilary. If only he knew I had the same smile on my face.

Chapter Eighteen

PREPARATION

I'd hardly slept that night, imagining what it would be like to finally feel Logan inside me—giving in to our deepest hunger.

I awoke early, went for my morning jog with no sign of Logan, and returned home for a shower. I was anxious to get the day going, and as I stood in my kitchen, staring out to the backyard, sipping some orange juice, I caught sight of Oliver in his backyard.

He wasn't alone. Natasha was at his side, helping him pack snow onto the front of a melting snowman. The smile on his face was hard to miss, and I had to admit Natasha looked equally happy.

Was there a chance she really just wanted her family back—to bond with her son and reconnect with Logan through sex, the only way most women did? The thought of her living in his backyard and bonding with their son left me conflicted, and only added to mission of the day—the day Logan and I would take the plunge and prove, once and for all, that we were better off friends.

With a thoughtful smile, happy for Oliver to have both his parents in his life, I set out to get dressed and start my day.

Hilary and I had spent the previous day shopping, and now there we were again. However, shopping for the perfect date accessories that would guarantee me the best sex of my life had me worried. Luckily, Hilary had it down to an art, and took the lead.

When we stepped inside the small boutique, I instantly surrendered the dress-searching part to Hilary and sauntered toward the lingerie section sheepishly.

Yes, lingerie. I hadn't worn it more than a total of two times in my life, but I felt tonight it was needed in the whole package Hilary was helping me prepare. And to ensure the night lived up to the pressure behind it, I felt lingerie was called for.

Tonight was going to be more than just a simple dinner date—it would be the end of the chase for Logan. After I was through with giving him everything he'd wanted the past few months, now on my terms, the sexual tension brewing between us would be sated and give us the closure we both needed to move on.

I found a black lace corset with garters attached to hold up the black sheer stockings. Perfect. It was everything I wasn't, which was exactly what I was going for. I wanted to have sex with Logan—to give my body and his everything they'd been craving, the release that was desperately needed at the other's hand.

It was my choice, my desires, and in my control. I plucked the hanger holding the corset from the rack and, with a smile on my face, headed over to find Hilary. Tonight was about letting go of my inhibitions and feeding the sexual need I'd been starving far too long. It had nothing to do with anything other than that, so Logan wasn't going to get the other side of me tonight.

No, he was getting the sexual, aroused, just-a-one-night-tryst Cassandra. The real, sweet, carefree me was getting locked up, sealed in with my emotions, tucked away from his alluring charm.

I had to admit it excited me, holding the fine lace in my hands, envisioning his expression when he saw me in it. Yes, it was definitely the right choice.

The smooth red dress Hilary found was not one I'd have chosen. I wouldn't have called it slutty or even sexy enough to accompany such vulgar lingerie, but she insisted it was exactly what I needed. It was very short, but that was the extent of sex appeal it exuded. In spite of the extra-tight fit and low cut (but not so low cleavage would show), the buttons running up the front gave it the look of a lab coat.

"I was thinking something more like this." I held up a tiny hot-pink dress that would barely cover a Barbie.

"Logan's been after you all this time for a reason. You're hard to get, and if you go at him too eagerly, he'll see through it. This," she held up the red number, "is what you need. Something with grace and," the corner of her lips curled up, "buttons."

"Buttons? Since when are buttons sexy?"

I wasn't feeling it until she stepped to the side, revealing a mannequin wearing said red dress and flicking her fingers over the top button, releasing it. She slid her hand down in a slow, caressing trail and flicked the next one open.

Oh yeah, we need buttons.

"Logan's going to want to take his time after chasing you so long. Let him slowly unwrap his present, and then you can greet him with the wonder of lace underneath. By then, he'll be drooling too much to stop, and he'll be putty in your hands."

I did like that, but it was hard to imagine Logan being putty in anyone's hands. He was always so cool and confident. The mission was to bring the man to his knees and give him all the sex he could handle until he was completely satisfied and ready to move on to the next girl.

A pang struck through my heart. Damn it, why did it hurt so much thinking about him moving on? We weren't good for each other, so I only hoped after that night we'd be nothing more than neighbors with a past who could say hi while getting the mail and experience no weirdness or enormous gravitational pull toward one another.

"Up next? Hair, nails, makeup, and...waxing."

I swallowed. *Waxing?* "Is that really necessary?"

"Yeah, you're right, your nails look great au natural. He'd know you were trying too hard if we did them up." She walked to the counter, handed over the dress, and took the lingerie from my hands.

"Oh, and I have the perfect heels you can borrow."

That was good, since I was officially draining my savings with the three hundred dollars' worth of clothing I'd never wear again, but it was worth it. It'd probably be the best three hundred dollars I ever spent.

With an anxious and excited smile, I handed over my debit card and watched the cashier wrap the items in tissue paper.

I leaned over to Hilary while waiting and whispered, "I'm not getting waxed."

With a bright smile, she grabbed the bag from the woman and gave me a we'll-see-about-that grin before strolling toward the door.

I took the receipt, blood draining from my face, and gave a quick thanks to the cashier before following.

The salon was one I'd frequented before with both Hilary and my mother, but that was for hairstyling, never makeup, and the only waxing I'd ever experienced was on my brows once. I couldn't imagine it being the same thing.

What was Hilary thinking? *Just my legs, or..?* I blanched.

"Hey, Maya!" Hilary greeted the receptionist. "I called last night for an appointment. Cassandra needs the full got-a-hot-date package!" Maya was a girl we'd grown up with, but still, Hilary didn't need to announce it to the entire salon.

"Good for you, girl! About time. So who's the guy?" Maya asked, stepping out from behind the desk.

My mouth remained shut. I wasn't planning on dating

Logan, so I wasn't sure what to tell her.

"Nobody from around here. Just a guy she met a while ago who's coming to visit her for the night," Hilary piped in, saving me. I gave her a grateful yet subtle smile.

"Oh really? Got to tell you, I was hoping to hear it was Logan West. That man is…mmm, dangerously hot. Not enough words to describe a guy that good looking. I'd give him a date he'd never forget if he asked, but from what I hear, he went from screwing around with most of the easy girls in town to not even buying a girl a drink. Figured it had to do with you."

Something about that brightened my mood.

"Nope, not me," I said softly.

I began to relax until she told me to follow her as she began walking through the rows of hairdressers toward a door in the back. Hilary shooed me away as she sat on the sofa in the front and opened a magazine.

I was on my own and had no clue what I was in for, so I just followed along, leaping in and hoping it was worth it.

"Everyone's been gossiping about how much you and Logan were hanging out in the fall," Maya continued as I stepped into the small quarters that held a long counter and massage-style table with a terrycloth towel covering it that reminded me more of the one at my OBGYN than the spa.

I sat with my hands shaking, fingers nervously kneading together while Maya sat on a stool, preparing materials and checking the temperature on a vat of wax as she rambled.

"And that sexy show you guys put on, on the dance floor at Haven on New Year's Eve? Damn girl, you had me hot and envious just watching! Hope you didn't think that went unnoticed."

I flushed, embarrassed. "Well, nothing's happening anymore with Logan. So where exactly did Hilary tell you to wax me?" I gulped way too loudly, a cold sweat breaking out over my forehead.

Her stool swirled around, a bemused smile covering her small, freckled face.

"Oh God, you look like you're about to pass out! Are you all right?"

"I'm not really into pain."

"Pain!" She burst out laughing. "Beauty comes with pain, but my goal is to keep you as relaxed and distracted as possible. Now get those jeans and panties off and cover yourself with this. I'll be back in a couple."

"Panties?"

"Mm-hmm. Part of the hot-date package, but no worries, I'll take care of you."

She walked out and shut the door behind her. Holy hell, was I really going to get fully waxed? Would she remove all the hair, or leave a little something? It was February, after all—too cold to go bare, right? Or was I just being crazy? I pulled off my jeans and looked down at my purple panties.

Yeah, definitely crazy. I needed Logan to have my body at its best, and a man like him would want all smooth sailing—quite literally.

I shimmied out of my panties and lay back down, covering myself with the towel she'd left.

"Knock knock, you ready?" Maya opened the door and stepped inside. She must've seen the apprehension on my face, or perhaps it was my wide eyes and hands clutching the side of the table that did it, but she blew out a breath and smiled.

"So tell me about this guy of yours. Hottie? He must be if he caught your attention, especially after Mark. God, I'm sorry, but your ex is a dumbass."

My hands clutched the table harder—not because of the fear of having my skin torn off, but from thinking about Mark.

"Yeah, he is," I grumbled through gritted teeth.

"You're going to show him, though. I don't remember you ever coming in here to get all prettied up for him." She giggled, and I relaxed instantly.

"All right, what you thinkin'? Brazilian, or—"

"Take it all! Just do it quick before I change my mind," I spit out, and she laughed louder.

"You got it." The heat of the wax being spread over a place few had seen left me uneasy, but Maya was a friend from elementary school and had been working at the salon since her aunt opened it when she was thirteen. If anyone was good for the job, it was her.

"So, this mystery man…you hoping to screw him at your place or his?"

"What—AHHH!" I bit my lip hard. "Damn! That hurt!"

"Yes, but you didn't see it coming. Mind over matter."

I closed my eyes, breathing steadily, ready for the next one.

———◆◆◆———

"Wow, you look amazing!" Hilary jumped from the spot she'd occupied for over three long hours and rushed toward me.

I was both sore and excited. Full Brazilian? Check. Smooth legs and underarms, and brows primped to the perfect arch? Check. Hair full of curls and sprayed with enough chemicals to outlast a tsunami? Check. And last but not least, makeup that screamed sexy, including a dark, smoky eye? Check.

I was all ready to go for the next phase, which included a grocery trip.

"Come on, I still have to get some food to cook for dinner, and then I gotta get dressed."

It was already pressing four o'clock, and he'd be there at six on the dot. I had no doubt about that—especially since I'd made it clear he didn't want to be late.

"Already done," Hilary replied, holding open the salon door for me.

What? When? I stared at her, waiting for her to explain.

"You didn't really think I could sit there and look at magazines that long, did you?" She smiled. "Go home. Everything you need is there."

Grinning, I gave her a big hug, relieved I was able to go home. "Thanks."

"No problem, but I expect to see you at my door tomorrow with full details!"

"Making no promises," I shot back, still smiling as I headed to my car.

Hilary's idea of dinner differed greatly from mine. The groceries she'd piled into my fridge included oysters, a cooked rotisserie chicken, strawberries, chocolate sauce, and four cans of whipped cream. On the counter was another bag, which included a box of biscuits and can of corn.

I shook my head, irritated but amused. I should've known better—or at least asked her before I'd driven all the way home. There was no time to go back out, so I'd just have to go with it.

After preparing everything in the kitchen, I headed for the bedroom with my new bag of clothes. Slipping my toes into the pantyhose, I began to feel it—the awakening of the relentless beast that lived deep in my gut and seemed to answer to only Logan. The garters were snapped in place, corset sewn up my front with a ribbon.

Standing in front of the mirror, I could no longer see the girl who was worried about heartbreak or love. I was a woman—a fierce woman about to have sex with a man who'd fulfill some piece of me that would give me my independence back. Give me back my empowering will to live my life without the need for a man...at least, until the right one came along.

I buttoned the dress, slowly covering the treat underneath, and let my imagination run wild with thoughts about how he'd unwrap me. A slow, seductive play of undoing button at a time, or a quick rip down the front, buttons flying in the air as he laid his eyes upon the naughty side of me, dressed in black lace just for him?

There I stood, fully dressed, including a pair of black six-inch pumps Hilary had left in front of my closet. The image reflected from my full-length mirror was overwhelming, powerful, and beautiful. I was a real woman, and ready for Logan to hear me roar.

I turned to my side, bending over to see exactly how much of a show Logan would be getting before the main event. The dress tugged up to show just a hint of the garters underneath. Logan was in for one hell of a surprise tonight.

The alarm clock on my bedside table glowed ten to six, and the butterflies were fully aware of it. As I turned to leave the room, my phone went off in my purse sitting on the bed.

I answered to Hilary's bubbly voice.

"Nice grocery shopping!" I complained instead of saying hello.

"What? It's exactly what I'd want." She giggled.

"I'm sure it is." I rolled my eyes, smiling. "I can't talk, he'll be here any minute."

"I know, but first look beside your bed, between the side table and your mattress."

Curious, I walked around the bed to find a hot-pink gift bag poking out. I picked it up and sat on the bed holding it. Tissue paper covered the contents.

"Should I be afraid to look inside?" I asked.

"It's five fifty four, hurry up and open it!"

"All right." Jeez, she was more nervous than I was.

I pulled out the tissue paper and gasped.

"Seriously, Hilary!?"

Her laughter filled my head as I dumped the rest of the bag onto the bed. There was the biggest box of multi-size condoms

I'd ever seen. Judging by the girth pressed to my backside the night we slept together, there was only one size that man was going to need.

"Two minutes left! Have fun! And Cassandra, whatever happens, it's okay to let yourself feel everything you do for him." With that, she hung up.

I knew she was hoping tonight would help me see how much Logan meant to me and be less one-night-stand, closure sex. She wouldn't say it straight out, but I knew she wanted me to forgive him.

I shook my head and pulled my attention down to the pump-style bottle of lube (which I was positive we wouldn't be needing), rhinestone-encrusted nipple clamps, blindfold, and pair of fuzzy handcuffs that were scatted over my comforter.

Yeah, aside from the condoms—the box of which I'd already ripped open and begun to pick through for the large and jumbo to go in my side drawer—the rest was not necessary.

I picked up the items just as the doorbell rang. My head shot to the side, staring at the six on my clock. I hurried, stuffing the items into the bag and dropping it back between the nightstand and mattress.

After one more peek in the mirror and a smack of my lips to redistribute my crimson lipstick, I was at the door, ready for the night to begin.

Chapter Nineteen

SEDUCTION 101

There are some moments in life you know you'll always remember: the warmth of your lips after your first kiss, the tingle on your skin after your first sexual embrace. And then there's the moment you open the door to the man who has dug a hole so far into your heart you wonder if he was always meant to be there.

Logan stood on my doorstep, reminding me to seal my heart away for the night as he appraised me with a thunderstruck eye, taking me all in. His grip tightened around the neck of the wine bottle in his hand, and it was then that I noticed the single lily in the other. His eyes feasted upon my hair, teased up and heavy with thick curls, down to my smoky eyes, until he reached the heels I wore with pride.

"You gonna come in or just stand there and stare?" I asked with a soft, seductive giggle. As it turned out, flirting when you had the sex appeal amped up was more fun than I'd expected.

He looked up with the confident charisma that had wavered for longer than usual during his assessment and smiled.

"You look...different." He walked inside, squeezing past me when I didn't move back. We were face to face, my breasts pressed to the chest of his wool coat, our bodies rubbing together with his slow steps...mine letting his know exactly what it was in for tonight.

"*Good* different?" I took the flower and bottle of wine from his hands and swayed my hips as I sauntered to the kitchen.

Logan followed. "You're always good, sweetheart."

I glanced back over my shoulder to catch his boldly handsome face smile warmly back at me as he removed his coat.

He was gorgeous—a true work of art—and for a fleeting moment, I wondered what his parents looked like. The shadow of his beard mixed with his striking features held a certain sensuality.

I ogled him openly, taking in his nonchalant stance and roguish handsomeness. I noticed his light, wavy hair had been cut shorter recently, and the jealously exposed in my gut from wondering who'd had the honor of running his or her fingers through his soft locks made me shudder.

His white dress shirt showcased the powerful set of shoulders hidden underneath, while his dark jeans hung casually around his firm legs. They were his wardrobe staples outside of work. He was a man who carried himself with a commanding air of self-confidence. I loved that about him.

I grimaced, turning away to dig a corkscrew from the drawer. *Not loved—it was one of the many things about him that turned me on*, I restated in my head over and over again.

Silence hung between us as I stood fiddling with the corkscrew in my hand for way too long, gauging the best way to go about opening the bottle. The fact that Logan never said even a silly quip about my gawking added to the electricity sizzling between us already.

Hilary always took charge of wine opening when we were together, and I didn't drink when I was alone. The few times I'd attempted opening wine bottles, I'd destroyed the cork to the point that it had to be dug out.

So not sexy.

"Need some help?" His warm, minty breath tickled my ear, startling me. I swung around on instinct, forgetting about the weapon in my hand.

He caught my hand, stopping the corkscrew from piercing his abdomen. His face didn't carry even a hint of worry—only a smile. "I'll open it."

Catching my breath from the adrenaline spike, I nodded and handed him the tool. "Thank you," I replied, pulling back on a heavy, sultry tone. He gave me a cynical once-over, but didn't say a word.

"So, how was your day?" Logan asked, pulling the cork free with ease. "I see you must have been busy." Two wineglasses were already set on the table, so he turned around, waiting for me to respond while filling them both.

Things needed to remain focused on why we were there, no matter how hard my heart boomed against my chest. It was only about sex.

I breathed a seductive murmur into his ear from beside him, placing silverware on the table. "Do you care how my day was?"

He straightened and set the bottle down, but before he could reply I was across the room, ready to serve the appetizer: oysters.

"Would you like one?" I purred.

He eyed them curiously. "An oyster?" I caught the humor flash in his bright eyes.

"Mm-hmm." I tipped one back and nearly gagged as the slime caught in my throat.

"You all right?" He strode toward me, patting me on the back.

I choked down the filth that was never entering my mouth again and nodded. That was my first and last oyster.

Brush it off and keep going.

"You should try one. They're…yummy." I nearly gagged out the word.

God, I was a horrible liar. And 'yummy'? What was I—five?

Even Oliver had a better vocabulary.

"Never really been an oyster fan," Logan replied with a knowing, tight-lipped grin.

With a cock to my head, I whispered, "That's a shame. I've heard great things about them." I winked.

Yes, I actually winked, and then ran my finger down his crisp white shirt, over the buttons I'd definitely have no for patience for later.

"Sit, I'm starved," I drawled, hoping he'd pick up on my double meaning.

Logan must've picked up on something, because his palm shot out over my forehead, testing my temperature. "You sure you're feeling all right?"

My eyes squinted. I was going for sexy, but wasn't sure it came through from the concern etched over his brow. I removed his hand, kissing the center of his palm.

"I'm better now that you're here."

He didn't say another word, instead sitting at the table and picking up his glass of wine. Standing beside him, I unsnapped my top button to reveal some motivation and leaned down to light the candles.

My arms brushed his, my body positioned at the perfect angle to give him an eyeful as I carefully lit two long, creamy candles in the center of the table.

When I stood back and flicked off the kitchen overhead light, I heard him say, "Interesting," under his breath.

Yes, tonight will be far better than interesting.

"I hope you like chicken." I pranced over to the stove.

When I set his plate in front of him, he caught my arm.

"It's fine. I think you know I didn't come over for the food." His voice was so raw and throaty I wanted to wrap myself around him and have him right there.

Oh he was feeling it, all right. I sat and crossed my legs, tightening them together to silence the quiver of lust.

Not yet.

"I came to spend time with you," he added.

"You don't say," I teased, resting my elbow on the table and swirling the liquid in my glass.

Dinner was eaten at a snail's pace. Our eyes were constantly fixed on each other, searching and challenging. I wasn't giving anything away. My lips nibbled the meat, my tongue playing on my lips longer than necessary to wipe away the juices. Logan barely touched his food, and I caught him shifting in his seat more than once.

After I finished all I could eat—which wasn't much, since my stomach was filled with horny butterflies—I set my fork down. Logan did the same and then leaned in, both elbows planted on the table, his fingers interlocking his strong hands together.

"I have to say, I wasn't expecting for you to be so…friendly tonight," he confessed.

"Well, despite what your big ego believes, you don't know everything about me, Mr. West." His eyes darkened at my use of his full name. "I have many sides that you've yet to see."

"It appears so."

I raised my brows, challenging him to dive in, and as I expected, he didn't let me down.

"Cassandra, you have until the count of five to either tell me what game you're playing at, or I'm coming to get you."

My lips curled up. *Yes, please come. I'm right here, waiting.*

I sat there waiting, and almost instantly he began the countdown.

"Five."

My pulse raced, anticipation heavy in my veins.

"Four."

I sat up straighter, my nipples hardening at his promising tone.

"Three."

My mouth opened just enough to release the breath I'd been holding onto unknowingly.

"Two."

Game on. I scooted my chair back and gave him a come-and-get-me smirk.

"One."

Logan stood and I did the same. But to keep the upper hand, I ran my wet tongue over my bottom lip deliberately and raised my brows.

"What are you waiting for? I thought you took what you wanted?"

Logan's lips attacked mine without warning. His stubble burned against my delicate skin when his mouth traveled down my jaw and then back up to recapture my pouty lips. His were as soft as I remembered, yet firm and demanding.

His kiss was greedy with hunger and radiating ecstasy. My tongue traced over his bottom lip, seeking entrance, and with a panty-soaking growl, his mouth opened and his tongue met mine in a fierce battle of lust.

Pulling back, I sucked in a deep breath of replenishing air, and then demanded, "Take me to bed—now!"

A loud squeal burst from my throat when he bent down and threw me over his shoulder, just as he'd done the day I got hurt jogging. This time, however, he was ruthless—one hand held me in place by my calves, while the other slid up my dress and caught my ass in his grip.

"You have no idea how bad I wanted to do that the last time I had you in this position." He kneaded and squeezed, walking leisurely to my bedroom, then dragged me back down the front of his body slowly. His manhood pressed into my stomach as I stood in front of him, swallowing at the size of it.

He noticed, and a cheeky grin crept over the lips that I missed already.

"You should have seen what you did to me then. Why do

you think I kept you up on my shoulder so long after we reached your porch?"

My face seared as my arousal plunged to unthinkable depths. I'd seen him checking out my ass that day, but the fact that he'd been sporting an erection was not something I'd even dreamed.

"I should have realized. I guess I still held out hope you were a gentleman in there somewhere." With an innocent smile, I went up on my tiptoes and placed a wet kiss over his irresistible neck.

"Always a gentleman for you, sweetheart. Only you."

"Shhh."

No nice words could be exchanged, or the heart I'd sealed up tight for the night would begin to uncover. I only wanted to prove this was all he really wanted—that he wasn't my happily ever after, and after tonight, we'd both be able to move on. It was the best kind of closure a girl could get: closure sex.

I silenced my thoughts as he kissed me again, my relentless hands tugging his hair, forcing him to remain quiet.

My face angled toward his, my fingers sweeping deftly over his scruffy jaw. He caught my pinky in his teeth, causing me to giggle. My laughter was caught in my throat when he released my finger and placed lingering, open-mouth kisses on the tips of each digit, one by one. He didn't miss a beat when he raised my hand, running his lips up my arm, his eyes holding mine in his steady gaze.

I'd never wanted someone so badly in all my life, and the realization that it was none other than Logan who brought that yearning out of me was terrifying.

"We don't have to do this." His mouth surrounded my ear, tongue flicking down over the lobe. My legs squeezed together, my sex clenching.

Oh God! The surge of heat rushing through me and pooling between my legs was too much to bear. I needed this. I needed him.

Without a reply, I pushed him down onto the bed and dropped to my knees. Logan raised his brows in approval, his lips pressed into a firm line.

Looking up at him, I bit my bottom lip and let it slip through my teeth. "You know you like me down here."

His eyes were a shade darker and half lidded. "Cassandra."

"Shhh. Stop thinking. Just feel," I murmured.

His black boots smelled of leather. I undid the laces slowly and pulled them off, followed by his white socks.

Gazing down at his beautiful bare feet, I smiled, my arousal influencing me to continue and eager to move on to the main event. Tonight was about fulfilling all the dreams of and desires for Logan I'd ever had.

With zealous ease, my hands slid up his jeans and over his calves, resting on his firm thighs. His muscles clenched, building my confidence.

Logan watched me with a stoic expression when I glanced up under my long, painted lashes and spread his legs apart slowly.

I smiled to myself as his bulge greeted me, proud I'd caused such a reaction from him. Gingerly, my fingers slid up his leg and traced over his hardness, continuing to the button of his fly.

I gasped, startled when he grabbed my wrist to stop me. When I tipped my head back to meet his gaze, my breath caught. The intensity staring back at me could never be matched. Heat prickled over my scalp, my cheeks burning under his scrutiny.

"Tell me you really want this." His husky tone was breathless.

My attempt at a smile was in vain. He could see right through me, and I found myself lost in the depth of his gaze. The strength it took to stretch up on the balls of my feet was nearly painful, but I managed with confident grace to lean into his ear, the warmth of his cheek pressed to mine while my hands braced on his thighs.

"I want this, Logan. And tonight, there is no place else I'd rather be."

Logan's eyes glistened. In that same instant, he reached down and scooped me up by my waist, flinging me up from the floor and burying me beneath him on the mattress. His hands held mine, pinning them to the mattress above my head.

"Tonight?" His teeth ground out the word, and I blanched. Before I could wonder if he'd read my mind or what was going through his, a flash of determination crossed his dark, shadowy eyes.

"Tonight," he repeated, as if testing the word in a new voice—a calmer one.

He released my hands and worked down my dress tediously, popping the buttons open one by one, torturing me with the deliberately slow pace of his fingers. I reached down to help, but he grabbed both my hands in one of his and, after placing a quick kiss to my thumb, returned them to their position above my head. My actions only deepened my need for him, as he slowed with now only one hand to undo the exasperating buttons.

After the final button, he looked up at me with a trace of the smirk I rarely saw anymore and released my hands. I remained still, anxious for his next move, but he didn't keep me waiting for long. His fingers drifted down between my breasts and he lifted one side of my dress slowly, revealing the shameless corset, eager to finally greet him.

"You're gorgeous, sweetheart." His hand moved slowly, undoing the ribbon just enough to reveal my breasts. "You don't need this."

His delicate touch unraveled the seal over my heart as his fingers worked with tantalizing finesse, as though I were made of glass. When he finally looked up at me, his eyes were filled with a concentrated emotion I failed to decipher. A shiver raced up my spine and wrapped a chill around my neck. It was something much deeper than lust, and it frightened me.

I squirmed, suddenly nervous. However, the moment Logan's mouth covered my nipple, all insecurities flew from my mind, replaced with the numerous fantasies that had filled my dreams for months. Finally, they'd become reality.

Logan's diligent and skillful tongue was warm and wet. His other hand freed my neglected breast and presented it with the same amount of stimulating affection.

His mouth released me after he'd had his fill and moved farther down, tugging the ribbon open, further revealing all that was hidden. He kissed as he went and stopped over my bellybutton, looking up at me with soft, unwavering eyes.

I flinched at the tenderness they held.

"I've never wanted anyone more, Cassandra. I wish you could feel how much you mean to me. How much I lo—"

"Stop, please don't ruin this." The nerves were back, pushing through the lust consuming me. Why did he have to go there? This wasn't about love. It was about closure—for both of us.

When his mouth moved down and landed over my hip, I moaned a deep, needy purr. His tongue swirled across my abs again, circling my bellybutton and causing my hips to lift off the bed just enough for him to snake one hand under me.

There'd been too many nights I'd lain awake, wondering what it would be like—what Logan could do to me. So far, my fantasies didn't even touch reality. I'd expected for things to go faster. Mark had been my only lover, and he wasn't one to waste time when getting things going for himself.

I couldn't really call Mark selfish in bed since I had no one to compare him to, but the moment Logan unsnapped the first garter and slid my stocking down my leg, setting them on the bed as if they were irreplaceable treasures, I knew I was in for a night I'd never experienced before and never forget. He did the same to the other side and then spread my legs just enough to reveal the lace panties covering my smooth sex, glistening just for him.

I waited, closing my eyes in anticipation for the moment to arrive—for him to remove his trousers and rest over me, pressed deep inside. But it never happened.

With bated breath, I peeked open an eye and glanced down. He was on his knees at the end of the bed, staring up at me, watching me. The moonlight illuminated his face.

My legs pulled together, insecurity and fear working against me. *Am I not good enough? Does he not want me?* Not again. I couldn't go through the rejection another time.

I sat up in a swift motion, but he was there pushing me back down, his hands on my knees, parting my legs further for him to rest between as I'd done to him moments earlier.

"Stay there." His words were nothing but a clipped rumble.

My heart thundered, stomach churning until he spoke again.

"You're so perfect."

Perfect? I was nowhere near it, but I wondered if I was to him. The longer I lay there, the more anxiety riddled me. He stroked the back of my legs that hung down off the bed, but didn't make another move. I needed to do something.

I sat up on my elbows and raised my brows. "You going to make me beg?" I hummed.

Logan's mouth twitched at the sides as his hands ran up from my feet and over my thighs, where he leaned down and placed a slow, sensual kiss over my scar.

He sat up further on his knees and whispered, "One day, I'll make you beg, but not tonight."

The smile growing on my face couldn't be missed.

"Not before I have at least one taste, anyway," he added under his breath.

Just one? What did that mean?

I opened my mouth to question it but fell back onto the pillows, speechless, as his mouth began kissing around the one place Mark had always neglected.

"Oh, God, Logan!"

My toes curled. It was unlike anything I'd ever felt before, and he hadn't even touched the main event. Just having him that close was unexpected and savage. He ravaged my inner thighs with his tongue, relentless and domineering. It was heaven. I relished the feeling, anticipation surging through me, fueling my high, his attention diverted from my center for longer than I could bear.

My legs trembled with desire when his fingers ran over the lace covering me and slowly pulled the fabric aside. His tongue worked closer, and when the scruff of his jaw rubbed across my newly bare area, I let out a full-on, hysterical scream.

"Wait! Stop! Stop! Stop!" I was on fire, and not in the way I'd planned.

I pulled myself up, bringing my knees up to my chin and fanning my hands over the raw skin while Logan stood and crossed the room, flicking on the light.

My eyes blinked as they adjusted to the brightness, and I watched in horror as Logan dropped back to his knees and spread my legs to examine me.

His eyes never looked away from my sacred area as he teased, "Well, I see you had more than a little makeup and hairstyling done today, sweetheart."

Kill me now.

"It's red," he continued in a matter-of-fact tone. "Looks tender."

The heat in my cheeks had to have been just as enflamed.

"You should have told me. I would have been gentler."

The man had been as gentle as you could get. I mean, his kisses were as—

"Ohhhh," I moaned, dropping my knees open and falling

back to the mattress as Logan blew a soft stream of breath over the fire burning between my legs.

He was right—he could be gentler.

"Better?"

"Mm-hmm." I bit my lip, hands covering my face but my stiff posture melting away.

"Tell me, does it hurt here?"

My hands slipped down, gripping the comforter below me as his tongue parted me down my center and slid over me with careful ease.

"Ohhh. Nooo. Perfect."

"It's gonna kill me to leave," he rumbled, and his tongue slid back down, careful not to brush the enflamed area.

Leave? What? Before I could comprehend, he was gone, my sex abandoned.

"Looks normal for being freshly waxed. You'll be healed up soon."

That was it? He was just getting started. And the fact that he knew what a freshly waxed vagina looked like turned my gut.

The bed dipped from Logan sitting on it, and he pulled my hand nearest him to his lips.

"I like you flushed. It's adorable." He grinned.

Great, I was adorable. Exactly what I was not *going for tonight.* I closed my eyes tighter.

"Do you have any aloe lotion, or—" He stopped abruptly.

"They gave me a balm to apply, but it hadn't hurt." To be honest, my body had spent the evening too aroused to think about the unfriendly waxing job.

Wait, why did he stop talking? And what was that ruffling—oh, crap!

My eyes flew open and I scurried up in horror, tugging at the bag in his hand, but it was too late. He pulled it out of my near-miss grasp and held up the handcuffs.

"Interesting choice." The corner of his mouth quirked up.

"You sure planned one hell of night. I hate to disappoint, but even if you hadn't been waxed raw, I wasn't planning on having sex with you."

"What?" I gasped incredulously.

He was lying. had to be.

"So, what, then? You would have just teased me and then left?" A hard laugh shot out. "You're lying!"

"That was exactly what I was planning on doing if you couldn't get out of your head long enough to see you were acting unreasonable." A serious scowl settled between his brows. "You think I couldn't see through your act all evening?"

Was he serious? I stood, wincing at the burn between my legs, glowering down at him with a harsh gaze through narrowed slits.

"Oh, I'm sorry, does that upset you? Would that have led. You. On?"

The sarcasm in his curt tone sent me over the edge. The bag of sex goodies in his hands was ripped away and thrown at his head. He ducked, a roguish chuckle filling the room at my outburst.

He was just going to tease me! I was floored. Logan always had to have control, and it pissed me off tonight.

"Tell me why that would bother you, sweetheart." He feigned innocence and sat back against my headboard, legs extended and crossed at the ankles.

He really wanted to know why I'd be upset that he was planning on walking out on me before I'd had my fill? Before I finally had a piece of him, like he did me?

"Why?" I snapped, exasperated. "I don't know…maybe it's because, yet again, you managed to manipulate me into calling the shots. Now that you finally got a real taste—" I recoiled and dropped my head, unable to face him.

"It's over," I breathed after a beat. "Whatever this was, you made your point. We aren't friends, and never can be again—it's too hard—and anything else is too ridiculous to consider. I wanted you, you hurt me, and yet I let you do it all over again. I thought I could do this. I thought I was stronger."

I slumped back down to the bed, pulling the blanket over my lap. I lifted my head just enough to peer over at him, and the intensity in his eyes hooked me in.

"You're gorgeous, okay?" I confessed. "Sexier than any man I've ever met, and I freaking hate you for it. There—is that what you wanted me to admit? That I'm weak around you? That no matter how hard I try, I keep falling over and over again?"

His eyes grew softer, and he let out an unexpected chuckle.

Humiliation stung my nerves and filled me with enough strength to push myself back to my feet. I tugged my dress closed. Before I got two steps from the bed, however, he yanked me onto his lap.

"Let me go!"

He must've seen the blood rushing to my cheeks when he ground against my ass, because he moved quickly and pinned me down on the bed, his arms on my shoulders. He smashed his mouth to mine, kissing me into oblivion.

He pulled back too soon, just enough to speak, his breath caressing my swollen lips.

"Do you honestly believe I could give you just one night? After everything we've been through, you think I can handle just spending the night inside you? And then what…you walk away feeling as though you bested me? Who's the one still playing games, Cassandra?" He released me and stood up, his jaw working hard.

Sliding forward, I perched myself on the edge of the bed with slumped shoulders. He knew what I was doing.

"Logan, we can't have more. I offered you friends and I offered you tonight, and then—"

"And then what!?" he shouted, startling me. "And then you expect me to leave? Disappear out of your life? You may think me a bastard for my past liaisons, but I've never taken a woman to bed who didn't know exactly what she was getting—who didn't know I wasn't available for a relationship. But you...you turned the tables. And although I admire that about you, sweetheart, I'm not playing." He stalked closer, kneeing my legs apart and standing between my open thighs.

I regarded him warily as the start of a smirk played on his lips.

"But if it's a game you need, sweetheart, all you had to do was ask."

What the hell did that mean? The whiplash of his mood was exhausting. I needed to end things—break it off before it went any further. Honesty was the best bet.

"I just thought that if we..." I blushed, then blurted out, "...if you finally just fucked me already, we could both move on...have some closure, and remove the tension destroying us."

He cocked his head to the side, frowning. "The problem with that is I don't want closure, nor do I want to fuck you." His eyes lit up and traveled down to my breasts, which were peeking out from my open dress. I closed it in a quick, tight clutch.

A sweet, unexpected smile formed over his gorgeous, kissable lips. "I want to make love to you, Cassandra. I want to hear you tell me you feel it, too. And when you're mine, body and soul, then I want you on your knees begging me to fuck you till you're screaming my name."

I shuddered, his words filling me with something I'd never felt before. I wasn't scared, but strangely aroused.

We needed to stay on topic.

"Logan, this is the end for me. It's over. Done."

"I'm sorry, sweetheart, but it's just the beginning. And after what you instigated here tonight, you've proven exactly what I'd been hoping for. You feel it too. You want me, but you're scared."

Scared didn't even begin to describe how I felt about letting

Logan back in.

"Please, just let this go. Why can't you forget about me and move on? We can't go back."

He either wasn't listening or couldn't hear, because he walked out of the room. I saw the glow of the bathroom light, then heard the sound of running water.

When he returned a moment later, I noticed a washcloth in his hand. He took my hand from my lap and pulled me to my feet in front of him.

"You're so beautiful, and yet you think you need all this to get me into bed." The warmth of the wet washcloth caressed my cheek, wiping away the layer of blush and bronzer. He continued cleaning it away until it was just me, fresh faced, staring back at him.

"There you are," he murmured with a sweet, caring smile. "Put on the balm they gave you and get some sleep. We'll talk about things later." His brows raised. "Unless you want me to stay. It seems as though you had been planning for me to, anyway."

I sighed, staring down at my feet sheepishly. "Logan," I sighed. Yes, I wanted him to stay, but I didn't know how to say it.

"I'll go." He surprised me with his gentleness.

His head tilted to the side, and I closed my eyes as he placed the most delicate kiss upon my cheek. "Good night, Cassandra."

With that, he handed me the washcloth, picked up his socks and shoes, and walked away.

I slid down to the bed, falling onto my back and staring at the dark ceiling. My heart was wide open, fully ready to consume my buried feelings he'd stirred back to life.

Chapter Twenty

SISTER ACT

Logan made his point that night, and I fell asleep with a cool washcloth between my legs and tears in my eyes as I accepted what I'd been denying for too long. His absence hurt worse than ever. At the end of the day, I wanted him there with me, and it was getting harder and harder to deny it.

He was in my bedroom, washing the makeup gently from my face. He saw me, the real me, and that crumbled the walls around my heart. I couldn't describe the final blow. I knew what was happening, and I couldn't stop it. I was plowing straight into the massive train called Logan, hoping he would detour before we crashed.

"Hey, what are you doing out here?"

I turned to see Julia walking over from Logan's yard, wearing a light smile.

"Relaxing. The sun feels good." It really did. I'd been enjoying my back porch lazily for over an hour, sipping hot cocoa.

"Yeah, hopefully it melts some of this snow. I hate driving in it." She sat in the empty chair beside me. "Mind if I join you? I'm waiting for Oliver."

"Sure. You guys going out somewhere?"

"The movies. Natasha wanted to take him, but Logan insisted I chaperone."

"Fun," I replied, not bothering to hide the sarcasm in my voice as I grinned at her. It sounded like hell.

"Not really the word I'd use to describe it," Julia said, making a face, "but Logan made it worthwhile." She pulled a wad of cash from her coat pocket, fanning it in her hand. "I'll be going shopping as soon as the movie's over and Oliver is back home with Jax. You want to come?"

"Shopping or to the movies?" I asked sarcastically.

"Either," she replied, chuckling as she stuffed the cash back in her pocket.

"I'll pass. Why doesn't Logan just go and chaperone?"

She shrugged, crossing her leg over her knee. "He said he had a meeting, but I think it's more about not wanting to be alone in a dark theatre with a skanky bitch who can't keep her hands to herself."

I recoiled. "Oh." The mere thought of Natasha touching Logan sent my stomach lurching.

She must've noticed, because she added quickly, "Not that Logan encourages it. You should see how he's able to tune the chick out. This morning, he came down for breakfast after his shower and was leaning against the counter drinking his coffee when she pranced in the back door, wearing an outdated black nightie. She went right up to kiss him, but he side-stepped her and strolled across the room to sit with me and ask about my plans for the day, as if it never happened. Natasha was fuming." Julia giggled at the memory.

Did I really want to hear this?

"Sorry, it's just hilarious to watch. My brother has more tolerance than I do. He's over there now, helping Oliver get dressed."

"So they don't get along then?" I spoke more quickly than I'd meant to, the words flying out, my mind desperate for the full picture.

"They don't fight, if that's what you mean. I've seen her try to bait him in an argument, but he doesn't care enough to get into it. He just lets her do her thing while he plots."

"Plots?" That perked me up.

"Oh, yeah. You didn't think he would really let her stay in his home and not use it to his advantage, did you?" Her eyes glistened with delight. "Logan was pissed when he called me back over after his birthday party to watch Oliver that night, yet the next morning he came back and explained that he was allowing Natasha to stay in the guest room and seemed okay about it. Said it might be for the best, you know—keep your enemies closer and all."

It made sense, but was still unnerving. I didn't say a word—only listened, digesting it all.

"Logan's determined to find out why she's back. He has his buddy keeping an eye on her at Haven, and even has Katie sucking up to her so she can try to get some info out of her."

"Your sister-in-law?"

"Yeah. Katie and Natasha used to be close, at least until Oliver was born and Katie realized she was friends with a selfish whore."

Natasha really had been part of his family at one time. The fact that she was back and living with him had to be affecting him in ways he wasn't admitting. The thought was ruining my mood.

"I see," I said softly and sipped my cocoa.

Julia turned in her chair, eyeing me. "Have you met Katie?"

"No, I saw her though. I guess she was picking up Oliver a few weeks back. She's pretty." I hated that I added that last comment, allowing my insecurity to shine through.

"I used to tell her she should model. She and my older brother Lawrence are amazing parents, and they adore Oliver. They know how hard Logan works raising him on his own."

I smiled. "I didn't know who she was when I saw her, so I thought…" *Why did I just say that!?*

Julia's head fell back from the burst of laughter thrust out of her mouth. "Shut up!" Her body flew forward, hands covering her mouth as she tried to calm her laughter. "Katie and Logan!? Oh my God, I can't wait to tell her that." She wiped a tear away. Was it that funny?

It took a minute or two, but Julia finally regained her composure.

"Katie's been dying to meet you. Oliver and I told her all about his new neighbor that has his daddy smiling whenever she's around. You guys will get along great. Think Martha Stewart meets Gisele Bündchen. Lawrence couldn't be happier, and I promise, Logan has never showed any interest, so you're safe from worry."

"I'm not worried."

"Whatever you say." Her grin was all perfect white teeth. "I should call her to come down this weekend and we could go out. A girls' night."

Being friends with Logan's sister was one thing, but adding in his sister-in-law was a little too close for comfort. It was getting hard enough resisting him.

"I don't know," I mumbled. What was I supposed to say— "Sorry, I can't because I'm afraid I'll have a good time and end up liking Katie"? Or maybe, "I don't want to go and get close to yet another person that will remind me how great Logan is"? I decided on a lie instead.

"I have plans this weekend. Maybe another time."

Her eyebrow arched, a stunned smile breaking over her face. "Wow, you really are a horrible liar, you know that?"

"I'm not lying. I have plans." I couldn't even look her in the eye. I *was* such a bad liar.

"With who?" she pressed, amused.

"Hilary." There. That sounded realistic.

"Tell her to come along. She *is* a girl, and we're having a girls' night." She laughed, watching me squirm in my chair.

"I don't know. I mean—"

"Cassie, I want to get to know you better, and Katie keeps asking to meet you. It will be a lot of fun. I mean, soon enough we'll be sisters, and—"

"What!?" I gasped, my jaw dropping open.

"Okay, now that's just insulting!" She feigned a pout and reached over to smack my chin up, closing my mouth.

"Sorry, it's just...what are you talking about, sisters?"

Julia laughed again, staring at me as though I'd grown two heads. "My brother is in love with you, Cassandra! Hell, I'd bet good money that I'll be attending your wedding next year."

With an awkward snort of a laugh, I had to remind myself to breathe.

"You are insane! Married? To Logan?" I wasn't sure whether I should laugh or cry.

Julia rolled her eyes. "You don't think one day you'll be my sister?"

"Sorry. You're great and I want to be better friends, but no, I don't."

"Then we bet!" she stated, insisting rather than asking. She and Logan were a lot alike.

Oh no. No more betting for me. "I've sworn off betting."

"Come on, it will make it interesting. I bet that within two years, you'll be madly in love and engaged to my brother. I should clarify, though—to my brother Logan."

My brow shot up. "You needed to clarify this why? In case Jax grew into a man I couldn't resist?"

"Believe me, I don't get it, but the girls love Jax. I have never had a single friend who didn't want to sleep with at least one of my brothers. In high school, a friend slept over and snuck into Logan's room when he was home visiting. He turned her down, of course—he never slept with my friends—and she ended up in Jax's bed. Disgusting." Her eyes rolled back and tongue choked out.

"Logan never slept with any of your friends? Not even one?" Why was that so hard to believe?

"God, no! He's seven years older than me, although most of the girls I hung around with would still try. Jax, on the other hand, couldn't get enough."

"How old is Jax?"

"Nineteen, same as me." Her eyes lit up. "We're twins! I thought you knew."

"No, but I should have guessed."

"So, what do you say? The bet's on?" she pressed, reminding me of the silly wager she insisted on dragging me into.

"Fine. And when I win, what do I get?"

"You won't, but if for some reason you do, then I'll…hmmm." She looked thoughtful for a moment until her face beamed, staring at me with a renewed eagerness. "If you win, I'll tell you what Logan said in his sleep this morning."

"What?" Did I want to know?

"Logan was sleeping on the couch when I came over, and I heard him talking," she explained, grinning with an I've-got-a-secret elusiveness.

I sighed. "Why would I want to know that two years from now, especially if I'm not even with him then?"

Her smile faltered as she thought it over. "I guess if it were me, I'd want to know."

What the hell did he say? She was right—I did want to know, and now I'd have to wait two long years to find out. I sucked in a deep breath and blew out a heavy sigh. "All right."

Julia sat up straighter, unable to control her excitement. "Great, and when I win, which I will, you have to name your first daughter after me."

"What!?" Oh, she had to be kidding!

"Ahhh." She wiggled her finger at my flabbergasted expression. "See, you *are* a little worried I'll win this."

"No, it's just…" My first daughter? A child? With *Logan*?

My head began spinning.

"Come on, at least the middle name," Julia drawled.

"What's your middle name?" Why did it matter? Logan and I were not having a daughter—or any kids, for that matter.

"Not telling." She gave a cheeky wink. "Got to be able to trust your future sister-in-law," she teased.

"You're positively insane!" I giggled at her antics. "But why not?"

We shook on it, and I slurped down the rest of my cold cocoa.

"So, any plans for tomorrow night—the big V Day?" she asked, leaning back in her chair.

"Luke, Caleb's brother, called earlier and asked me to hang out for the night. He's bringing over pizza." Her head snapped back in my direction accusingly. "As friends. He's dateless as well," I clarified, not that it was needed. I was very much single, although I felt far from unattached.

"Really?" I noticed the pink of her cheeks deepen. God knew Luke liked her, and he hadn't even been officially introduced. Did she have an eye for him as well?

With an inquisitive stare, I regarded her with a crooked, knowing smile. She caught it, then looked down at her lap sheepishly. Who was this girl, and since when was she bashful?

Picking a piece of invisible lint from her jeans, she added, "I mean, he's cute. I guess I expected him to be in a relationship."

Yeah, she was interested, all right. It was a shame she was still dating my ex-dumbass. Or was she?

"Nope, he's single. It's a shame, though, because he's a really nice guy. He just needs to find the right girl," I said.

"Yeah. So, does Logan know?" She looked up and out at the row of trees across my backyard.

"That Luke's single? Not sure he'd care." I lifted my shoulders and made a face.

Julia shot me a smile and giggled. "That you're not his date for Valentine's."

Oh, that. He might care about that, but then again, he hadn't asked. "No, but he never asked."

"You wanted him to."

"I never said that."

"You didn't have to." With a wider smile, she added, "Next year, he'll make up for missing it."

"Next year, he'll have moved on to another girl," I retorted immediately.

The moment she opened her mouth to reply, Logan appeared from around the corner of my house.

"Oliver's ready to go," he said, interrupting our challenging stares.

Did he hear us? He had to have heard at least my last statement.

Julia stood. "I'll be calling Katie to set up a night out, or maybe a girls' weekend to Vegas this summer."

I didn't have a chance to do anything other than laugh to myself before she was skipping away happily, humming.

"Hi," Logan said softly, looking down at me wrapped in a flannel blanket on the porch chair.

"Hi," I repeated with the same thoughtfulness. He looked amazing as always in his black wool pea coat with a dark work suit underneath.

"How are you feeling this morning?" His blatant glance to my crotch heated the blood in my cheeks.

"Better," I replied softly, regretting looking up to meet his humorous gaze.

"That's good to hear." The corner of his lip twitched. "I wanted to ask about Valentine's, but I overheard you have plans already."

I took in his intimidating stance in front of me. He held himself with such grace, strength, and power, and here I sat with bedhead and a crotch slathered with balm. It suddenly felt like we were polar opposites, defying the odds by enabling our attraction.

He was watching my every uncomfortable move as my mind reeled back to wondering how long he'd been listening to his sister and me. The idea of him overhearing us put me back on track with words ready to aim his way.

"You were eavesdropping? How shady is that!?" I said, clearly offended and overly appalled.

He caught the amusement in my eyes. "I came out just as you mentioned Luke's name."

Thank God he didn't hear the bet I placed.

"So what do you have planned for tomorrow? Maybe finding a waitress to seduce?"

His smile grew, eyes twinkling. "No, I have other ideas."

Other ideas? I didn't want to think about what they were, and the longer I sat there with him staring down at me, waiting for me to respond, the harder it was to ignore the throbbing between my legs that had nothing to do with the waxing. He'd been there, and my body was begging him to return.

"I have to go shower. I have an appointment at noon." Setting the mug on the small table beside me, I stood. A shower was exactly what I needed—a cold one.

"Can I ask a favor?"

"I guess." My heart raced faster as he stepped closer.

"Jax is supposed to be over in the next couple hours to watch Oliver for the afternoon. Can you see to it that this gets to him when you return from your appointment?" He pulled a white envelope from inside his coat.

"Can't you just leave it on your counter for him or something?"

He shook his head once. "No. It needs to go in his hands today. It's extremely important that he gets it, and I can't risk anyone—meaning you-know-who—getting ahold of it."

Natasha? "Um… okay."

He trusted me. I saw it clearly in the deep-blue pool of his eyes. My heart skipped a beat as his hand placed the envelope in mine, then he kissed my knuckles before releasing.

"Thank you," he murmured, hooking me in with his minty warm breath and intoxicating scent of clean, soapy perfection.

We were so close, standing face to face, our eyes interlocked, searching.

"Logan," I breathed. What was happening? Why couldn't I move away—step back and go inside? I was locked in place, inhaling his virility.

"Yes?" he crooned, his breath caressing my lips.

I closed my eyes. What was I trying to tell him?

"Please." It was said in a breath, and I had no idea what I wanted.

"Please what?"

My eyes fluttered, unable to hold his gaze much longer. On cue, his tongue poked out, moistening his flawless lips, pulling my eyes straight to the movement. It answered the question.

"Kiss me," I panted, barely above a whisper.

My eyes were still on his lips when they pulled up in a charming smile.

"Gladly."

Instantly, I was in his arms, his lips claiming mine, our tongues dancing together. My hands encircled his neck as I fell into the moment, with no questions or insecurities. I just went with what felt natural—what felt right.

It was Logan who pulled away first, looking undeniably pleased when he placed one more soft kiss on my lips and then my hands after he slid them down from his neck.

"Cassie!" Oliver yelled, running around the corner with a cheerful grin covering his face. He raced straight toward me and didn't stop until his tiny arms were hugging my waist.

"Hey, how have you been?" I asked, hugging him tightly.

Logan watched, a relaxed smile on his lips.

"I'm gonna see a big movie!" Oliver buzzed with excitement as he stepped back. "You can come too."

"She sure can," Julia chimed in, walking over with Natasha.

I shot her a tight, contrived smile, keeping my eyes off Natasha.

"I would, but I have an appointment today. Maybe another time," I replied, my smile turning up into a genuine one when I looked down to Oliver.

Natasha walked closer and took Oliver's hand. "We don't want to be late, baby. Let's go so we can get you a giant popcorn before the movie starts."

"I love popcorn. So does Cassie." He snickered, and I knew what he was remembering. How could I forget that night? I still felt bad for the housekeeper who was faced with cleaning the theatre room the next day.

The bittersweet laugh that caught in my throat couldn't be helped as I glanced at Logan, his expression pained, staring down at his son.

"I sure do," I replied. "You have fun today, and I'll come see you soon."

"'kay, bye."

"Logan, can you walk us to the car?" Natasha asked, her eyes on him.

He nodded once. "I'll be right there," he answered to Oliver, not her. I watched them walk away, leaving Logan and me alone.

"You're so good with him," Logan said, stepping closer to me.

"He's a great kid."

His smile grew. "I wish I could stay. I could spend all day just standing here with you, but I have back-to-back meetings that can't wait and you, sweetheart, are not ready for what I want. I want all of you."

He was right—I wasn't—but I couldn't continue to push him away, either.

He leaned in and gave me one last kiss.

"Have a good day, Logan."

"I will now," he replied, earning him a soft, blushing smile. "Good luck with your appointment, sweetheart. And thank you again for seeing to it that Jax gets that envelope."

I nodded, holding the thick mystery packet in my hand as I watched him disappear back the way he came.

Chapter Twenty-One

INTEREST

My appointment at the bank had my nerves on the fritz the entire drive there, and the longer I waited past the hour for a so-called Mr. Jefferson to call me back into his office, the more my thoughts drifted to Logan, as always. I wondered if he was still thinking about the kiss we shared only an hour or so earlier. Could he still feel the tingle over his lips as I could over mine?

Blinking twice to shove the memory back in its secret box to pop out later in my dreams, I shifted in the uncomfortable blue upholstered chair surrounded by three other , all waiting impatiently as well. A row of customers in line for tellers stood off to the side, and I smiled, watching a young girl snatch a lollipop from the same fishbowl I had done so from growing up.

I couldn't help but wonder what Logan would have to say about me coming down here, pleading with the bank for a loan, when he had more than enough money to help me himself. I didn't want to know, and was going to make sure he never found out. I didn't tell anyone other than Hilary, and I trusted her with my life to keep the secret.

A woman in a grey suit with bluish grey hair walked by with a stack of papers and smiled. I smiled back, but it was bittersweet. The old woman reminded me of my grandma, and just like that, my guilt trip began. What would my grandma think of me being down here, using her home to pay my bills and buy a car? She was a strong woman, and I'd like to believe she'd understand. "You got to do what's best for yourself," she'd once told me.

"Miss Clarke?"

With a deep inhale through my nostrils, I plastered on my sweetest smile. *Here goes nothing.*

I looked up in the direction my name was called to see a silver-haired man walking toward me, glancing down at his watch. I stood, grabbing my purse, and approached him.

"Hi, Mr. Jefferson?"

"Yes, sorry to keep you waiting." He shook my hand with a firm grip. "A board meeting ran late. Please, follow me."

He led me to his office, a room with a giant glass wall that overlooked the front of the bank, complete with a massive desk, and two upholstered chairs matching the one in the makeshift waiting room facing it.

"Please, have a seat." He held out his hand, gesturing to one of the chairs, then walked around his desk and sat, typing something into his computer. "So you're here for a loan. Can I ask what it's for?"

My pulse quickened at remembering the night that started it all, but none of that mattered. It wasn't about the why—only the outcome.

"I was involved in a car accident last month and am unable to return to work for a few more weeks. I need to purchase a car, and just need a little help putting things back together."

He glanced up from the monitor. "I'm sorry to hear that. Well, we can definitely see what we can do to help. It says here you own your home."

"Yes, I inherited it from my grandparents."

"Do you have any other collateral?"

"No, just the house." I swallowed, sweat beading over the back of my neck. Could I really do this—risk losing the home my grandfather had built with his own two hands?

"That should be more than enough," he said, offering a warm smile. "We'll need some information, and I—" He looked past me, his brows knitting together. "I'm sorry, would you excuse me a moment?"

"Of course, take your time," I said, wiping my hand over my forehead subtly. The room was getting hotter, my breathing harsher as my throat began to close up.

It felt wrong being there, sitting there. If only my grandparents could see me now. They'd understand I had no choice, right?

Fidgeting in the chair, struggling to get comfortable, I heard Mr. Jefferson reenter the room.

Okay, I just need to stay focused and get this over with. They left me the house to look after me. I need to calm down.

Pulling my smile back into place, I looked back, my lips melting into a confused frown when I saw it wasn't Mr. Jefferson. The man standing behind me wore a dark scowl, with anger radiating off of serious, tense shoulders.

"What are you doing here?" I asked, standing up, stunned to see Logan.

"I told you I had meetings today, one of which was here at the bank." His voice was hard, with a menacing edge I didn't recognize. "Now, let me make this very clear, Cassandra: you are not getting a loan."

"What? How did you…"

I backed up as he stepped closer, the backs of my legs smacking against the chair I'd been sitting in.

"And you sure as hell are not putting your house up for collateral." The darkness in his eyes brought a tremble to my knees.

Why was he so pissed? It wasn't his business. My chin jutted out, ready to take on the beautiful man staring me down.

"Mr. Jefferson told you? That is completely unprofessional. I should report him—"

"Mr. Jefferson knows his place, and you, sweetheart, need to see that you have a man willing to help you in every way possible. If you need money, tell me—don't run off to the bank behind my back."

"Screw you, Logan! You don't get to tell me what to do! You're not my boyfriend, so back off!"

It felt wrong yelling at him after our memorable exchange earlier, but he was out of line getting involved in my personal affairs.

Frown lines etched over his forehead as he did just that— he backed off, running his hands through his hair, a soft growl rumbling in his throat.

"Why are you doing this?" he asked a moment later. His voice was barely above a whisper, eyes soft and rueful. "It's my fault you're here. Let me take care of this for you."

My anger melted at his kindness, and my shoulders relaxed with a heavy sigh. "I need the loan, Logan. Don't make this any more difficult for me than it already is, please. You think I want to be here? You don't think I feel horrible using my grandparents' home?" I sucked in a sniffle and urged the tears beckoning to stay at bay. "I need to buy a car and pay to keep my house heated. I'm down to my last twenty dollars. I barely had the gas to drive here."

"You don't need a fucking bank for that!"

"Yes, I do!" I yelled back.

He stood there in silence, his jaw clicking. "Twenty dollars? Tell me you did not just say twenty dollars!" he all but roared. "Why the hell didn't you tell me sooner? Huh?"

He stared at me, waiting for me to respond, but his strong voice had silenced me. He walked over to the office door and slammed it shut, giving us privacy, but through the glass window, I could see most of the people in the bank were staring. With a flick of his wrist, he yanked the blinds down, ending the free show for the gawkers.

I watched his back rise and fall with each deep breath before he turned back to face me. In an eerily calm voice, he asked, "How much did you spend on that new outfit for last night? The fancy lingerie? The lovely wax job that only ended the evening early?" Slowly, he walked back toward me.

"What about your hair and makeup—did you pay for that, as well? Spend money to impress a man you already have enchanted? You didn't need that shit, Cassandra. You're gorgeous without it, and I'd have preferred you in something you already owned. Or, if you were truly looking to seduce me, you could have opened the door nude rather than draining the remainder of your bank account."

He stopped directly in front of me, staring down into my eyes that were filled with humiliation at how irresponsibly I'd acted with the last of my money.

"Answer me. Is that why you're down to twenty dollars?" he hissed.

Embarrassment consumed me. My head fell forward and I was unable to even look at him any longer, but from the corner of my eyes that were cast on his expensive black shoes, I caught him moving his hand to his suit jacket. I glanced up to see him pull his wallet from the inside pocket and grab a handful of cash.

"I don't want your money. Don't you understand?" I told him in a weak, defeated breath.

"You think I don't know that?" With a frustrated groan, he grabbed my hand, stuffing the cash into it, pleading with me. "Please, Cassandra, see my side of this."

"You need to see mine. I need the money from the bank, and borrowing it from you is… complicated. And we have enough complications."

I set the money on Mr. Jefferson's desk when Logan refused to take it back.

"That we do. If you won't take the cash, fine."

A triumphant smile began to crack over my tight lips until

he shoved the cash back into his wallet and added, "But I'm not allowing you to risk a loan. Go home. The money you need will be deposited into your account by the time you get there."

"No!" I wanted to stomp my foot. This was going nowhere. I stormed past him and threw open the door. "Mr. Jefferson!" I called for the man staring dumbly at the grey carpet, waiting outside his own office.

He didn't make a move or even respond, but instead stared past me to Logan. I slammed the door shut again and turned back, glaring at the man in front of me who was working my last nerve. Why couldn't he let me do this one thing?

"If you are determined to take out a loan, then we'll compromise: let me cosign for you instead of using your house for collateral."

Was he serious?

I huffed out a laugh. "Cosign? I'm not an unemployed teenager looking to buy her first car, Logan. I'm a grown woman."

He leaned in and whispered, "Believe me, sweetheart, that's no secret to me." He pulled back, a deviant smirk tempting his lips. "Either I cosign, or I'll inform Mr. Jefferson's superiors that if they proceed with your loan, I'll be forced to end all business with this bank."

"You're kidding!" My jaw fell open, completely appalled at the length he'd go to.

"I never joke about finances. Now what will it be?" He knew he left me with no choice, and the twinkle in his eye rubbed it in.

I wanted nothing more than to escape that room and find another bank for help, but it wasn't worth all the trouble. "Fine, cosign the damn loan."

"Fantastic. Now go home, and I'll have Mr. Jefferson draw up the papers for me to bring by later for you to sign." His hand landed on the small of my back to lead me to the door.

"What? No, I'm staying. I haven't told him how much money I need."

"How much?"

"I was hoping for five or ten."

"That's all, ten thousand dollars?" He let out an arrogant snort, and I wanted to reach out and slap the smug grin off his face.

"Yes, to most people who aren't egotistical asses, that's a lot of money." I planted my hands on my hips, narrowing my eyes.

"Forgive me. It's just frustrating that most women I've met would be asking for that amount for a new handbag and would eagerly accept cash from me at their first chance. You astonish me, sweetheart." His fingers swiped the tendril of hair that at some point had fallen over my eyes.

I flushed. He must've dated a lot of gold diggers. I shouldn't have been surprised.

"Material items won't make me happy, so your money has never mattered to me."

"Yes, which is one of the many reasons why I love you."

"Logan, don't." I whispered my plea. I couldn't hear that, and he knew it.

He tugged my stiff arms from my hips and held them against him.

"Shhh, go home. I'll have the loan drawn up and bring it by in the morning."

"All right," I relented in a ghostly whisper. There was no winning this.

He leaned in and placed a kiss to my cheek. "Don't forget the package for Jax. Remember: in his hands. The last thing I need is for Natasha to get ahold of it. He knows you're coming. I messaged him earlier."

I nodded and walked out, giving Mr. Jefferson a pitiful goodbye in the process.

A text chirped my phone to life the minute I pulled into my driveway, and I couldn't help but smile as I read it.

You are a stubborn and enigmatic woman, Miss Clarke!

I smiled to myself again, rereading Logan's words.

Not as stubborn as you, Mr. West!

I dumped the phone in my bag and stepped out of my car to find Jax's flashy convertible parked in Logan's driveway. The envelope was hidden at the bottom of my purse. I didn't know what was in it, but felt it was safer to keep it on me.

Buttoning my coat, I trudged across my yard through the melting snow and cut through the bushes to Logan's yard. When I reached the front door, I rang the doorbell.

"Come in!"

It sounded like Jax, and Logan had said he was expecting me, so I opened the unlocked door and strolled right in. I didn't see Oliver anywhere, so I assumed he was still out with Julia and Natasha. I figured Jax was probably playing video games, or whatever else nineteen-year-old boys did.

"Hey, Logan asked me to give this to you," I called out, following the muffled voices to the kitchen.

"Harder! Damn it, Jax, harder!"

"Like that, baby?" a needy growl answered, its voice forceful, freezing me in place as my gaze hit upon Jax pistoning his hips into the lean body of a redhead bent over Logan's granite countertop.

"Oh my God!" I jumped back, whirling around, and slapped my hand over my eyes.

"Hey, Cassie!" he panted. "Logan said you had the instructions for me."

He was not serious! Time to leave.

I threw the envelope down on the counter, and caught it

slide to the floor from the corner of my eye.

Crap. Logan said it was important.

Assuming Jax had the decency to cover himself, or at least cease and desist, I ran forward and snatched it up from the floor, holding my hands over the side of my face, blocking my eyes when I heard the mystery girl cry out.

"Yes! Like that! Don't stop!"

Oh, for the love of God.

"Here, take it!" I demanded, holding my hand out in front of me, my mouth pursed, with my other hand still shielding my closed eyes as backup.

I heard Jax chuckle, and then felt the envelope being removed from my grasp.

"You're a pig, Jax. And you, miss, should have a little more respect for yourself!" I yelled as I stomped out of the room.

"I thought you said she was coming to watch," the hussy said.

"Guess not." Jax chuckled louder.

The woman must not have minded my judging, based on the breathless moan that followed.

I slammed the front door shut behind me as I heard Jax yell, "Come on, Cassie! Don't be mad! It was just a joke!"

Mad did not even begin to describe my emotions. I was furious and embarrassed for the girl who, from the glance I'd had of her, looked no older than eighteen.

My phone fumbled through my fingers as I pulled it out and hit Logan's number.

"Cassandra, what a surprise. Are you calling about the loan? Because it's—"

"No, I'm calling to let you know the next time you need a favor, ask someone else!"

"What happened? Did Jax say something to you?" His voice was ice.

"No, but that was because he was too busy screwing some

bimbo! And by the way, don't ever expect me to eat anything served off your kitchen countertop!" I hung up and tore open my front door, storming inside.

It was past five so I called Hilary, hoping she was home from school and not out with Caleb already. I needed someone to vent to about what I'd just witnessed. I shouldn't have been surprised when the girl couldn't stop laughing about Jax's little rendezvous. Other than asking if I'd seen anything noteworthy, which I hadn't, she thought I was overreacting.

The more time I had to cool down and think about it, maybe I was, but Jax could've at least stopped his thrusts for a moment. The girl, whoever she was, had no shame. I had no idea where the West men found their sluts, but I hated to think they all came from Harmony.

"He's young and just trying to get a rise out of you," Hilary said through her laughter.

"Well, it worked."

"So, enough about the younger neighbor. I'm still waiting to hear how the date went with the older one—you know, the guy you spent all yesterday getting ready to blow away with the night of his life. Was it as good as you hoped?"

"Things didn't exactly go as planned," I answered, sinking further into my couch.

"What? Why?"

"Because he figured out my vagina was waxed raw. Not really the night I had planned."

"Didn't she give you some balm? Shit, I totally forgot about that."

"Yes, I had the damn balm. It doesn't matter, I'm over it and don't really want to talk about it at the moment."

"All right, later. And hey," she said, her voice rising, "tell Jax I said hi next time." She laughed. "He's cute."

"I'll be sure to let Caleb know you think so."

"Oh shush, Caleb's perfect and all mine. He has nothing to

237

worry about, but I have to say, Jax has created quite a stir with some of the younger teachers at school. They look forward to the days he picks Oliver up from school. The guy's as charming as his big brother, from what I hear."

"Lovely." I rolled my eyes. "Bye."

She chuckled. "Bye."

I settled into the couch, my legs stretched over the cushions, with Scout on my lap I closed my eyes and let the day's events clear away.

The doorbell awoke me what felt like minutes later, but the sun setting through the window told a different story. Annoyed my time home was resulting in far too many naps, I sighed, setting Scout on the floor as I stood.

After a refreshing yawn and wakening stretch, I strolled to the door, unsure whom to expect. Logan had said he'd be over in the morning. Surprised, I was met with a red-faced Jax.

"Hey, Cassie. I just wanted to apologize for earlier. I knew you were stopping by and should have made sure I was finished fucking her by th—ahhh, SHIT!"

My eyes widened at his pain-laden scream as Logan stepped out from the side, grabbing Jax's arm and twisting it around his back.

Jax hissed in agony and muttered, "I'm sorry, okay? Really sorry, and it won't happen again, ever. I was just screwing around."

"And?" Logan hissed in his ear.

"And the countertop is being sterilized by professionals first thing in the morning." Jax let out a heaving breath when Logan released him.

"Damn, dude, you got it bad for her," Jax grumbled, shaking out his arm.

"It's fine, Jax. I'm over it," I said, hiding my smile.

"See? I knew she was a cool chick." Jax chuckled to Logan, than turned back to me. "It really was a douchebag move, but what can I say?" His shoulders rose. "You're fucking hot, and the idea of you watching turned me on."

Logan reached out, but Jax was already halfway down the driveway. I'd never seen anyone move so fast.

"Let him go," I laughed, watching Jax turn back and wink. "I'm over it. Besides, I think he only did it to get under your skin."

"Well, it worked. You shouldn't have had to witness him…with some girl." His hand reached up, kneading the back of his neck, his jaw set tight.

It was sweet seeing him so upset, defending my honor. I opened the door for him to enter and headed into the kitchen.

"I should expect it by now when I go over there. How many times did I interrupt you?"

His jaw clenched impossibly tighter, lips set in a firm line. "That was unfortunate, but a long time ago." He stood beside me as I slid into a chair.

"Only a few months back."

"Cassandra, it feels like another lifetime, and one I'd rather not bring up again."

"Whatever. I thought you were going to bring the papers in the morning," I said, motioning to the folder in his hands.

"I changed my mind."

"All right. I don't see why I had to deliver something to him if you were going to see him anyway."

Logan took a breath, his expression suddenly bordering on irritated. "I needed him to do me a favor this afternoon—one that he has assured me went off without a hitch, but we shall see."

"Okay." I replied. *Elusive, much?* "So the loan was approved with no issues?"

"Of course." He smiled with an authoritative confidence only he could pull off so effortlessly. "You need to sign next to every X." He pulled the documents out of the envelope, setting them on the table and handing me a pen.

"Oliver wasn't home, I hope," I said after a few minutes, eyeing the contract. I couldn't imagine Jax being that irresponsible.

"No, he was still out, thankfully, or Jax would have gotten it a lot worse from me." He pulled up a chair and sat beside me. "Here," he said, pointing to the first X awaiting my signature.

"I need to finish reading it first," I replied, pushing his hand away.

"You don't trust me?" His soft eyes drew me in when I glanced up, but the smile on his lips brought out a need to lean over and kiss him. He was so sexy when he was playful.

"For all I know, these are papers signing my soul over to you."

"I tried, but it turns out the bank isn't into selling souls." He chuckled and smoothed back my hair that had fallen, creating a curtain between us.

I read through the first document and shot my head up when I saw the amount of the loan.

"I said ten thousand!"

"And I felt it wasn't enough."

"Logan, I'm not signing this!" I pushed the papers back to him and set the pen down.

"It's only five thousand more than you requested. Now sign." He pushed the papers back at me.

"What if I can't afford the monthly payment due to that extra five grand?" I was not giving in this time.

"Then I'll pay it for you."

"No," I sighed, reading down further. To my surprise, the payment wasn't bad at all, and I wasn't about to ask how he got it so low. "What's this?" I tapped my finger on the line below it.

"Part of the arrangement as cosigner."

I read it again, making sure I was understanding it clearly, then looked up to meet his firm gaze. "If I don't pay it by the first of every month, it will be drawn from your account and paid in full?"

"Yes," he said, as though it was nothing.

"I'm not going to win this, am I?"

"No. Now sign." His lip curled up.

Beautiful, infuriating ass!

"Fine," I grumbled, signing my name. "But if you pay this off, I am still paying you back, with interest, just like I plan to do for those medical bills."

"I would expect nothing less."

A grin grew over my lips as I looked up at him, extending the pen back to him. "Good."

I stood and handed him the papers. "Thank you for your help—not that I needed it—but to be honest," I said, looking down awkwardly, "I was terrified of using this house to secure the loan. I mean, I know I could have made the payments, but…"

"But things happen, and it's how good people lose what they've worked their entire lives for. This is your home. I'll never let you lose it."

He cradled my chin and lifted my face to meet his eyes. I didn't fight him when he leaned in and placed his lips on mine. It felt good, comforting, short and sweet—just enough to leave me craving more.

"You should go," I murmured before stepping back as I cleared my throat, searching for my voice. "Or stay—"

"Soon, Cassandra."

With that, he walked out, leaving me reeling. I couldn't go much longer without him. All I could do now was head in for my second cold shower of the day.

Chapter Twenty-Two

CUPID

I smiled, peeling myself from the couch when a knock sounded at the front door. Luke was right on time, which was great, because I was starving. He promised to bring pizza and wine while I took care of the movies. The plan to spend Valentine's at home, without romance, was exactly what I needed.

When I opened the door, I was instead met with a bouquet of red roses and a cocky smile that did not belong to Luke. My face fell, confused.

"Happy Valentine's Day," Logan said, placing the flowers in my hands and leaning in for a quick kiss to my surprised cheek. He was dressed in light faded jeans, and his wool coat was open, revealing a casual black V-neck T-shirt.

"Um...happy Valentine's Day to you too, but why are you here?" My face had to have shown how surprised I was to see him. "I told you I already have plans tonight...with Luke."

"Yes, I remember, but I thought I'd stop by on the off chance that he canceled."

I snorted. *Canceled?* "Yeah, didn't happen, but thanks for the flowers, they're beautiful."

He looked pleased, standing there watching me as I struggled with telling him goodbye. If Logan wanted to spend time together, he should've asked. I did eat lunch alone a few hours earlier, and wouldn't have shot him down had he asked to join.

"Luke will be here any minute, so if you don't mind, I'll see you around," I said with a soft smile.

As I began to close the door, Logan's hand flew up, holding it open.

"Wait, can't I at least come in until he arrives?"

My plans for a romance-free evening were not starting off very well.

"Logan," I sighed, dropping my head, staring down at the bouquet in my hand. "I'm sorry, but if you wanted to—"

My phone ringing from the coffee table cut me off. I looked back to the table where it sat, and then to Logan.

"You can get that," he said, smiling a little too brightly.

I eyed him carefully and walked over, snatching it up to see it was Luke.

"Hey Luke, you on your way over?" I asked, grinning cheekily at Logan, who was bent down petting Scout wearing a smug smile he didn't even attempt to hide.

"Actually, something came up. I need to take a rain check."

Was he kidding? I turned away from staring at the gorgeous man looming in my doorway and dropped my voice to a whisper. "Why?"

"I'm sorry, it's just that…I was driving over when I saw a car on the side of the road about a mile from your house. I stopped to help, and it was Julia West."

I sighed. What were the chances? A quick over my shoulder told me it wasn't a coincidence, by the raise of Logan's brow. *Damn it.*

"Long story short, her car just needed a jump, but she insisted on taking me to dinner as a thank you for helping her out."

"You don't say."

"I hate to cancel, but it turns out she and Mark broke up, so I figured why not?"

"Broke up?" That was news. I'd just talked to her yesterday, and she a thing. Not that we were BFFs.

"Yeah, she didn't say much aside from that she hated being single on Valentine's, so I took that to mean they weren't together anymore. Listen, I got to go, she's coming back from the restroom. Sorry, I'll make it up to you. Bye."

Luke hung up and I did the same slowly before turning back reluctantly to face Logan, who was now strolling into the house with a paper bag in his hands that he must've had sitting on the porch. He shut the door behind him.

"Hope you're hungry, sweetheart. I plan on making you a meal you'll never forget."

"If Julia's playing with him, I swear to God, Logan, I will hurt you both!"

"Calm down. She and that scumbag Mark broke up last week. She won't say why, but I did happen to catch the way your little friend looked at my sister when we ran into him and Caleb the other day." He walked toward me, his breath warm over my cheek as his voice lowered to a husky murmur. "Hate to break it you, sweetheart, but it's not how he looks at you."

With a ragged breath and raging hormones, I shoved past him, annoyed at how easily my body responded to his and that he knew it. I shook off the butterflies flittering through me.

"I told you—Luke and I are just friends."

"And I believe that. It's obvious he's interested in my sister, and everything I've heard about him from Caleb tells me he's not so bad. I figured why not help the kid out?"

I followed him to the kitchen, where he removed his coat and began emptying the bag of food onto the counter. He had no issue making himself at home.

"So, then, you admit to putting your sister out in the cold on the side of a backcountry road with a dead car?" I stared at him crudely, waiting for his answer.

"No, that was all Julia." He gave a cunning smile. "She was

244

more than eager to help me out tonight. I merely suggested distracting your date."

With a shake of my head, I opened my small pantry in search of a vase for the flowers he'd brought.

"You're both horrible, and that better be one delicious meal, or—"

I stopped, cut off as I stared at the rows of vases Hilary had brought home from the hospital. I knew she'd cleaned them up and put them in there, but what I hadn't noticed was the largest vase closest to the door still had the unopened card perched on top.

It'd taken everything in me not to open it at the hospital. That damn thing had called out to me from my bed every minute of every day since it'd been delivered with the first round of beautiful flowers Logan had sent. I'd spent countless hours telling myself that whatever Logan had to say, it didn't matter. Staring at it now, I couldn't find that reason, and my curiosity was piqued.

I grabbed the vase and popped the small card into the pocket of my worn jeans before walking back to the table to set the vase next to the flowers.

Logan already had pots removed from cabinets and the stove fired up as I brushed past him in the tight space by the sink, where he was rinsing a bowl of the largest shrimp I'd ever seen. My mouth watered at the sight of them, and when I glanced up, he was staring across at me with the sweetest lighthearted smile.

"Sorry, I just need to fill the vase," I explained.

He turned the faucet to reach me and I held the vase as still as I could in my hands that were unsteady as his gaze bore into me.

It was going to be a long night.

"Thanks," I said after it was filled, and headed back to the table.

Carefully, I unwrapped the bundle of classic red roses. With a pair of shears from my junk drawer, I began cutting the ends off each one and arranging them in a perfect bouquet.

"So, where's Oliver tonight?"

"At my mother's with his cousin, Charlie. Jax will bring him home in the morning before school."

"And Natasha? How did you escape her?"

"Thanks to your help with giving Jax the information, Natasha is halfway to Aspen right now," he said, looking positively pleased with the thought.

"Why, exactly?"

"Because she believes that I was heading to my home there to stay a few days to think over my feelings. Jax tried to convince her she was wrong after a performance where he *accidentally* informed her of my plans the afternoon she got back from the movies with Oliver. As I expected, she purchased a ticket and left this morning in the hopes, I presume, of surprising me there."

"But you're not going?" I asked, unsure what to think and still not clear what the envelope I gave Jax contained. From the weight of it, I'd assumed cash.

"Does it look like I am?"

I turned to focus on the flowers and he stood at the stove, our backs to each other.

"Do you know what Caleb has planned for Hilary tonight?" I asked, breaking the silence hanging around us.

"I do."

"Care to tell me?" I prompted, a smile on my lips.

"I've been sworn to secrecy," he replied, still busy at the stove.

"Well, what time was he going to surprise her?"

"About now."

"Then she's probably already enjoying the surprise, so there's no reason not to share now, right?"

"Possibly."

I turned and chucked a piece of stem at the back of his neck.

"Still not telling you," he said, and I couldn't stop the laugh I released at his nonchalance.

Focused back on snipping another end from a beautiful rose, I felt his breath tickling my neck. I didn't move, my entire body still as his fingertips caressed a trail back and forth under my shirt, over the bare skin at the small of my back. A chill raced up my spine, and a heated shudder wracked my body.

"I love how you react to me."

"I sometimes hate it," I replied quietly.

"Understandable, with our history, but never again. I want you to love it as much as I do."

His moist lips drew over the back of my neck, my head tilting to the side to give him better access as his tongue peeked out and ran up to the tender flesh behind my ear. Before I knew it, a sensual moan was pouring from my open mouth, my legs trembling with desire.

"Grab some plates. It will only be another minute before dinner," he murmured. And then he was gone, back working at the stove as though he hadn't just worked me up and left me famished.

I closed my eyes and took in a deep breath, then let it out, my legs clenching tight to quell the heat pooling.

Yeah, it was definitely going to be a long night.

The flowers were set in the center of the table, with two plates on each side of the vase. However, when I looked over to Logan, he was shaking his head.

"What were you and Luke planning on doing tonight?" he asked.

My brow cocked up as a provocative grin played on my lips, teasing him with what could've been with Luke.

"Funny, sweetheart, but you can't fool me. Let me guess:

dinner and a movie on the sofa?"

I allowed a pout to play on my lips before answering. "Maybe. Why?"

"Because if that was your plan, then that's what we'll do."

Did I hear him correctly? "You want to sit and watch a movie with me while we eat this amazing meal you just cooked?"

"Yes, it's not like we never did so last fall."

I couldn't disagree—we had watched a few movies together before the crash, but it was at his house, with Oliver, in an enormous theatre hidden in his basement. This was different— friends territory, for sure—but then again, how long could I deny that we were already there again?

Grabbing the plates, I took them over to the stove. He filled them both full of shrimp linguini, and I carried them out to the living room. Logan came in while I was debating which movie to watch between the two I'd rented, and set a glass of wine in front of my plate on the coffee table.

"All right, we got *Scary Movie 3* or the new *Texas Chainsaw Massacre.* That one was Luke's request."

He raised his brows. "Was there a theme you guys had planned tonight?" he all but laughed, sitting down on the couch with his glass of wine.

"Yes, anti-romance. Clichéd but timeless, and these movies definitely have no love story to tell. I don't think, anyway."

"All right, put in whichever you'd like."

"Hmmm, let's start with scary and end the night on a comedy. I hate going to bed after watching a horror flick. I need something nice in my head or else I'll have a chainsaw freak chasing me through my dreams."

"I could always spend the night and help with distracting your nightmares." His brow rose suggestively, but the gleam in his eye was all humor.

"No, but thanks," I scoffed.

"Anytime, sweetheart." He shot me a boyish smile that

made my knees wobble just the slightest. Turning away, I glanced out the window at the setting sun casting an orange-ish hue of light through the window. It was going to be a long night.

After loading the DVD in, I flicked off the lights and plopped down on the opposite end of the couch from Logan, watching as he slipped Scout—who was at his feet—a piece of shrimp.

I shook my head. "You're gonna regret that. He'll never let you eat in peace again," I said, lifting my plate to my lap.

"Is that your way of saying I'll be enjoying many more meals here in the future?"

"Let's not get carried away with the *many*s." I shot him a teasing smile.

The first bite of the shrimp and pasta with a creamy sauce he'd prepared from scratch was heaven, as was the closeness of Logan's body as he set his wine glass down, lifted his plate, and moved over just the slightest bit. I fought back my smile, focusing on the dark screen as the previews began.

An hour or so later, my plate was empty, as was my second glass of wine, and I had a terrified death grip on Logan's shirt. I was scrunched up in a ball with my head buried in his chest, peeking out occasionally when the chainsaw stopped roaring.

"Did he get her?" I asked, my voice trembling.

The rumble of laughter in Logan's chest shook through me, yet my tight grip never faltered. I was going to have it out with Luke for telling me to pick up this movie. No comedy was going to remove it from my mind, ever.

"Not yet, she's hiding," Logan said, his hand stroking my back.

I peeked out just as the chainsaw rumbled back to life on screen, followed by a blood-curdling scream from the girl who shouldn't have been having sex in a horror movie. I shoved my head back into Logan's chest, my feet on the couch pushing me into him as close as I could crawl until the horrible sound was gone. The room quieted.

I glanced up to see Logan had switched off the television. I sat up with a cool shrug. "You could finish it, I don't mind."

His head fell back from his boom of laughter, and I took that as my cue to crawl back to my side of the couch, slightly embarrassed at my inability to sit through the movie without having an aneurysm. However, Logan held me close—one hand around my back, the other sliding over my warm cheek, not letting me get away.

"How about we stay away from scary movies?" he offered.

"I guess. They really don't bother me that much," I lied, smiling.

He laughed again and then stood, holding me close to stand with him. The room was dark. The only light now shining in was from the bright moon outside.

"I don't like seeing you so scared, but I do love being the one you cling to."

My teeth caught my bottom lip to hide my embarrassment and control the spread of my smile.

"Wait here." Logan released arms and walked to the kitchen, coming back a second later with something in his hand that he set on my bookshelf. He pressed buttons, and music began.

He turned back and walked over, his eyes glittering in the dark.

"Dance with me," he said.

I couldn't resist. With an easy smile, I gave him my hand and allowed him to pull me into his arms. He held me close, one hand on my lower back, the other wrapped in mine but tucked between us.

Ed Sheeran began singing "Give Me Love", the lyrics hitting deeper than ever before. It was beautiful and easy, and by the time the song finished, I was lost in Logan. I smiled up at him as "Echo" by Jason Walker began playing. Memories of the many Christmases I'd watched my grandparents dance in that very room as music played through an old record player flashed through my mind.

A sweet smile and tightened grasp around my waist was Logan's response. By the time the song finished, I had tears in my eyes that were soaking through the shoulder of his T-shirt.

"I hate this feeling," I mumbled, more to myself than him, before angling my head a little to catch his gaze. "I just want it to be the way it was before things got—"

"Real?" he chimed in, our bodies still swaying as one as a new song began to play.

"I was going to say heated." I let myself smile, relaxing further into his arms.

"I'd never start over, even if I had the chance, but I wish you could trust me again. Give a fresh start to your confidence in me."

I wiped my eyes and then placed my hands on his shoulders, stretching back just enough to look into his own eyes.

"Logan, we tried the fresh start before. You only get so many do-overs."

His smile faltered, not quite reaching his eyes as he processed my words, but it was only a brief second before a sinfully sexy smile broke out. "If I screw it up again, then I won't ask for another."

I raised my brows, unconvinced. "Really? So if you mess things up, you'll walk away and never ask to start over again?"

"Oh, no." He grinned wider, shaking his head once and running his hand up my spine. "I'm never walking away, sweetheart. I just won't ask to start over. There are so many enjoyable ways I am sure I can think up to earn your forgiveness."

I released a breath of laughter. "Why not just try harder to begin with?"

His brow shot up. "Hmmm, very interesting. Do tell me

more about that plan." He leaned in, bringing me closer, and chuckled softly.

We continued to dance, no more words needed as we fell comfortably in sync with the music through another song until he dipped me down in a graceful move.

Where my next words came from, I didn't know—perhaps it was the sincerity in his eyes and tenderness of his hold on me as he raised me back up into an embrace that I truly believed wouldn't ever let me go.

"You don't to have ask," I breathed.

He held me firmly, a smile tugging at the corners of his lips right before he leaned in and claimed mine.

For song after song, we danced in the center of my living room, his lips only straying from mine to slide down over my jaw throat, and back up to my cheek—anywhere they could reach while we danced.

I know if it was the music, the holiday atmosphere, or just good timing, but my hands were suddenly moving on their own, tugging at his shirt, pulling it over his head and going to work on the buckle of his belt.

It was frantic, as though a ticking bomb was suddenly set and about to detonate within me if I didn't bring him as close as possible, touch him as I only had in my dreams. I wanted him more than anything, and it wasn't something I could deny any longer. I didn't want to.

"Cassandra." His voice was a deep, strained breath against my neck as his belt fell open, and my fingers slid back and forth over his waistband.

"Don't stop this, please," I begged, my lips running over his broad, rippled chest. My tongue darted out in hunger as I brushed over his nipple.

"Tell me first," he demanded, his finger under my chin, drawing my head back up.

I looked up under my lashes his eyes, dark and hooded.

"Tell me you're mine. Tell me you trust me again and that you'll still be in my arms when the sun comes up. No regrets, Cassandra. I won't take you until you're mine."

His? Didn't he already see it? Or was I that good at hiding how I felt?

"I've been yours for longer than I've been able to admit."

Logan's smile stretched so wide I couldn't help but grin back.

I didn't see it coming and wasn't prepared when Logan leaned in and, instead of kissing me again as I'd anticipated, yanked me into his arms.

I sucked in a deep gasp of air as I was expectantly lifted in the air—one hand on my ass, the other in my hair, tugging out my hair tie. My unruly waves cascaded down around us as my legs locked around his back.

Logan's lips were on mine, soft and slow as he carried me out of the room and, a moment later, placed me gently down on my bed.

Hovering over me, his hands gave a tight squeeze to my ass before releasing it, earning him a muffled giggle from my busy lips. Our tongues danced together, taking our sweet time stroking and nipping. He tasted of mint and sweet wine—a taste I would never forget, and could only dream to experience again.

Logan pulled back after a few minutes, drawing me up with him, never once breaking our kiss until he dragged my shirt over my head. Slowly, he reached around me, and with one flick of his wrist, my bra fell forward and he was pulling it away.

"Gorgeous," he murmured.

Out of nowhere, I was hit with a moment of shyness. The way he looked at me, stared as though he'd never seen anything like me, took my breath away.

His hands cupped my cheeks, pulling my gaze back to his. "You're stunning. You should know that and never forget it."

Smiling, I placed a kiss to his scruffy jaw, snaked my arms

around his neck, and brought him back down with me as I fell back onto the pillows.

Logan's hands were everywhere, caressing me, hauling me closer around my back, and then wandering down between us. I wasted no time raising my hips for him, spelling out what I wanted, my jeans aching to disappear.

"Not yet." He kissed my chin and smirked, a mischievous glint in his dark-blue eyes as he sat up on his knees.

My breath was heavy, my body surging to life and anxious for more when Logan dipped down and sucked my nipple into his mouth.

My head fell back, eyes slamming shut with my wild moan. The pads of his fingers worked over me delicately, memorizing every curve of my breast. I gripped his shoulders as he sucked harder, my legs moving closer to wrap around his waist, locking my ankles to hold him in place.

With a flick of his tongue, a loud, foreign moan escaped from my mouth, and I caught the pleased smile on his perfect swollen lips as he ran his tongue across my chest and over to my other breast. Back and forth, he showered his kisses and adoration down over me.

My legs locked tighter around him, begging for friction between my legs as I ground my hips into him at the feeling of his growing erection. Kneading my breasts together, he buried his face between them, inhaling so deeply my cheeks flushed.

"So sweet, mmm," he growled. My insides tightened at the sound, the fire in my center burning stronger than ever.

Logan's thumb and pointer finger flicked and tugged on my nipples as he brought his lips back to mine, kissing me from one corner to the other with slow, soft pecks before claiming my mouth in one quick movement.

My hands were clammy on his back, caressing, running my nails over the powerful strength he possessed in his perfect body. The groan that escaped him pushed me to continue, knowing he was enjoying my exploration of his body.

Slowly, I trailed my hands down his side and up and down over the muscles in his solid forearms. I couldn't control myself—my body wanted him in every way, grinding against him to the point that my legs were painfully tight from the feeling of his erection pressed into me.

"Soon, sweetheart," he whispered against my neck, reading my mind.

Before I knew it, he was unraveling himself from my hold and sitting up, smiling down at me.

"Don't move," Logan said as he stood from the bed and walked around to the end, where he spread my legs apart and settled between them. Slowly, he leaned down while my hands covered my stomach. I was unsure what to expect when he unsnapped the button on my jeans and drew down the zipper.

"Lift your hands over your head. I want to see all of you," he instructed, and I did so immediately.

His eyes darkened as I lay there stretched out, my hands twisted above my head. I clutched the bottom of the headboard with a tight grip, needing something to hold onto as my body waited in anticipation.

"There, yes, just like that."

Undeniably aroused and not afraid to express it, I ran my tongue over my parched lips as Logan placed his hands on my hips, digging his fingers into the hem of my jeans, his thumbs circling and teasing my searing flesh.

His head dipped down and placed a slow kiss across my stomach as his hands ran down my legs until they were holding my ankles. I felt his fingers grip the fabric of my jeans there and slowly begin pulling them down my clammy legs, my body stretching out with each tug. The rush of the last rapid movement before my jeans were tossed on the floor was exhilarating, leaving my body pulsing in waves on the bed as it settled back down.

"Oh, sweetheart." He looked pained, his voice stressed as he stared down at me.

Realizing I was there in nothing but panties I'd thrown on the morning after my shower, my cheeks warmed and my head shot up to do a quick peek to see what panties I was wearing. To my relief and his obvious approval, I relaxed back down after seeing the white lace.

Logan took me in, inch by inch, his tongue wetting his lips. In the darkness, with only the light of the moon filtering in through the curtains, he stood tall, a broad chest of rippled muscles and beautiful dark features regarding me as no man had before.

"You have no idea what you do to me—how long I've wanted you, ached for you in ways I never imagined." He shook his head, his eyes closing as he continued. "So many incredible fantasies have overwhelmed my thoughts, my dreams, night after night for months now." He opened his bright eyes. His lips were straight—serious. "Yet none of them can compare to seeing your beautiful body stretched out over this bed now, waiting for me. Only you, Cassandra—you're the only woman that has made me feel like this."

Logan's eyes halted their appraisal as they focused on my thigh. Without a word, he traced his finger over my wound, now practically healed but still slightly tender. I winced not from the sting, but from the impact of his gentle touch there.

His eyes shot up, searching mine. We'd come so far, and I wouldn't let past events dictate our future together anymore. Offering him a soft, reassuring smile, I watched as he bent forward, placing a lingering kiss over the scar I'd carry forever.

Caught in the moment of his loving act, I gasped when his fingers slid over and hooked inside my panties, then slowly peeled them away. The thin fabric hung around my ankles for a moment, and then it was gone.

"Let go," he said. I released my hold and brought my arms

back down beside me.

The longer I lay there, the harder it was to control my eagerness to feel him against me as he stared down at my naked sex, his hands roaming up and down my thighs.

"I won't be able to stop this time," he said, eyes moving slowly up to mine.

There was no chance to reply. As I processed the weight of his admission, he dropped to his knees on the floor, grasping the backs of my thighs and tugging me down until my legs were propped over his shoulders. I could only see the outline of his frame, but it didn't matter.

My back arched up, hands fisting the sheets as he ran his tongue over me, exploring me as no one else had before. I could feel the spring tightening in my gut, the uncontrollable need growing and growing until he removed his mouth.

I jerked back, ready to complain, but I didn't have to. He knew what I wanted, what I needed, and was set on giving it to me. My entire body stiffened as I felt his finger slide inside, and then his lips were back where I needed them.

"Logan! Please!"

My body jerked up to a sitting position as he slid his finger around, my hands flying up into his hair, fisting it as my release drew closer and closer until I was screaming his name and my body was falling back, bucking wildly until I was left soaking wet and ready for more.

I lay there, my head swimming with absolute bliss when I felt him release my legs from his shoulders and climb over me. He pulled me into his arms, bringing me farther up the bed until my head was resting on my pillow.

I hadn't even seen him remove his pants, let alone his boxer briefs; however, his erection pressing at my entrance got my blood pumping again and heart racing, reminding me there was more to come. Much more.

His lips were on my stomach, kissing, when I heard him

speak. "Condom."

Condom? No problem there, thanks to Hilary's goodie bag. I reached over into my nightstand, pulled one out, and tore it open with my teeth.

He smiled, taking it from me and rolling it on. The darkness and my sated hangover left me unable to see his manhood, and I couldn't deny the disappointment in that. But then again, the night was still young.

"I'm shocked Mr. Playboy doesn't keep one handy."

I wanted to slap a hand over my mouth as the smile fell from his face. But he seemed to shake it off, hovering back over me and nipping at my nipple.

"My plans tonight involved spending time with you, doing anything you wanted as long as we were together. This incredible turn of events wasn't expected, so no, I didn't feel the need to keep them *handy*."

"I'm sorry." I shook my head. "I didn't mean—"

"Shhh, I know." With that, his lips were on mine as his erection pressed against me again. "Tell me you really want this. That you want me—us."

I couldn't help myself as I cupped his face and held his gaze.

"Us. I want us...ahhh."

I winced as he slid into me, stretching me. He was so big it took a moment to adjust. I clutched his shoulders, my nails digging into his flesh.

"Are you all right?" he asked, his eyes wide. "You're so...tight. I've never felt anything so..."

"Please, I'm fine. Move. Just...I...I need more," I pleaded, clawing at his back, pumping my hips up to meet his thrust.

"Cassandra."

With each thrust of his hips, I melted into him, my mouth roaming over the swells of his arms, his tight muscles. My hands couldn't get enough, digging into his hair, bringing him closer.

The moans that spilled out of me were like no other—strong, fierce, and full of life. I'd never felt so wanted, so needed, so adored.

Making love to Logan was something I'd never get used to. With each thrust, he held me as though he'd never let go, kissed me as no one else ever could, and when he could stand it no longer he brought my legs up higher, deepening the angle and taking me to a climax that rivaled the first one.

"Us. Always," he panted, driving in once, twice. Then, with a deep husky groan, I felt him still inside me, his lips breathless against my cheek with his release.

Logan's arms were on each side of me, palms planted firmly against the mattress, caging me in. I'd never felt safer or more wanted.

When we began to sit up, I pulled him in closer, not ready to lose the connection. I wanted to stay there forever with him inside me. I wondered if he felt the same, because when he rolled over, he took me with him so I was on top of him, resting on his chest, still connected as his lover.

"That was…"Logan was panting, a sheen of sweat covering his warm body. "Unbelievable."

I nodded, smiling to myself as I placed soft kisses to his chest where I lay.

"Extraordinary." I laughed lightly, and his chest rumbled under me with his own soft chuckle.

His hands caressed my back and I could feel his subtle throbs inside me. Slowly, I sat up, the movement sliding him out of me. It was then I noticed the card peeking out of my jeans lying beside the bed—the card from the flowers.

Logan must've followed my gaze, because before I could stop him, he reached down and snatched it.

"What's this?" he asked.

"Nothing, give it here," I pleaded as he eyed the envelope.

He wasn't listening to me. Instead, he was pulling out the

card from inside. Slowly, his gaze landed back on mine.

"You keep this on you?"

"No."

"Then why was it in your jeans?" he asked curiously, watching me as I lay back down on my pillow.

"I found it in the pantry earlier. Hilary left it in the vase after she cleaned it for me."

"Did you read it?"

I swallowed. "No."

A small smile drew over his lips as he leaned down and handed it to me. "Well then, I think it's about time, don't you?"

I had no reply, so I took the card and inhaled a deep breath that caught in my throat as I read:

My soul aches with regret for what I have done to you. I'm at your mercy till the day I take my final breath. I am yours, and can only hope for the honor to someday prove myself to call you mine. I love you, Cassandra. Yesterday, today, and forever.

Releasing a ragged breath, I tore my glossy eyes from the card and looked up at him sitting beside me.

"Logan, I—"

"I love you, Cassandra. I think I always have," he said with a confidence so strong I felt his words rebuilding the final pieces of my mending heart.

"I love you." *Did I just say that?* The look on my face must've told him I was just as surprised by it as he was. He kissed me, smiling against my lips.

"Say it again," he demanded.

"I do. I don't know when it happened or how, and I know it took me so long, but I love you." I swallowed a sob, tears blurring my vision, emotions rushing through my veins. *I love him—Logan. I love Logan!*

Unable to control the grin growing over my lips, I threw myself into his arms and held him tight, placing a long, gentle kiss to his ear. His arms encompassed me, his breath tickling my searing cheek.

"I never want to let go," I confessed. "I love you so much. I didn't know it could feel like this. It's painful and beautiful, and it consumes me like nothing else." I pulled back just enough to look into his eyes to tell him what he longed to hear. "I'm yours, Logan. I always have been."

A tear glistened in his eye. I placed my mouth over his cheek as it slipped free, licking it away.

"I'm sorry I doubted you over and over again," I said, tears slipping out.

"Shhh, nothing matters except that I absolutely love you with every fiber of my being and want to spend tonight showing you that."

"Stay with me tonight," I said, hopeful.

"You couldn't get me out of this house without you."

I laughed again as he readjusted my legs to straddle his lap.

"Good, 'cause I'm not ready for tonight to end."

"We're far from the end, sweetheart." Logan's arms pulled me down, and he crushed his lips to mine.

Chapter Twenty-Three

TESTING

The next day, I awoke in Logan's arms, warm and loved. Was this my life now? Would it always be like this?

Logan placed a soft kiss on the side of my head, and I lifted my chin to his chest just enough to be greeted by his delicious, relaxed smile.

"Morning, sweetheart."

His arms wrapped around my waist and dragged me over to lie on top of his body fully, my lips over his. The thought of morning breath had me struggling to retract, but he was having none of it.

"Get out of that head of yours," he said, his hands loosely on my hips, thumbs stroking over my bare skin.

With a smile, I leaned down and placed a small peck on the center of his inviting lips, then peered up at his deep blues. They watched as I placed another short kiss on the corner of his lips, then slowly kissed my way down his scruffy jaw.

I made my way down to his neck, where I ran my tongue over his salty skin and then placed a lingering wet kiss and looked back up. The grin creeping over my lips couldn't be helped, as my hand trailed down his side and found him ready for me.

With one stroke of him in my hand, the blaring of my alarm sounded, and Logan reached over casually to turn it off. It was seven a.m.—time for my morning jog, and then it was off to meet my mother for breakfast before her shift.

"Please, continue," he said, resting his arms behind his head and watching me with a pleased eye.

And I did. Even knowing we needed to start our day—the man had to work, and I was supposed to meet my mother in a couple hours—I took my time. With my eyes on his, I slid my body down the length of his, my grip firm around his erection, stroking until my mouth was over him.

"Oh fuck," he groaned, his hands in my hair. "God, I'll never let this end."

I peeked up through my lashes, releasing him from my mouth just long enough to reply. "Me neither." With a smile, I ran my tongue down his length.

Logan's eyes lit up and his grin beamed. He looked the happiest I'd ever seen him, and suddenly he was pulling me back up and resting me over him. I wasted no time connecting our bodies, my lips on his as I rode out a morning of his love—our love—together.

—◆◆—

"I'll be late!" I giggled, squirming out of his arms that were locked around my back, his mouth suction-cupped to my nipple.

He let out a fierce, possessive growl and bit down gently before releasing me with a pop.

"Fine, go if you must, but I want to see you tonight. Every night."

"I'll be here."

"Damn right, you will." Logan sat up, releasing me so I could head to the shower.

It didn't take long to realize he was following.

"Go!" I laughed, standing in front of the shower. "I'll be late if you get in there with me."

"And?"

"And my mother will be waiting."

"Better her than me." Logan's finger circled my breast as I stood nude in front of him. "I hate to wait for anything, yet for you…" His head dipped down and he placed a kiss over my nipple, then looked back up with a slight smirk. "For you, I'll always wait."

I smiled. "Tonight. I'm all yours tonight."

"Fair enough. I need to go make sure Jax remembered to bring Oliver home with him from the city in time for school." a long, lingering kiss, Logan walked back into my room, dressed, and came back for one more kiss before leaving.

It was strange. Here I was, a month and a half after the accident, finally able to allow myself to feel what I'd been denying, avoiding. I loved Logan, and for once I wasn't going to overthink it.

—◆◆◆—

My mom was already sitting at a booth with a plate of scrambled eggs and hash browns when I strolled into Haven, feeling like my world had been finally set right. Any lingering doubt I had about Logan was somehow washed away by his affection that morning. I loved him, and without a doubt, I knew he loved me.

"There you are. Thought you forgot," she said, smiling. She stood and pulled me in for a big hug, then stepped back, looking me over.

"You look beautiful, honey. How you feeling?" She slid back down into her seat, and I did the same across from her.

"Wonderful." I couldn't help the grin that was stinging my cheeks.

The waiter approached, and I ordered some pancakes as my mom's stare focused on me, a slight furrow to her brow.

"What?" I asked, my lips twitching.

"Nothing, it's just good to see you smile. Been too long."

"I agree. So how's work going?" I asked.

"Fine, but I wanted to meet you to talk about something other than work."

That didn't sound good.

"I heard you went to see a loan officer at the bank."

"Mom…" I drawled, popping my elbow on the table.

"Now listen, I told you—"

"Don't worry about it, Logan helped me out. The house isn't involved."

She sighed, relieved. "I'm glad to hear it, but surprised. Does that mean you are actually on speaking terms with him?"

I nodded, the grin back in place over my lips. *Definitely on speaking terms.*

"I see. Well, I don't know what you and him are doing, but be careful. I like him—a lot—but I also know he has an arrest on file that has me a little concerned."

"An arrest?" Shock was heavy in my voice.

"Yeah, I'm sure he'd prefer me to keep it to myself, and because I believe that man is in love with you, I'll do just that. Everyone has a past, but stay clear of that ex-girlfriend of his."

"No problem there," I grumbled.

"How's Oliver?"

The waiter set my plate down and I poured on some syrup.

"Honestly, I haven't seen too much of him, but that's about to change."

"So you and Logan West," she said, more to herself, smiling. "I wondered how long it would take him."

"You were convinced I wouldn't be able to resist?" I half chuckled, slightly offended.

"Can't resist the inevitable, honey."

I took a bite, realizing she was right. I was through resisting anything when it came to Logan.

We finished eating, chatting about her boyfriend and the

bombshell that I should've been expecting: they were moving in together. It was easy to see how she felt about him in the way she spoke. A peaceful feeling settled over me. After years alone, she was finally happy.

Now came the part I was dreading—the part that should've happened before or during breakfast, but it hadn't felt right. So as she pulled out her wallet, I knew I had to do it now or I'd regret it all day. I reached into my tote and pulled out the hat box, setting it on the table.

"What's that?" she asked, smoothing a twenty through her fingers.

"For you. I found it in the attic."

Her brows pulled in as slid it closer to her.

"I never knew about him and Nina. I had no clue."

She gasped, her eyes darting up from the box to me in a panic. "Why would you? You were a child."

"I'm so sorry." My heart broke for her.

"So am I. You deserved a better father."

We sat quietly for a few minutes as she read my grandmother's letter to her and then pulled out the picture of my father and Nina.

"I was blindsided when he left... especially with her. She was barely an adult. Her father was livid, to put it mildly." She put everything back in the box and the lid, looking up at me softly. "It was...horrible. A bad dream that took me weeks to realize wasn't ending. I never told you because it wasn't my place. If your father wanted you in his life, he could have visited you. I never would have stopped him."

"It doesn't matter. It's been too long now. Wherever he is, I don't need him, and neither do you," I told her as I reached across the table and took her hand.

Giving mine a squeeze, she smiled. "How did I raise such a strong woman?"

"I have no clue," I teased, then drew in a breath. "I take

after my mother: the strongest woman I know."

"All right, I got to get to work before you having me tearing up." My mother grabbed her purse and stood as I finished my orange juice. "Give me another hug, and drive carefully. Those roads are slick out there. This winter doesn't seem to want to let up."

I nodded and stood as she took the box.

"Maybe we can double date sometime," she offered, hugging me tightly.

Double date with my mother and George? I grimaced, but something told me it wasn't negotiable.

"I'll be looking forward to it," I said.

My mother released me with a knowing smile. "Still a terrible liar, Cassie."

She laughed and I watched her walk away, happy.

———◆◆◆———

The drive home was at a grueling pace due to the thick snow drifting over the road, but I made it safely. I spent the rest of the day cleaning a little and lounging around a lot. Stir crazy—that's how I felt. I missed school, and I missed Logan.

By four o'clock, I was showered, lotioned up, and throwing on an easy dress—easy for Logan to remove, anyway. I pulled my hair into a loose bun and stared at myself in the mirror. The reflection that greeted me was one I hadn't seen in a couple of years—before the accident, and before Mark's betrayal.

I was deliriously happy, and I could've sworn I was actually glowing. My phone chirped and I all but skipped over to it. I hadn't been able to control my urge to text him throughout the day, and he hadn't seemed to mind.

Still miss me?

I laughed at his reply to my text from an hour earlier. He'd told me he'd be in meetings most of the afternoon.

Maybe

Liar. And for the record…I miss u…BADLY.

Good :) Show me how much when u get here.

Butterflies roared to life in my gut, fluttering around with anticipation as the phone sounded with his reply.

Nothing could stop me

It was just after four thirty when the doorbell rang. It was so unlike Logan to not just waltz right in, but I was too excited to drag him back to bed to give it any real thought.

I opened the door with an eager smile, only to be greeted by the swollen red eyes of Hilary.

"Hilary, what's wrong?" I asked, hurrying her inside and out of the icy weather.

Her face was pale, her bottom lip disappearing between her teeth as she gnawed at it, clutching a brown paper bag in her hands.

"I went shopping today," she replied eerily and nodded down at said bag, crinkled in her hand as though she'd held it the entire drive over.

She held it out and I took it, hesitant to open it by her pained expression. It was more supermarket shopping than boutique.

"Before you open it, you have to swear not to tell anyone."

What was in there? "Of course."

Nervously, I unrolled the bag that had been nearly worn through from her handling of it, and peeked inside.

"Hilary." I sighed, pulling out a pregnancy test that was piled in the bag with a dozen more of every brand.

She plopped down on the couch and shrugged out of her coat, not saying a word. I didn't press her—just placed it back in the bag and sat beside her quietly for support, unsure what I could say or do.

"Caleb's going to kill me," she said finally after a few minutes.

I pulled my legs under me. "Are you sure about this? I mean, have you taken a test yet?"

"Not yet. I was waiting till you were with me. Didn't want to do it before school. " She ran a hand over her eyes and down her face. "My cycle has been regular since I was thirteen, yet I'm two weeks late."

"Did you guys use protection?"

"I'm on the pill, but I may have forgotten to take them every day."

"You forgot?" I hadn't meant for that to sound as judgmental as it had come out.

"Yes, forgot! Seeing as my best friend was laid up in a hospital, unconscious, I was a little stressed last month, all right!?"

"I'm sorry. I didn't mean…" *Crap.* What a good friend I was. I took a deep breath and stood. "There's no reason to sit here freaking out until we have an answer."

I dumped the bag over the coffee table, spilling the tests out.

"Did you need so many?" I chuckled, then bit the inside of my lip. Not the time to laugh.

"I grabbed every kind off the shelf and made a beeline for the register. Had to throw in an extra twenty to swear Mr. Tanner to secrecy." I caught the twitch at the corner of her lip.

"Seriously, you're worried old Mr. Tanner's going to spread gossip?" There was no way to hold in my laughter at that. The man was pressing ninety-five years old.

"Shut up!" She giggled, throwing a test at me. "I was panicked, all right!?"

"Whatever you say." I grinned.

"There has to be an easier way," I said through my hysterical laughter.

"Come on, hand me another."

I was nearly bent over, standing in the doorway to my bathroom. I handed her another test as she sat on the toilet. She dipped it into her stream of urine before setting it on the counter.

"Another, hurry!"

"You have eight more. There is no way you have that much pee in you!" I shook my head in disbelief, holding out another test.

"Shit!"

"Told you."

"Okay, well, we have the first seven tests, and I'll drink lots of water and take the rest next."

"You sound crazy. You know that, right? You only need one—maybe two, tops."

Hilary flushed the toilet, stood, and pulled up her jeans. The tests were thrown all over the counter, and all she could do was sigh as she turned on the faucet and washed her hands.

"I know, I just want to be sure. So please just let me have my irrational freak-out."

My attention was now trained on the instructions, reading to see how long we needed to wait, when my head dipped back in a fit of laughter.

"What now?" She turned back, staring at me. "I get it. I took too many tests. Haha."

I shook my head and read back the new knowledge I'd learned. "'Place a clean cup in the urine stream to collect sample, then dip the test for five seconds.'"

She gaped at me and sucked in a deep breath, blowing it out

270

and rolling her eyes. "Well, now we know for the next time someone, maybe even you, has a pregnancy scare."

"Watch that mouth of yours!" I cracked a smile and tossed the paper in the trash with all the others. "Besides, there's no cup of mine I'd have let you piss in!"

Hilary laughed and followed me out to the living room. Five minutes later, all seven pregnancy tests were spread out on the small coffee table over a long sheet of paper towels. It was hard to watch as she anxiously placed each one out, her hands trembling, gnawing on her lip as the timer counted down the minutes.

The buzzer jolted her up from her seat, absolutely terror-stricken.

"I can't look! You do it!" She walked across the room and began pacing.

"You sure?"

"Positive. I mean—just do it, no positives. Please!" Her nails were being chomped to bits in her mouth, her eyes glued to her feet.

"Whatever these say, it's going to be all right. I'm here for you, and Caleb will be, too. He's a good guy."

I looked down at the first test and then ran my eye over each one in the line. They all revealed the same results.

"Well?" She was facing me now.

"Congratulations—you're going to be a mother, and a damn good one!"

"Oh…I'm going to be sick." With that, she sprinted from the room, slamming the bathroom door shut behind her.

This may not have been how she'd planned it, but she loved Caleb and he loved her. I knew they'd make it work. He wouldn't leave her.

I'd started cleaning up the table when my phone rang.

"Hey," I answered.

"Hello, sweetheart. Sorry, I'm running late. Oliver had a

karate class after school, but I'd love for us to have dinner. Can you come over in an hour?"

Hilary walked back in the room then with a washcloth, wiping her mouth. She was as white as a ghost.

"I'm sorry, Hilary's here and she isn't feeling well. How about tomorrow?"

There was a beat of silence before he spoke. "You're not backing away, are you?"

"No, I told you last night and this morning. I'm yours."

"Good, then I'll come see you tonight after I put Oliver to bed. Jax should be home by ten to keep an eye on him while he sleeps, then I'll be there."

"I'll be waiting," I said before hanging up.

"You and Logan finally worked things out, huh?" Hilary smiled.

"Yeah, it appears so." I placed the phone on the side table and continued cleaning up, walking into the kitchen.

"If you have plans, I can go."

"No, stay and hang out. We can try another hand of poker and see if our luck's improved," I said, opening the junk drawer by my fridge.

"Seriously," Hilary said, her eyes darting to her stomach, "does it look like luck's on my side?"

"How about a movie then?" I chuckled, tossing the cards back in the drawer and heading back to the sofa.

Chapter Twenty-Four

BLINDSIDED

That night, after Hilary left, Logan was there just before ten and had me wrapped around his body before the door was shut behind him. We spent the night making love and talking about nothing important, and yet it meant more to me than anything. For the first time in a long time, I felt the connection I'd been longing for.

The next day, I went out to get groceries for dinner. I wanted to make something special for Logan and Oliver, and found myself walking blissfully through the grocery store when I felt the hairs on the back of my neck stand.

I looked back, feeling eyes on me, only to see the back of someone's legs as he or she left the aisle. I shook off the shiver and continued until I had a cart full of groceries and was on my way home.

The roads were icy and snow-covered, so I took my time, my nervousness about driving after the accident amplified even more by the weather. As I drove down a back road, I noticed a pickup truck behind me. It was close to my bumper, and then it was swerving.

I slowed, watching the scene unfold as the truck lost control and flew across the other lane into the ditch. I pulled over immediately and ran over, opening the driver door, when I noticed the man inside clutching his head.

"Are you all right? Did you hit your head?" I asked.

Slowly, his hands lowered, and I found myself staring into the familiar, menacing eyes of Kurt, my blind date who, last I heard, was still in jail.

My stomach dropped, but I tried to play it off. Maybe he wouldn't remember me.

"I left my phone in my car. I'll go grab it and call for help," I explained, smiling, hoping he didn't recognize me. I was about a quarter mile from my house and knew the tow truck wouldn't be there for at least twenty minutes with the condition of the roads.

"Thank you," he said with a smile, then dropped his head back into hands. "I hit my head on the steering column."

"Just stay there. I'll be right back."

It was a lie. I'd get in my car, drive away, and then call for help. His head looked fine and so did his car, but I'd still call for help—I just wouldn't leave myself out there with him, in case he did suddenly remember me.

As I walked to my car, I heard him step out, then slam his door behind him. I quickened my pace and made it to my car, rushing inside and grabbing my phone.

With a trembling finger, I shot a text to Logan.

Kurt near house.

The knock on my window startled me, my phone slipping through my hands as I looked up to see Kurt staring in.

"I just phoned the local garage for a tow truck. Do you want me to call for an ambulance?" I asked through the glass as I gripped my keys tightly.

"I can't hear you!" he yelled through the glass.

"I said, do you want me to—"

He shook his head as though he still couldn't understand me. I rolled the window down half an inch. I still wasn't sure if he was a threat, since he didn't appear to remember me. I reminded myself that I needed to calm down.

Lifting myself up slightly, I spoke through the open crack of the window. "Do you need me to call the paramedics?"

"No, thanks, that won't be necessary…Cassandra!" His smile faded into a snarling scowl.

A scream shot out of me when his arm connected with my window. I flew across the seat as he beat on it again and again. My keys fell from my hands and I struggled to cover my face while scouring the floorboards to find them.

Glass showered over me with his final blow. His hand encompassed my ankle, while his other reached in through the broken window and unlocked the door.

"What's the chance that I run into you before leaving this shitty little town, huh?"

Glass tore into my stomach as he yanked me across the seat. My feet were relentless, kicking, beating down as hard as I could manage while I clawed against the seat, fighting to reach the other door handle, desperate for an escape.

"Let me go!" I shrieked, finally grasping the handle.

"Why? I did nothing to you, yet I found myself sitting back in jail anyway! I thought I was helping you that night, but you're just like every other woman out there!"

His hands were up my skirt, gripping the thick black leggings I was thankful I wore. In one painful move, he ripped them down my legs.

"Now I'll get what I have coming to me! Take what I want, since being a gentleman isn't what you're looking for."

His fingers gripped the band of my panties, and my adrenaline spiked into full-blown panic. With all my strength, I yanked my leg free and kicked back as hard as I could, landing my foot right on his face.

Kurt stumbled back, releasing his hold as blood gushed from his nose.

Taking full advantage, I pushed open the passenger door and scrambled out, darting into the dense forest beside the road.

I knew I was close to my house and Logan's house, so I ran, never once looking back through the heavy snow. It was bitterly cold; my leggings hung around my waist in pieces.

Over fallen trees and through dense, thorny brush I raced, my heart pounding against my chest. I could only hope I was going in the right direction. Rows of fat pine trees blocked the path, and in desperation, I slipped between them. The needles scratched my legs, and a frozen branch sliced into my cheek, but I never stopped. My pulse was racing and body trembling when I heard his sickening cackle.

"You can't hide out here, Cassandra! You'll freeze to death before you find help, because I'm not going anywhere until I have what was mine that night!"

I ran faster, tripping over a hidden pile of rocks covered by the snow. It didn't slow me. I was back up and going.

Kurt's voice was a constant, his words only growing angrier and nastier as he spouted out exactly what I had coming to me. The man was out of his mind—worse than a menace to society. He was psychotic!

Finally, hope was near. My house. I wasn't sure if Kurt knew I lived there or if he'd only followed me from town, but it was my only shot. Nobody would be home at Logan's, aside from the off chance that Natasha was back, but she'd be little help.

I needed my house, my phone, and my gun.

The instant my body collided with the back door, I scrambled for the small porcelain bird to the side that held an extra key, and with shaky hands, slid it into the lock.

"Where you going?" Kurt voice washed over me.

He was close, his voice no longer a yell. Still, I wasn't looking back to see. The knob turned and I pushed myself inside, then twisted the lock back in place, only to come face to face with his black eyes staring at me through the glass.

"Well, this will be even better—I won't have to freeze my

ass off fucking you!"

I stepped back, eyes wide in terror as his foot connected with the door. There was no time to grab the phone on the wall. No time for anything.

Tears heating my eyes, I raced into my bedroom, slammed the door, and fell to my stomach, digging around under my bed for the safe. It only took a second to grasp the box and pull it out.

The shattering of glass echoed through the room, adding to the pulsating trembles wracking my body as I yanked open my side-table drawer and dumped it onto the floor.

Papers, books, and miscellaneous junk were scattered around, yet with luck, the small gold key fell out on top.

His pounding on my bedroom door had me focused on the safe, bent over, on my knees. The key unlocked it with ease. There, exactly where my grandfather had left it, was the gun I'd only used during target practice years earlier.

With the gun in hand, I opened the accompanying box of bullets and spilled them onto the floor in front of me.

Another pound at my door followed by his gut-wrenching snicker had my clammy hands in a fit, unable to place the bullet in the revolver.

"The fun's over—here I come, baby!" With those final words, the door flew in, busting off the hinges.

I ducked down, the bullets further scattering over the floor with my rushed movements.

"There you are. Getting ready for me?"

I held up the unloaded gun, threatening him to stay there, and hid two bullets in my other hand.

"Leave! Now!" I yelled.

His smile broadened into a wicked grin. "Why would I do that? So you can call the police? Send me back to prison? No, I think I'll stay."

He took a step toward me and I swallowed, struggling to

hold the gun steady.

"It was more than a coincidence that I saw you in the supermarket today. I mean, here I am, my first day out on bail, grabbing a carton of cigarettes before skipping town, and who do I see? The girl I thought I was trying to help that night. The girl I thought I was being a gentleman with." He shook his head at me and ticked his tongue.

"I never pressed charges." My palms were sweating against the weight of the gun in my hands, yet I never let the barrel sway from its aim at his chest. "It was a misunderstanding, that's all."

"Yes, I agree, it was. Except your so-called boyfriend didn't think so. He *did* press charges, and he also paid off some guards to make my life hell the past couple months!"

"I'm sorry," I practically sobbed. "I didn't know. I haven't thought about you since that night."

"Funny, considering I thought about you every. Single. Night I was there. With every fist I took to the gut, elbow to the face, knee to the groin, I saw your face. And now I'm going to make it all worth it."

Kurt ran at me and I darted to the side and around the bed, focused on loading the gun, but he was fast, knocking me down to the floor the instant the bullet slid in. The gun fell, and I rolled to my stomach, scurrying to reach it.

"Come on, it doesn't have to be like this. It doesn't have to be painful," he drawled in my ear, his body lying flat over mine as I lay on my stomach.

His erection pressed into my ass, and tears began to stream down my cheeks.

This wasn't happening.

Kurt's hands grabbed mine and buried them under my chest, then he pressed his palm down between my shoulder blades, using my body to lock them down. His other hand was tugging at my skirt, lifting it over my hips. Then his weight shifted, and I heard the earth-shattering sound of his zipper.

I kicked my feet, but it was useless. He was on his knees, his elbow now digging into my back as I felt him pulling his pants down. I needed to move, get a hand free, something. I couldn't let this happen.

He leaned forward over me, his elbow lifting only to be replaced by his forearm resting over the back of my neck, forcing my face into the carpet. Tears and snot covered my cheeks, but the pressure removed from my back now allowed me to wiggle my hands.

It was the moment his palm slapped down over my ass before he tore at my panties that I managed to rip my hand free and grab the gun. The weight of his entire body dropped onto me as he began grabbing at my outstretched hands gripping the gun. He snarled, trying to reach it as his bare erection rubbed over my backside.

A loud, piercing scream escaped my throat at the feeling of him there, so close, and my body burst into an uncontrollable tremor, rolling from side to side.

I closed my eyes, crying, screaming, begging for the strength to move the gun at the right angle to shoot. But on my stomach with him on my back, it was impossible, until his weight was suddenly gone.

My body flipped over and I pointed the gun up, only to see Logan holding Kurt against him, his arm around his neck.

"Logan!" I cried, the gun shaking in my hands.

"I'm here, you can put the gun down. The police are on their way."

My breath had abandoned me, a cold sweat pouring down my face. "He...he..." I sobbed louder, my gun never once moving from the target.

"I know, sweetheart. It will be okay now, put the gun down."

With the inhale of a deep breath and then another and another, my head spinning, lungs empty, I couldn't loosen my grip on the weapon.

"He...was..."

"Shhh, I'm here."

"Son of a bitch! I'll fucking kill you both!" Kurt roared, and with indescribable ease, Logan released Kurt just enough to whip him around and connect his fist to the side of his head so hard he fell unconscious to the floor.

Logan was beside me instantly, his hands covering mine and removing the gun slowly. My body fell into his, grasping handfuls of his shirt as I unloaded my sobs onto his chest.

"It's all right now. I'm here." He stroked his hands down my back, his heart beating against my ear. "I'm sorry. I didn't know they released him. Caleb called right before I got your text. One of Kurt's friends bailed him out."

He sighed, and his body fell back against the foot of my bed. "God, I'm sorry, Cassandra. This never should have happened. I promise I'm here now. I'll never let anything bad happen again."

I wasn't sure how long I lay in his arms crying until the police knocked on the front door, but when they did, my entire body stiffened against him, not ready to let go.

Logan called out that the back door was open and drew me closer. My back door was more than open—it was destroyed—yet instead of letting that fact and the images of watching the events unfold tear me back down, I found solace in the firm embrace of Logan's arms that never let me go.

The police entered the room moments later, guns drawn. After they assessed the scene, paramedics followed.

"Can you talk to them?" Logan asked, lifting my face up gently to meet his pained stare. The pad of his thumb ran over the cut on my cheek, and I winced. "I'll have you cleaned up soon. They'll need a statement, but if you're not ready—"

"I'm ready," I interrupted, sniffling and wiping away the final tears. "As long as you'll stay with me. Don't leave. Not yet."

His eyes softened. "Cassandra, I'm not going anywhere, ever."

Logan stood and brought me with him as I relaxed against him. Face to face with him, I leaned forward and placed a soft kiss to his lips.

"Thank you," I murmured into the gentle kiss.

"Don't thank me. It's what a man in love does."

"Miss Clarke?" An officer stood behind us, clearing his throat.

"I love you, too," I whispered, then took a deep breath before turning around.

Kurt was lying on a gurney, wearing a neck brace in the all-too-familiar scene. He was alive, but was going to be in some serious pain when he woke up.

"We need your statement, ma'am."

"Of course. Let's go in the kitchen," I said, my hand wrapped around Logan's.

He was my strength, my rock, my everything, and I was never more confident than with him at my side. We could take on anything.

Chapter Twenty-Five

COLLATERAL
~NATASHA~

Two days—that's how long it had been since I'd showed up at Logan's vacation house, sneaking in the back, waiting to surprise him. To have him alone and remind him how good we once were—how we could be again.

Yet here I'd sat for two long days. Alone.

As the sun set over the snow-covered mountains, I picked up my phone and dialed.

"I figured you'd be back by now," Jax chuckled. "Good thing you have the looks, 'cause baby, you're not the smartest."

"Where is he?" I asked, anger lacing my tone.

"Logan? Oh, you know, out." He laughed again. "Actually, he's probably *in* Cassandra as we speak. You know, the pretty blonde that lives next door—the girl he actually enjoys hanging around."

"You played me!"

"No, Logan played you. I simply got paid to make it happen. Having his ex-fiancée around on Valentine's Day didn't sit well with him, so I'm sure you understand. And by the way, no rush on your return."

Rage consumed me, surging through my veins. Logan wasn't coming. He was never going to give me a fair chance—at least, not with that woman around.

"I'll be coming back soon, Jax. And when I do, you're going to help me win him over."

"And why would I do that to my own brother?"

"Because if you don't, I'll tell him all about this past summer in Miami—every juicy detail of how you tracked me down for Oliver, only to spend the week in my bed!"

"I was out of my mind that week! Whatever you gave me—"

"I gave you exactly what you wanted. It wasn't my fault you couldn't handle it." I smiled to myself.

"I went looking for you in the hopes that you'd changed—that you could be his mother. But like I told you the day I left Miami, you're nothing to this family, and Oliver doesn't need you. He was happy enough before I got involved and dug you up!"

"No, he wasn't. You said so yourself. You asked me to return—"

"No, I told you to stay as far away as possible when I realized what you were into! That week is still a fucking blur to me."

A blur to him, perhaps, but an eye-opener for me. Oliver wanted his mother, and it was the push I needed to return to him.

"I want my son, and I want Logan where we once were: heading for the altar. And you will help me!"

"Logan won't even speak to you, and you think you can convince him to marry you?" he scoffed.

"I think, with a little persuasion, Logan will see exactly what I want him to."

"He loves her," Jax said, sounding a little too convinced for my taste. "He won't screw that up again, so if you think you can break them up now, you're too late."

"Who said anything about *me* breaking them up?" I grinned as I hit the 'End Call' button. After surfing the web on my phone, I found the number I needed. After one ring, a man answered.

"Twenty-Four-Hour Pawn, how can I help you?"

I looked around the lavishly decorated room, smiling. "Yes, do you buy furniture?"

"If it's in good shape, we buy just about anything."

"Good. Send out your largest truck, because I have plenty to sell." After giving him the address, I hung up and walked over to the window.

This wasn't the way I wanted things to unfold. I tried to be what he wanted, what Oliver needed, but I was running out of time. If Logan wouldn't listen to me, then I'd just have to make him see things my way.

Look for Book Three of the
Harmony Series,
the conclusion of
Cassandra and Logan's story,
coming early 2014

About the Author

Angela Graham resides in Tipp City, Ohio with her loving husband and three beautiful children. Her first novel, Inevitable, was released in early 2013 and is part of a three book series.

Visit her at Facebook

www.facebook.com/angelagraham.author

Acknowledgments

I have to admit, writing this was harder than I expected. So many kind and generous people have entered my life since I released Inevitable. I am awed by the support I have received and I don't really know where to begin, so I'll start with my family that have dealt with my preoccupied state the last few months.

First and foremost, I want to thank my husband, who has stuck beside me and watched from the sidelines, helping out more than ever as I've pursued my dream. I love you, babe!

To William, my handsome son, the genius artist who inspires me to dream bigger, I love you. No matter how tall you grow, you'll always be my little baby.

My little darlings, Tinsley and James, I love you both so much. Hugs and kisses every day.

I also want to thank Maureen and Tom for all their support while I wrote most of this book hidden away in the cottage. You gave my kids a summer to remember, so thank you from the bottom of my heart!

Through this journey, I'm blessed to have Stephanie, my CP and friend, still by my side. She has been my writing rock.

There has been one person welcomed into my life that I can't imagine not having, and that is Whitney. She keeps this new world organized for me, and in doing so keeps my mind clear so I can focus on writing. Thank you for everything you do.

Another wonderful addition who has come on last minute has been my fabulous new editor, Jen. She has helped me pull this book together to give you the best reading experience possible. I look forward to many more books with her on board.

To my beta readers—you know who you all are—I'm so appreciative of your honest feedback and patience. It was beyond helpful, and I look forward to hearing your thoughts when the third book is ready.

Now here comes the tricky part—the part I'm terrified I'll forget someone if I start naming names. I have *never*, in all my life, met anyone as generous with their time and kind with their hearts as bloggers. It's because of all you guys out there supporting indie authors that readers discover our work. My gratitude is indescribable. I wish I could start from day one of publishing and list every blogger with a heartfelt comment for each, but the fear of missing even one person is too much. I hope you know who you are. To everyone who has reviewed, shared, and promoted my work, as well as spent precious time answering my e-mails, giving me invaluable advice, and helping me navigate down this unfamiliar path: thank you, thank you, and again, thank you!

Lastly, but most importantly, I want to thank my readers. From the very beginning, you have amazed me with your kind words, filled me with happy tears, and lifted my spirits when 1 was overwhelmed. Your constant support amazes me daily, and is more than I ever could've dreamed of. I hope to someday meet you all and wrap you in a tender, warm embrace, as that is what each and every one of your e-mails does to me. There have been so many amazing readers who have gone above and beyond to support my books, and I hope you all know that I see it and am extremely grateful. Thank you!

Playlist

Plumb—"Cut"

Ed Sheeran—"Give Me Love"

W Temptation—"All I Need"

Jason Walker—"Echo"

Ross Copperman—"Holdin On & Letting Go"

Christina Perri—"Jar of Hearts"

Alex Band—"Will Not Back Down"

Birdy—"Skinny Love"

The Fray—"Never Say Never"

Florence & The Machine—"Never Let Me Go"

Sum 41—"With Me"

While you wait, be sure to check out

Embrace, Book 2 in the Evolve Series

by S. E. Hall, releasing Oct 1, 2014!

You can also visit her at
https://www.facebook.com/S.E.HallAuthorEmerge

Chapter 1

Dear Laney

~Evan~

My phone is burning a hole in my pocket. Ninety percent of me wants to respond to the text Laney had sent about an hour ago, but the other ten percent, the shred that still has some dignity, is winning. As much as I want an exact explanation, I simply can't bear to hear it right now.

Sawyer's a godsend, shoving beers in my hand and attracting every lady in the bar over to our table. He's doing a better job than anyone else could at distracting me, including the brunette currently perched on my right leg... Manda? Mandy? She's hot with long dark hair, full lips and huge tits that she's not afraid to let play peek-a-boo. She even smells decent and her hands know no boundaries, but all I can think about is the one who got away; a beautiful blonde with a quick wit, smart mouth and devastating smile.

"Dude, you need another one?" Sawyer's question drags me from my mental misery, and I'm almost sure he's asking about another beer, not another girl.

"Sure," I respond with no feeling whatsoever. It's sadly the correct answer no matter what he was asking.

"Want me to get it, sugar?" Man—whatever asks with a syrup to her voice that I just noticed and don't particularly like.

"Two, Amy," Sawyer directs her and hands her some money.

Amy? Shit, I wasn't even close. Good thing I hadn't spoken to her even once.

"She's hot, bro." Sawyer raises his brows and motions to Amy with his head, to which I shrug noncommittally. "What is it, you need a blonde? I figured that'd be too much, but I can—"

My hand shoots up, cutting him off. "I appreciate it, man, I do," I stop and take a swig of beer, "but a parade of girls isn't gonna help me tonight. I just need to crash; wake up to a new day. You think you can take me to my truck?"

"Nah, but you can bunk with me." He throws some bills on the table and stands. "Let's go."

We leave the bar, not collecting our beers he'd already shelled out money for and not saying goodbye to Amy. I appreciate the hasty retreat.

"Why are you going out of your way for me?" I ask him as we drive back to his dorm—her dorm.

"Real talk?"

"Please."

"I'm not just helping you. I mean, I feel for you; damn do I feel for ya." He chuckles and reaches over to punch me in the arm, offering a grin covertly lined with sympathy. "But it's more than that. Laney's my girl, and I know she's probably worried as shit about you right now, so I'm partly looking out for ya cause she'd want me to. She'd feel better knowing you're not off crying in your beer alone." He laughs again. "But mostly, Dane's my boy. Not only is he my employer, but he's one of my best friends, and he loves Laney. So I'd be lying if I pretended this wasn't a little about distracting his competition." He parks his car and turns to me, waiting for my reaction to his honesty.

"She texted me." I have no idea why this is what I'd chosen to respond.

"Oh yeah?"

"Yeah." I rub my eyes with the heels of my hands, fighting off the beginnings of a headache. "I didn't answer her. I have no idea what to say."

"Don't ask me," he says as he gets out of the car. "I'm terrible with women. Well... I'm terrible at talking to women about important shit." He opens the door to the dorm, letting me walk in first. "Never saw the need."

I crash on Sawyer's couch, resting another beer nightcap on my bare chest, thoughts of how differently I saw things panning out swirling in my head. She'd warned me, I knew this Dane kid was creeping in; I'd gotten here as soon as I could. Just not soon enough.

How naïve I'd been, thinking Laney and I were forever, that distance wouldn't affect our closeness. The thought of Laney coming out of the box she keeps herself in long enough to meet someone, to actually fall for them, shutting me out—I'd have bet you all the money in the world it would never happen. Well, there goes that safety net. You know what they say—take care of your woman or another man will.

I don't even know how to proceed with this—I certainly don't know how (or if) to respond to her messages. I'm definitely not qualified to write the manual on Plan B, since Plan A, plunge head over ass into a year of ineligibility for the girl who is now with another guy, blew up in my face. Delirious with grief, jealousy, and a million other things, I rudely dig around Sawyer's living area until I find a pen and paper. Who writes letters anymore? This guy, apparently. It just feels more personal than a text, and if Laney and I are even one single thing anymore—it's personal. No matter what Dane has with her now, he can't undo ten years of us.

I can imagine what she demands of him, what she expects. I helped set those precedents. I proved to her there are guys that will listen and treat her like a queen. Since she's been a little girl, I showed her how a man should treat a woman as special as her.

So he's getting a real lady…

You're Welcome, Asshole.

I want to know why? What had he done, so well, so quickly, that I'd been forgotten; replaced? Is there anything I can do to get her back? Do I want her back?

It's around 4 am when I finally finish my letter to her, calmer now that I've gotten some of it out on paper, the racing questions in my mind slowed down enough that I can finally fall asleep.

No sooner than I finally fall asleep, I'm awake, sun streaming obnoxiously through the curtains and straight into my eye. The microwave clock says it's 9:12. Ugh. I wanted to sleep so much longer than five hours.

The least I can do is run out and grab breakfast. Sawyer's been pretty cool, and since I'm starving and he's got twenty pounds on me, he's got to wake up ravenous. I get up and dressed, checking my phone out of habit. There's six texts waiting, all from Laney, the last one from around midnight. I didn't answer her then and I don't answer now, heading out with my letter and appetite.

I hit the nearest drive thru and curse myself for not grabbing Sawyer's keys. I wait about fifteen minutes in front of the dorm, holding bags of breakfast in my hands, before a cute co-ed lets me back in the door. I thank her and walk slowly down the hall, giving her a chance to gain some ground. I don't want her, or anyone, to see my pathetic next move.

I'm not sure how I remember, but I find Laney's door easily. Pulling the letter from my back pocket, I bend to slip it under her door, shocked when I hear her sweet laugh from the other side. She's here? She's not with him anymore? My heart suddenly lifts, as does my hand, ready to knock, when his voice reaches out and rips my heart out of my chest.

I should walk away. Definitely the right thing to do. Fine, open a spot in hell for me, like it's so much different than where

I'm at right now anyway—I'm not moving. Their voices are muffled and I'm straining to do so, but I hear it.

"So you forgive me?"

"Yes, caveman, I forgive you, but I'm still not ready to forgive myself. I mean it, though, don't ever do anything like that, ever again."

"I promise, baby. I love you."

"Me too."

Ah fuck. Me too? Whatever does or doesn't happen now, no matter what words she says to me, it's those words, those last ones to him, which will ring in my ears.

How could she love him? I've had ten years with the little girl, the young lady, and apparently the "I love you as a best friend," but in the span of only months, he'd taken the woman. This realization sends a wave of nausea and loneliness through me, but I muster the energy to move my feet, not wanting them to open the door and catch me standing here like the loser I've become.

I turn to head to Sawyer's room, and with every step I take, a new fervor flames inside me. Yes, my face grazed tits, and she'd gotten a picture of it. Sure, her best friend woke up in my room, her only clothing mine...but I never told anyone I loved them! I never gave my heart! I transferred schools for her, gave up a scholarship, fought like hell with my parents about it...damn right she shouldn't forgive herself. I flex my hands in and out of fists, rolling my neck, fighting the urge to punch a hole in the wall. Nostrils flared, chest heaving rapidly, I take a few deep breaths before finally knocking.

When Sawyer opens the door, I have only one thing to say. "Last night was a bust. Think we can do better tonight?"

He smiles and fist bumps me, which I take as a yes.

Fuck this. Disney movies suck anyway—bring on a porno!